Contents

I have too many people to thank, and not enough space. Y'all know who you are.

"For those who love the deepest and regret the most, our greatest punishments are our memories.

Because they never leave our hearts and especially not our dreams.

For my memories were all I dreamt about.

I used to hate the dreams because whenever I woke up they ended.

I could never go back and fix them.

And the memories hurt the most when you knew how they ended.

I thought that was as bad as it could get.

But now the nightmares follow me into my reality without any chance of correction yet every possible chance of failure.

I think I'm beginning to forget how good my dreams were once."

The Depths of Man

ACT I

Deeper

People never talk about how easy it is to lose everything.

One of the biggest things I lost was my personality some years back. Stripped away. Ripped apart. The dreams made it worse. All the dreams I hated dreaming and all the dreams I dared to dream were locked in my head, only to be opened at night.

All my beloved bridges were burned. It felt wrong to feel happy too. Spending so much time being driven by loneliness and pain made it all normal.

The result of all of this? An emptiness. I'd been empty for so long that I forgot what it was like to feel.

Until now. Unfortunately for me, under the guise of "feeling", the mind that operated this hollow husk of a being had decided to build an enigma around itself at this moment. An intricate, thick construct I couldn't understand. A thick construct I'd mostly avoided to prevent the horrors of my imagination from leaking into my reality. The horrors of everything I lost begging to come back into my life.

Despite having just opened the email a few minutes earlier, I was already feeling regretful. I was happy with the way I was living. I was content with what I had. *Was I?* Yet it was that email, that deluded, desperate email, that already started me down the path of desolation.

While I had the remotest idea of what it was thinking and the various instances it fed me, my mind never let me find the "Why". What some would call the root of the problem. I didn't even know if it was a problem.

My mind refused to conform to reason and instead hung on to the email. That deluded, desperate email still distracted me now, when it was most important. The lady interviewing me sat there, waiting to see what I'd do. I wish I could open my mouth and assure her I did not know about what was happening to me, either.

My eyes settled on her gray pupils. She smiled at me, but there was something behind that smile. The clarity was sufficient. She wasn't happy with me. A small part of her already decided that I wasn't going to get the job. It was fine by me. Six figures were in my retirement and savings accounts. Nevertheless, the thrill I felt was a rather intense emotion. I hoped there was a way I'd get to experience that again like I had the privilege of experiencing at Gilbert.

At least that's the story I've repeated to myself. I had a hard time bolstering even that lately.

It didn't occur to me that she was waiting for my reply. "I'd like to hear from you." She offered before I could embarrass myself by asking what the question was. It was clear she was still prodding me, trying to figure out what else I had to offer besides my resume.

This was one of the quirkier offices, something I noticed while my eyes wandered without aim or focus. The greenness of a start-up, naïve and playful, was all too visible. The office was more decorated for the aesthetic, rather than functionality (defined by the mossy yellow cabinets that held nothing, yet complemented the beige walls behind them). Accordingly, I couldn't record anything that occupied that space. It looked great, but I couldn't identify with it. I felt blind to my surroundings. I didn't like it.

My seated position was cross-legged, with my arms over my top knee. Fingers interlocked. "Right-"

"Speak a bit louder, please."

I didn't even get to say anything. "Right. Sorry. Anyway, what do you want to hear?" I regretted the question. Made me seem too defensive. *Coffee would've helped.*

"I mean, I can't argue with your past. Your history. I knew you'd entered the building before the elevator even closed." I couldn't help but smile at the compliment. A fake smile, done with the lack of another response.

"But we've seen many qualified candidates. So, tell me, what drives you to be different from everyone else? What do you feel makes you different?" She spread her hands along all the resumes that littered her desk, presumably to expand on her thoughts. Each ray of sunlight that made it past her body made an effort to touch the lines of text gently.

4

I asked myself some similar questions. Would anyone in my situation do anything different? Would they go where they fear to go?

My thoughts caught up to reason. At this point, there was no point in this interview. I found myself unable to answer her questions or do anything that wasn't involved with my dilemma.

I smiled, hoping not to sound indifferent. "You know, I don't know if this is what's best for me right now." I trudged my words through the mud, pausing in between every word, trying to see how she'd react. But it just reeked of hesitation. I knew that if it were a few years ago, she'd be crawling all over me, salivating that she had her hands on someone with "Gilbert blood". She would've been offering all kinds of starting bonuses, trying to get someone of my caliber to join her team. But it just wasn't the same now. *Nothing was.*

Only way it'd be worse was if you went back. Confirmed it.

I sighed. "So, thank you for your time and consideration, but-" My mouth stopped moving. Once more, my brain had different ideas than what it initially intended. Oozing with awkwardness, I tapped the chair with more hesitation. *Maybe I'm trying to learn some Morse code on the spot.* The hesitation soon went away as I jumped up from the chair and barreled out the door.

Sitting outside was a corral of other prospective candidates. Their white shirts stank of sweat. Mine was more defined by its wrinkles than its sweat, sleeves rolled up due to the lack of A/C. They looked at me with their nervous and expectant faces. Some even looked in awe.

That was me. A lifetime ago.

At that moment, I realized that I left my coat on the chair inside the interviewees' room. It wasn't worth it to go back inside.

The white, reflective hallways gave me enough time to think about this decision. *Visit Greg.* Then maybe Dan. Robin. *That's it.* A day or two. More time and hallways passed, and I started to doubt even visiting Robin.

I, thankfully, didn't doubt that I needed to avoid Aubrey at all costs. Shannon, too, if the rumors were true.

My first thought about her in a couple of days.

The blue tie seemed to get tighter around my neck. *Why was it getting tighter?* Cruising, I pulled it off and around my neck before shoving it into the small pockets of my dress pants. It fell off after a few steps. I didn't bother to get it.

The sweat poured in torrents and my shirt began to slow me down. If it wasn't for my unceasing wiping, the sweat would've rooted me to the spot, gluing my shoes to the floor. I wouldn't have combatted it.

The car was parked outside. It looked terrible, to put it simply. I didn't care too much when I bought it. As long as it could hold my things. Or at least the ones that didn't remind me of what happened, which left the car empty.

Over time, the car had become my abode. I still owned my house on Cherry Hill. The loan, the mortgage, and anything else I needed to pay were taken care of until next July. But the memories plagued me too much over there. They seeped into my nightmares constantly, especially when I slept in our bed. *My bed.* So, I forced myself to grow accustomed to sleeping in the car. Of course, I was still haunted. I was too hurt inside for such an easy transition to work. But the frights came in a languid, more governable manner.

My hair reached out to further touch the wind as my fingers felt around my pocket, fishing out the keys and unlocking the car.
Leaping inside, I looked behind me at the brown suitcase, struggling to hold back a wave of clothes eager to be worn.

That wasn't the only mess I'd bothered to make. The dashboard was littered with food I'd eaten in a panic as I read the email at first. Crumbs were all over the place. The plastic water bottle in the cup holder had been there longer than I could remember.

The only greater mess would be the one I saw in the rearview mirror. I hadn't bothered to shave or cut my beyond-overgrown hair. To make matters easier, I refused to look down and see what horrendous shape hid behind my shirt.

Somewhere in the car was my laptop and my charger. Once found, I pulled it out and waited as I gave the breath of life to the computer with the press of the button.

It whirred to existence. I was already signed in, which meant the first thing that assaulted my eyes was the latest in the long string of emails, filled with vague exposition and purposeful distance.

Cal,

Dad's getting close. They haven't told me how long he's got, but I can feel it coming. Stuff happened to us, I get it. But please.

Dan

We knew each other enough to the point where "stuff" didn't have to be elaborated. Nevertheless, the summary of all the trauma I'd been through to just "stuff" made it annoying. It was apparent he never even had the chance to experience that "stuff", mostly thanks to me. Sheltered. Protected like a cub in the forest. Part of me wishes that I was a cub, too. But because I wasn't, I was able to see things as they were. Dan still defending Greg on his deathbed made him stink, but of the protection he received. It almost made me question if we'd even been through the same "stuff" together.

OK. You looked at it again. You wanna come up with a decision now? It seemed obvious, yet not quite at the same time, what I had to do. Still, I forced my mind into deep thought. About whether I was ready to get all those secrets dug up.

I couldn't hear anything outside the car, so I was thankful for the quiet, peaceful environment around me. Unlike what was going through my head. Personal dilemmas and past feelings were dug up and weighed. My mind had long waded deep into the pros and cons, the sacrifices I'd have to give, and what I'd get in return. Either way, I went about things, I was going to sacrifice something. The more I thought about it, the less I wanted to go. Just too much pain had occurred. Above all, the air conditioning blasted wet, cold air into my nostrils. *Why does it smell?*

At the end of all the deliberation, I sighed. My brain had settled on a decision. I was going to do this. To find out if anything was left for me to salvage. If I could find out the "Why". *Maybe I can stop the nightmares.* If this could be a way for the voices in my head to shut up, I needed it. I couldn't let them haunt me anymore.

But I knew it was not for Greg. *Never.*

As I set aside the computer and started the car, I muttered a silent prayer to god. Not one in particular, just any god that existed, who was up there and sympathized with my situation. For comfort. Maybe for some luck, so that I wouldn't lose anything I hadn't lost already.

I really hope I don't lose anything else.

Beginning

I held my hands up and shielded my pupils. The lights. Hints of blunt-force trauma forked its way to my head. I looked away, though the harsh blue light synonymous with Chicago from the windows didn't help much.

I shuffled back, into the darkness. Almost allergic to anything but. I looked around my surroundings, unaware of where I was.

There was an advertisement for a hotel plastered up on one of the walls. A projector screen was right next to it, sitting without use. Tables with cheap cloth and even cheaper candles were pushed off to the side to make room for a red carpet that ran through the middle of the room, all the way up to the projector. Flower petals littered the walkways. Most of the tables had their chairs relocated to either side of the carpet, all once again facing the projector.

In the back with the tables that still had chairs, sitting and chatting among the small collection of our mutual friends were Robin and her wife. Happy, yet wary at the same time. Robin's bright blue dress went effortlessly along with the blue-highlight aesthetic she always maintained in her hair. The yellow heels did their job as well. Her wife had on a dress and heels. Similar colors, not exact but enough to cause comments from everyone else at the wedding.

A sharp, deep, breath of remembrance filled my mouth. *It'd been a long time since I dreamed this dream.*

Robin's dad forbade their wedding. So, she resorted to moving the location here to Chicago, a decent flight length away from her family's influence. She'd been stressed the night before, worrying that he still might do something on their wedding day.

Her wife said something out of earshot. Robin turned and laughed, that easy and carefree face returning to her once more.

If I dreamed this dream before, then she was behind me right now.

"They seem happy." A voice from behind pointed out. The room and everything in it seemed to warm up. Even the blue haze from the windows disappeared for the time being.

I didn't have to turn to know who said it, but I did anyway.

Shannon. The girl that made every movie "It-Girl" jealous. The girl with personality leagues above any movie adaptation of the "It-Girl". The girl with a unique genuine - and actual - personality. The girl in a beautiful blue satin dress. The girl who didn't need a blue satin dress to look beautiful. *She didn't.*

Her hand, was sifting through her hair, showcased her multi-colored family bracelet, whose meaning would endlessly perplex me.

She always perplexed me. Even with something as simple as her face. One I'd once yearned to wake up to. With hair that I wished lay gently on my skin.

The temptation to form memories with her that would never be tainted arrived. The temptation to push her away and forget every memory I had made did too. In a life where I did my best to forget everything, she was the one I tried to forget the most. *You never could.*

A different perplexity entered then entered the room with us upon my realization. Her blue eyes weren't directed to me. They were staring at . . . me.

A severe questioning began to occur as I began to register that version of me that stood in front of me, taking in the attention that Shannon gave him with a hidden giddiness. *This was new.* His hair showed evidence that he still cared enough to take care of it. He had no beard.

The newlyweds got up from their table and made their way to the exit. They moved and lit up the area in a distracting joyous manner, with no care about the lack of pace with which they moved. I took a step back, feet still echoing its mind's dazedness. When Robin and her posse reached me and Shannon, they cut themselves in half and filtered around us. Almost as if we had this forcefield, impenetrable to all.

I had to reconfigure my mind before my headache elevated to an untold extreme. *They. Not we. Him. Not me.*

Their eyes couldn't help but meet through the contained chaos. Awkward smiles surfaced.

Robin's face loomed in front of him. A whisper. "Enjoy yourself." She and her wife then strode their way to the door at a blistering pace. Whether that was supposed to make him hopeful for some alone time with Shannon or to make me wince in pain, I wasn't sure.

All the noise left the room with everyone else when the door closed. There were only three people left in the meeting hall: me, me, and Shannon. All stuck to the ground.

Shannon tore apart her attention from the door and met his eyes again. I looked into hers, trying to figure out what was stuck in there that caused me such anguish. I couldn't help but see the stars woven into the blue.

Robin never failed to drive it home that we were perfect together during high school. It didn't matter, as no matter how many times I tried to spend some time with her, or how many hours Robin spent trying to match us up, I'd never even get to talk to her.

A forcefield was around her, constantly omitting me. Shannon's friends always grouped around her, every single second of every day. If I wanted to see what she thought about something, my queries were answered by them. Almost as if I wasn't worthy enough to be graced by her speech.

Junior prom. I couldn't help but stare - along with a few other guys - at just how carefree she was at prom. How attractive whatever she did was, even as she messed up the lyrics to the songs playing over the speakers. I wanted in some of that infectious fun. *Badly.*

For about ten minutes her friends had abandoned her. She was sitting on a table at the edge of the dance floor. Legs swinging, eyes looking around, and waiting for someone to talk to her.

Shannon later told me that her friends never thought that she could make her own decisions. Combined with her parent's approval of them, the possibility of any move of mine working was high. *I could've saved her.* Yet I was always worried about doing something wrong back then. Making the wrong decision. Before I successfully talked myself into the fact that I had a chance with her, she was gone. I was frustrated that she chose that moment, out of the ten minutes, when I was actually about to talk to her, to walk away.

It wasn't the first time. It wouldn't be the last.

She got a boyfriend at the tail end of junior year. Chosen by her parents. It didn't matter. Her perfect surroundings and tailored life began to make me envious near the end. Immature as I was, the jealousy even induced some actual rage within me. Amongst the other rage I felt towards my naivety. The rage made it easier when I left. Those feelings went away, and she drifted into my subconscious.

He didn't realize the loose end he left behind until that moment. *This moment?* Even with all we went through after this fateful meeting, the youthful innocence, and naivety I'd contained around her that'd made life easier now returned.

I felt myself back up, the fear inside resurfacing and evoking a physical response. "Shit," I muttered. To myself, but louder than I wanted it to be. I looked around. But no one batted an eye.

I sat down in a random chair and stared at the impossibility of this scenario. An impossibility I hadn't realized up until that point, as I saw the pores on her face as surreal. Astonishment, that my brain had managed to create such a unique simulation. It felt real. *Painfully real.*

Meanwhile, he smiled. This wasn't high school anymore. The newfound confidence - though it often crossed over into arrogance - was something he could use to great effect here. "Didn't expect you to be here." His fingers adjusted his cufflinks with a virtuosity that suggested they were reaching under his skin with its silky tendrils, almost as silky as his voice.

"Yeah." She agreed, "After you left, I didn't think I'd be seeing you again. No one did." I resisted the urge to bring back the pain that caused my premature departure, or any such reminder of it. Yet her face morphed into something of confusion like my very presence wasn't possible. But then she regained her smile.

He shrugged. "Well, there wasn't much left back there anyway. Besides my family. My Mom." *You.* I could almost hear his thoughts. *Or it was me thinking of them at the same time.* Pretty soon, the light wasn't the only thing giving me a migraine.

Shannon smiled once more, though this time it was forced, a feeble attempt to make this conversation more than just small talk. "Well, do you want to just stand around awkwardly or do you want to sit down?" She gestured over to any empty table.

The comment surprised me a little. *Like she actually cared enough to stop and talk to me.*

Stop there. Don't give yourself that hope. I remembered repeating that once more in my mind. Nevertheless, he smiled back.

A certain transfixion continued to keep me rooted in the chair. Curious, my mind was, to see where this all began.

The curiosity disappeared with ease. I couldn't help but get irritated by how long I sat watching the two talk. I was surprised then too, to the point where I was almost timing how long she was sitting beside me, and how many glasses of champagne we went through. I'd always imagined time alone with her, with no one stopping me from loving her. No one trying to convince me otherwise either. But I never thought those desires would come true in this lifetime. I'd dreamt about it so long that I was convinced it'd stay a dream.

The conversation flashed by in a blur. An actual blur. The memory before me sped up until our mouths and actions were exaggerated and cartooned.

The audio was muted too. Like someone sat on the remote. But I knew what was said. Entire epics about our lives were summarized in a few short paragraphs. We laughed, and our glasses clinked often. We joked about our past lives. Our futures. Even our present state. She joked about how guys thought that facial hair made them look cool when in reality a lot of girls hate it. I laughed at that and thanked myself for shaving earlier that day.

Her eyes remained stuck on me, in fascination. *For some reason.*

The memory gradually decelerated. "Well good for you." She raised her glass.

"Where do you work?" He asked.

Shannon nodded. "Well, right now I'm just interning. Trying to get my act together and see if this is something I want. Plus, I'm currently working to get my master's." At that, he smiled. I got my master's the year before this encounter. It was that tiny boyhood jealousy coming to fruition like I had finally gotten the best of her in something.

"Of course, you probably already got yours." That inner jealousy died then and there. Those words, simple and sincere, made my feelings just feel wrong. I never wanted to see her as someone capable of such wrongdoings to me again.

Shannon began twisting open a new bottle of champagne that had sat in a bucket at the edge of the table, hoping for some usage. I watched as she executed some magical maneuvers with effortless ease until the pop echoed throughout the room.

If Robin were by my side and it was still high school, I would've leaned into her ear and said, "She's so hot." I knew I would because I did the very same at the most menial of tasks she did. Robin would then smack me and make fun of what Shannon did later in the day when no one was watching.

Shannon motioned the bottle to him, snapping me out of the past. He waved her off. "You don't have to be nice."

She nodded, taking a sip straight out of the bottle. "No, I'm serious. You were one of the smart ones back-" A nod behind her. "You know." Her mouth and face contorted in an unholy way. "Yeah, let's not drink that."

He smiled at the remark and considered her thoughts. "I mean I had good grades, but you had a bit more emotional intelligence." I figured that a compliment might make her sit here longer. Only I saw the desperation, not Shannon and not even me.

With a lack of knowing how to react, she smiled. In a flash, her awkwardness and her disinterest returned to force her eyes to the windows.

He knew that he couldn't let the disinterest overrun her, so he grabbed the bottle and took a sniff. The nasty aroma hit and the gag reflex announced itself to Shannon.

Her face was straight for a second. A laugh began to overtake her, and soon we were both engaged in the affair. I didn't know why, but I followed along anyway. Amidst the short breaths, I plugged the champagne bottle closed and put it back in the metal bucket with a quiet slosh from the water inside. Just like that, our faces were straight.

Yet they weren't. A smile spread across her face. "Told you so."
She shook her head in pure joy. I remembered the thought that became
buried in me. *Was she flirting?*

"Well, it's gonna take more than that to get me to listen to you."
Probably not.

Right? "Yeah? What'll it take?" The way she looked at him was
scrutinized even more by his bulging eyes, straining to spot a hint of
anything.

Without waiting for an answer, he said it. "A date would work."
Seriously? Aubrey? Joseph? Are you really ready for it all? If it happens again?
Yes. At the moment, I didn't realize the extent I'd be stretched.
If I did, I'd say no.

"I liked you. A lot." She opened her mouth to respond, but my
words stopped her train of thought. "You can ask Robin. I don't think it
was bad, though. Otherwise, she would've handed my ass back to me."
More silence. "I never acted on it. But I think I'm done staying quiet."
Before long, the words tumbled out of his mouth.

Looking at it at the moment, I realized it also served as a
goodbye along with the obvious love declaration. We weren't close
enough for one, but for me it was necessary. *Just in case.* No matter the
delusions, I knew she wouldn't like me. It wouldn't change, no matter
what. It was as though a certain side of me wanted to come to terms with
it.

Her face was frozen. For a long time. A smile escaped her mouth
but disappeared just as fast. Her eyes seemed cloudier and more aware.
Like a seriousness was awakened within her.

"Oh."

She looked down at her feet, through the table. I could almost
hear them shuffling along the carpet. "How long-"

"High School."

Shannon nodded. "Now I see why you ran out of whatever room
I walked into." She chuckled. *I should too.* He did.

The smile then dissipated from his face once the necessity left
the room. He waited for her to leave too or throw that awful champagne
in his face. His worst suspicions would be confirmed, even if he had a part
in creating those suspicions.

15

She stayed put for the time being. "If I'm being honest, I don't know."

"I mean you're nice and all," Luckily, I never gave her a reason to dislike me. "But liking you as something more," A pause. "I just don't know." She looked at the windows, this time more consciously than before.

Fortunately, I didn't have to look for signals for long. "Alright. How long are you in town for again?"

It was silent.

Then the thoughts arrived. *Holy shit! Who saw that coming?* He shrugged, though, trying to play it cool. "Like I said, my job's here." Even though the giddiness inside him almost caused an eruption. Back then, not scaring her away became my main commonplace goal. "So as long as I keep that, I guess." A smile sneaked its way past my thoughts.

"Right." Shannon scrunched her mouth. "You're kinda lucky." *I was.* "The place I'm interning at is only an hour and a half away. I have a month until that ends, and I'll have to find something somewhere else. We can go out for dinner. See what happens."

"Well, what if I'm a rapist or something?" *Stupid. Way too creepy.* Not as sarcastic as I'd hoped for.

Nevertheless, she shook her head. "I guess we'll find out. But you probably expected something along those lines. Didn't you?"

He smiled and let out a short chuckle. She nodded once more. I deduced it was more playful this time around. *Or was it?*

My surroundings crumbled, and I was soon in a black void. No thoughts dominated my head, choosing instead to scream in terror as my stomach turned over and over and over. My fists were still glued to the chair I'd decided to sit in. It didn't want to let go.

A burst of light. The void was no longer devoid of color. A barrage of images replaced it. Different from the scene I was just in. But I remembered these all too well after a few seconds of thinking.

Tears flew out of my eyes, though I wasn't sure if it was because of my fall and the thunderous air that'd decided to roar past me. Or the regret as the images conjured up the memories and thoughts attached to it.

A skyscraper-sized Robin, in her apartment back in New Mexico, hunched over her phone.

She'd helped me plan the conversation topics I was going to bring up. One for the appetizers, a couple for the main course, and one for the dessert, if I still had her attention. She went over every aspect of what I was going to do - as well as what I wasn't going to do - with meticulousness, even though we were hours away from each other. Our phone bill was no doubt reaching the ceiling, but I wanted it to be perfect. I even thought about making a set of notecards.

My sedan and its faded gray exterior.

I had picked her up in my car for our first date night. She was staying with a friend. We drove in silence, and I talked only to say an awkward joke or two.

Her face. That smile.

It was the sky. Distorted and elongated. I was still screaming. Whatever thought surfaced in my mind about that drive, appeared in front of me. A car crash we'd encountered along the way now was all around me, a cop car at my legs and a flipped-over sedan at my head. Only for a moment, however, as I fell further.

A plate full of spaghetti which took up the entire sky.

It was a small Italian place. While we - mostly her - were eating, I couldn't think. The scenarios I played to myself at night, and the ones Robin trained me with flew away in the hot spring breeze. I thought it was all over. But Shannon whispered something to our waiter, who came along a couple of minutes later with a set of children's menus. Half the date was us laughing over the children's games and their triviality. I had no idea that we could bond over something so silly, but the spontaneity worked. It was a dumb sort of love I didn't know she was capable of. The questions as to whether she was the same person I saw from afar, or if she'd stay if she knew everything, arrived. It was valid. Having someone who used to look at me and see nothing that turns around and suddenly sees something. But all the words we exchanged felt warmer than anything I experienced before. Warmer than all the intrusive thoughts. Suffice it to say, the evening went well. I had even made her laugh a few times. It wasn't until a few minutes after I dropped her back at her apartment, that I realized how important she was to me, how I used to hold so close to my heart the fact that I'd managed to make her laugh.

We left after she found a hair in her lobster. *Stay. Order dessert. Maybe another plate of spaghetti. Ignore the hair. You won't get another first date.* My thoughts had no choice but to stay in my head while I spiraled deeper and deeper through the air. The chair was long gone. But I kept falling, my screaming following close behind.

An old Ferris wheel that creaked with enormity and two lonely riders.

A couple of days later, she called me to go to the state fair with her. It was in the middle of my lunch break. But I didn't care, because she cared enough to call. We forgot our responsibilities and met up in a desolate spot smack dab in the middle of the banking district. That day was the last day the fair was open so many of the shops ran out of their treats. Dust flew in the air when we walked on the metal steps and ramps. It was still fun. The creaking of the Ferris wheels and the other various instruments almost formed an entire orchestral concert, and we were the only ones who truly experienced it. It was the first time I could smile. Truly smile, without having to ponder what tribulation life would throw at me to wipe the smile off my face.

The secret smile Shannon shot me as she walked back into the apartment with her friend standing outside, her gleaming white teeth filling up my entire eyesight.

Just as it started, the day ended. That smile added a climax to the wonderful day I thought was unattainable. It was the first smile that made me truly melt inside. It was still a bit awkward between us, yet it felt like we both were aware of it. Almost accepting it in a way. *Our own way.*

My new flip-phone, its keypad directly in my minuscule eyes.

I decided to christen it by calling her for a third date the week after. She accepted. The fourth came soon after. Two weeks passed as we found more excuses to meet each other, each more spontaneous than the last.

A crowded movie theater, a luscious park, and a rundown building.

Images of each flew to the sky in speedy succession. Like so, the meeting place varied from time to time. Before the end of the month, we met more times than I could count. If we were preoccupied, our schedules changed to make some more time. The more we met, the more we chased that time. I noticed that she laughed more around me, the more we found ourselves near each other. I almost thought she was growing more comfortable. We even held hands as we waited in line for our movie tickets. It was the first time someone held my hand, and I wanted to scream for joy from the rooftops. The race we went on to catch more fleeting moments like those grew more desperate as the month drew to a close. That was when her internship was terminated.

The colors around me settled into an actual environment. Once enough details had been filled, I was decelerated until my legs were safely perched on solid ground. Instead of the boiling swirling blood weaving its magic panic as it should've, my blood settled when it realized where I was now.

The hug.

Shannon's unusually hot apartment. Her friend had stepped outside to smoke. I was happy initially that we were alone, but the phone call about her termination had to interrupt us. It hit her hard. So, I hugged her. It was a split-second decision. Maybe to show her what she meant to me. Shannon's arms didn't complete the embrace for a heart-stopping second. But she didn't resist me, and she didn't reach for the pepper spray. When her arms finally came around my side, my insides froze, yet turned themselves inside out simultaneously. The room grew even warmer.

The kiss.

We pulled away. Without hesitation, she flew onto her toes and pecked my cheek. Settling back down onto her heels, I saw tears in her eyes still. But a wide grin was on her face. A grin I'd always hoped to see. A hope I'd lost for a long time, which ruined me. I didn't think any of the butterflies and all the other insects in my stomach would go away at that moment, but her next words accomplished the impossible. "You gonna just stand there or what?" Everything was empty inside of me.

The kiss.

It was my first ever, so there was nervousness that I'd be bad at it. But her lips were soft. Comfy, even. I didn't want to stop. My right hand went up to her cheek, and I pulled her as close as she could get to me. Her arms grabbed me and pulled me to the wall. I was half-worried when I heard the thud of her head, but she didn't relent.

The kiss.

We pulled away. Just a few inches. "I won't leave you like they did. If you still wanna take me as a chance. I know your worth. Even if they don't. I'll look out for you." *Don't fall for that. Please.*

Silence. "Our trial tun ends today." I hoped that she didn't notice that.

"Yeah. I noticed. So do you still wanna give me a chance?"

She didn't speak for a few seconds. Finally, she broke the silence. "Everything you just said about my worth?"

"Yeah?"

"You beat me to it."

"Oh."

"Yeah. You expected something along those lines. Didn't you?"

"Why do you keep saying that?" I let out a snort before sighing it away. "I mean, as long as you did."

"I did."

I pulled away a bit more so I could see her beautiful face in its whole, tucked her hair behind her ears, and kissed her again. But at the same time, I would've been equally content if we did just stand there in each other's arms. Breath on each other's faces. Her eyelashes touched my skin.

We stopped when we realized that her roommate's dog was watching us.

After we escaped our lips, our faces stayed lingering a few centimeters apart for a few moments. Our eyes were deeply entranced with each other. With a few minutes of intense thought, Shannon came back with a plan to stay with me while she found something permanent.

That was the deciding factor. It was enough to convince myself that I could begin to love her again. *I'm ready to go through it all again.*

My eyes fluttered. For a moment, though, I didn't know where I was, but the confusion subsided fast enough for me to finally pay attention to the honking. I jammed the accelerator and sped through the intersection before the light turned red once more.

With a few glances at my surroundings, I figured out where I was. I was about to take the highway to the interstate. I saw the sign a bit further up the road. Out of the corner of my eye, a gray circle appeared on my phone's map. Even it seemed hesitant. My mind threatened to use that as an excuse not to go. But I stormed forward regardless.

Half a mile before the exit. After that, I knew where I was going. It was more or less a straight shot. Whatever I forgot could be easily remembered with a bit of digging into the details of every little bit that I'd gone through to get here.

Just a quarter of a mile away. After a few seconds, I'd crossed it.

That evening at Robin's wedding was the first time I felt true purpose. *She saw me and still said yes.* That was a bigger moment for me than my proposal.

The proposal. We were on vacation near Edisto Beach. The entire weekend, I couldn't shake the negativity that was just 3 hours away, so Shannon dragged me out of the resort at one - disguising it as a late-night coffee run - for an impromptu visit to the beach. The raging waters and clear night sky had their beauty elevated only by the uninterrupted moon. I couldn't think of a better place to pop the question. Privately. Surrounded by beauty. *Asking her.* Unfortunately, the sign that warned people away from climbing on the slippery rocks was too dark to see. I fell into the ocean and the romantic atmosphere was drowned out by her laughing. Yet, as I crawled back onto the beach, with the crackling eggshells under my feet, I took her breath away when I asked her. She said yes then too. *For some reason.*

Even though we'd interacted before, Robin's wedding was the night we met. The one everyone talked about. *The question was, did she want to go back to it like I did?*

I had no idea why that meeting, that interaction with Shannon, and what followed afterward came up in my mind. I often didn't. Especially in such a vivid way. *Why did it all feel so real this time?*

I found temporary solace in the fact that it was over. Still, I had a feeling I was going to encounter more such instances more often on the way down.

I crossed over to the second lane from the left without much else thought. Once in the middle of the highway, I leaned back as much as I could in my seat.

My senses took a pause. All the thinking, doubts, and insecurities ceased to exist. Hours passed in seconds. I liked that about driving. I could've easily flown, but flying didn't have that sense of ease. That sixth sense, where my mind was given all the creative liberty to wander the fields I passed, yet still struggled to remember the past.

My right hand juggled my phone to shuffle up my Shoegaze playlist. Turning up the volume - the car didn't have Bluetooth - I tossed the phone into the passenger seat and the pile of fuck-all.

The road began to slip under the hood of the car. I often looked in the rearview mirror to see just how much distance I covered. Pretty soon, the Chicago skyline was a thing of the past, almost far enough to become one with the clouds.

I didn't realize you were stupid enough to fall for that bitch. Out of nowhere, the thought arose. My brain was humbled by the venom and bitterness it contained. Desperate to get my mind off it and prevent any other savage thoughts from flooding my conscience one more, I looked out, hoping to find something distracting in the landscape.

Roads, cities, counties, and states were passed, but nothing was worth noting. There were still no trees. *I could've sworn there were more trees.*

As evening turned to night, the number of headlights ramming their neon red in my face disappeared, and my lone, yellow headlights illuminated the road in front of me.

My thoughts took the empty backseat - with the clutter from the opened suitcase - as the serene experience washed over me.

A Question's Fragility

But the thoughts soon realized that they had enough, and the memories decided to plague my mind again.

The warm-plastic water didn't help the drowsiness. *Coffee would've definitely helped.* My eyes began to run away from my grasp, down the straight sleep-inducing highway. My last thoughts as the steering wheel escaped my grasp, and my feet lost the pedals.

I landed on solid ground. An empty forest lay around me. The fragility of the silence made us feel intrusive, similar to someone encroaching on another's private property. Thankfully, the leaves under my shoes didn't crunch.

The sun shone on us a harsh grayish-blue, with absolutely no protection from the canopy. A harsh grayish-blue that was easy to remember.

Finally. Something I can enjoy. This was one of my favorite memories. One of the only dreams I wanted to remember every single detail of, even if I couldn't bring myself to dream it more often. The only one left that wasn't tainted.

Some movement to my right helped me resist the urge to still look up at the blinding light. There I was. Little Me chewing the string from my sweatshirt and in deep thought on the trail in front of him. Mom walked along with us, crunching more leaves. I couldn't help but gaze at her with my mouth open. It was the first time I'd seen her in a long time. In this dream she was young. *Immensely beautiful.* Anyone with eyes could see the pure soul she held within. She saw me staring, and she smiled. "How's it going?"

My throat collapsed momentarily with the thought that she saw Adult Me. My windpipe rebuilt itself as I realized she was talking to Little Me.

He shrugged. His eyes were glazed with a weary face that contained a slight hatred. "It's going. I'm just tired. And boored." He murmured the last part, with the desire not to talk screaming for him.

Mom shook her head, her brown hair ruffling around with ease. "Alright. Just missing a big opportunity." The bait was laid.

Little Me's eyes were kindled, a sparkle noticeable. Her invitations were always tough to ignore, even if I was in the worst of moods. "What do you mean?"

She shrugged back. "I'm just saying, there's absolutely nothing in this forest. Think about it. Besides these old trees, it's just you and me. No one else can hear you. You can talk about anything." She dramatically whispered the last part.

Little Me stared back at her, clueless. Mom sighed, staying silent for a couple of seconds to think of another way to approach the situation. "Ok look. Your father and I have been talking." Her tone grew serious. No more happy-go-luckiness. "You've been a little too silent these past few days."

"No." The pessimism won. I couldn't help but think there was a reason this dream came up now, after so long. The way things were going in my life, I couldn't help but see this dream getting dragged through the mud. *No.* I'd heard enough. I refused to be trapped.

Leaving the two behind, I started to sprint back the way we were walking. My feet hurt in the dress shoes that twisted and turned alongside the uneven rolling hills. My white shirt was turning not-white with the amount of branches I was hitting. The cold inserted itself into my eyes, and tears started falling out with ease.

No matter how much I ran, the trail kept getting longer and longer. I couldn't see anything past the trees. No sign of civilization. With a stop that threatened to break my knees, I halted to lean up against a tree nearby. My chest could no longer take the physical stress. My right knee, which hadn't flared up for years, hammered itself with a thousand tiny hammers. My breath was running away from my mouth as well with tiny white wisps. I looked all around for another way out. "Maybe if I cut across. Take another trail." I tried not to let the intrusive thoughts distract me from my search. Yet nothing else was to be seen.

I blinked. Mom and Little Me were back in front of me, walking. "Fuck me." After a long silence, I came to terms with the fact that there was nothing else to be done except catch up with them. My eyes still drifted back onto the tiny white wisps that - unlike me - had managed to escape what was going to happen next.

Little Me's face, now back beside my waist, had returned to a state burdened by a lack of energy. At the time, both Mom and Greg were stuck to Dan, feeding him, changing his diapers, shaking him to sleep, and doing whatever else they were doing. Unfortunately, Little Me knew whenever they did so when the noise filtered with ease through the already-thin walls of our home. Once awake, his neck made itself sore by craning into various positions, trying to reconjure said sleep.

"Really? You're still gonna stay silent?" Mom's smile crept back to her lips and all else faded away. Little Me couldn't help but laugh. I didn't know what was funny about it, and even I almost chuckled.

"It's nothing Mom. I'm just tiiired." Little Me yawned, as if on cue.

"Really?" She asked. "Why are you tiiired?" Her blue eyes sparkled with a curiosity that compelled Little Me to shout it to the world. Even I felt perplexed by her eyes. A perplexion that wanted me to spill my guts as well. "I am tired Mom," I whispered.

"It's okay." Mom turned to me and smiled.

I blinked and she was back to pretending that I didn't exist. *What?*

Little Me sighed before I could think of anything else. "Weeeelll, Dan's being annoying, and every time y'all feed or change his diaper, I can hear it in my room. And in school, my wife's not talking to me anymore."

Mom was ready to supply me with advice regarding the first problem, but it was interrupted by her laugh and the shake of her head about the second problem. "Your wife. Huh."

"SEE? This is exactly why I didn't tell you guys." Little Me stretched that last word out as I let my arms both rise and fall in a state of desperate exasperation.

25

I winced even harder. I never knew exactly how childish I was until now. Yet Mom just kept smiling. No matter what I'd do, she'd always smile.

Mom realized my emotional state and morphed her face into something straight. It was amazing how she was able to change just for me. As she shook her head in the blistering cold, her brown hair whipped around her some more. She took a deep breath. "Ok. So, what's my Daughter-in-law called?"

"Gracie." Little Me didn't know what a daughter-in-law was back then, but he told her his wife's name anyway.

"Ooh." She sounded delighted, but I wasn't able to tell if it was genuine or fake. It mattered very little to my opinion of her. "That's a pretty name." Little Me smiled. So did I. *She knew me so well.*

"And how long do you guys plan to be together?" Her tone started to change into a more playful suggestion. The pupils in her eyes seemed to dance in the brisk climate, and her hair continued to hop along with her joyful stride.

Little Me kept smiling. "Maybe forever." How naive.

"But isn't she the girl that's going to be in Florida next year?" Little Me's feet stopped, so I did too. His eyes trembled as his brain struggled to reach the possibility that it had forgotten. The foolishness of his actions became abysmally deafening to Little Me. Said foolishness began to flow to his eyes as Mom started to giggle once more, walking past both of us.

But she stopped as soon as she saw the first tear. Little Me closed his eyes in shame at caring for the wrong person so easily. *Get used to that bud.*

"Hey. Hey, listen." Mom walked back to kneel to his face. There was an awkwardness in her movements, grabbing his shoulders with a massive hesitance.

Only when she was certain that his eyes were closed, did she let out one tear. Just one, as if that was all she allowed herself. With a smile, any trace of it disappeared. Any indication of why it was there in the first place did too.

Mom wiped his face of any impurities. I remembered her hand was frigid, and if I hadn't known better, I would've thought that it was frozen.

Her arms tried hugging him. She didn't. Despite being a mom, she never hugged Dan and me before. Almost like she couldn't. *Or she didn't want to.*

Stop. Don't. He opened his eyes again and looked up as she put her glove on. She walked ahead and waited. "Girls are just trouble, man. Just stay away from them, 'cause they're always up to no good."

He looked up and sniffled. "But Mom, you're a girl." The distraction worked when I realized our legs were working once more.

"Hmm. Really? Didn't know that." She looked back and smiled. The smile of a musician, who'd manipulated their instrument to their favorite melody. Both versions of us smiled. *When was the last time I smiled?*

"But I'm glad that you told me. Whatever you need, I'm your man. Don't think trees can speak, so they won't tell anyone obviously. And I'll take it to my grave." She assured me.

"Your grave." I muttered. *Almost like she knew.*

"What about anyone else around us? What if they were close enough to hear?" Little Me asked, looking around in the sudden fear and realization that came along with the fact that his voice was carrying along with the freezing wind.

She just shrugged. "I guess we'll never know." Mom smiled. "There's a lot of stuff I haven't told you guys too." She didn't say that before.

A mist of unfamiliarity came over the vision. "Like what?" Little Me implored, his hand now holding a stick. Long and thick, but not too long and thick. The right size for a sword. His hands grasped the thickest end and started to swing it on trees. Slowly at first, gauging its durability. After a few whacks, the stick began being wheeled into anything that appeared tangible.

One of the strikes went straight through me as if I wasn't present. I touched my waist and was stopped by my flesh. The perplexity of this scenario just kept confusing me.

I looked up. Mom's face morphed into concern. Concern, though I wasn't sure it was for Little Me's playfulness. I could tell by the way she pursed her lips that there was a temptation to use it as an excuse not to answer. But she didn't want to let me know that. She warned, in a half-serious, half-joking tone. "Stop before you hurt yourself."

Little Me pretended not to hear her. "If you tell me, I'll stop." He smiled, trying to shoot back that same face that'd manipulated him moments before. It wasn't the same. *Nothing was.*

The very tip of Little Me's branch, which held many similarities to the tip of a snake's tongue shattered mid-stride against a lonely rock and shot out splinters in all directions. We still kept walking, as I waded deeper into the unknown waters with each precarious step.

Both of us looked at her face at the same time. The sun bouncing off of the multitudinous clouds prevented us both from fully seeing her eyes. The mistiness and uncertainty were only seen by me. Her attention was on something far off in the distance. The focus at which she stared, the intensity in her pupils threatened to scare me even now.

She took a breath, not deep but long. Like someone preparing to go underwater. When Little Me registered this, he stopped swinging the branch. It seemed important, what she was about to say.

Except it wasn't. "It was a few months back. Dad stayed behind when we went to Grandpa's place for Christmas. Do you remember it?"

Confused, Little Me nodded. Even though nobody saw me, I nodded in remembrance as well. A blizzard had hit us. The fact that the town had finally seen snow after so long was momentous. I played a lot that day. So did the whole of Gaines Elementary, evident by the fact that it was as though they were unable to stop talking, the way they spent the whole week afterward bragging about what they did. *I wonder if they remembered that now. Do they even remember me?*

Little Me could barely stay on my heels, his blood no doubt pumping. Pretty soon, he bounced while rambling through shortened breaths about how many people he hit with snowballs. "It was amazing! So much snow! Why would I forget?"

She ignored my question with a slight head nod as if she had a very good reason to forget that day. That face went away with a smile. "Yeah. You got so tired you went to sleep at seven. I had to carry you upstairs." She said the last part like she was in pain.

A small stream suddenly sprinted up to us. It wasn't more than a few inches deep, but it was treacherously wide. The rocks tumbling and rolling down the stream showed no faults, no divides. Just perfection. One trickled off the water and to my feet. Little Me had to let the stick go as Mom grabbed his hand. A slight sadness hit his face. "You're gonna have to get used to that too." I muttered.

We all crossed the stream, step by step on the bigger rocks that seemed like they would stay. At least the two of them did. I just drifted along through the water.

When I looked down, the water that flew past my ankles left no impression on my dress pants. The cold water that managed to make its way into my toes was numbed. *Am I not supposed to pay attention to this stuff?*

I crossed over to the other side of the stream moments ahead of them. Looking back, I wished Mom was there to help me even though it wasn't necessary for a grown man like me. Her hands were soft, yet strong. I couldn't help but feel safe whenever I held them.

As we jumped over to the other end of the stream, Little Me grabbed a rock and threw it into the trees with a triumphant roar. Mom giggled, and that joyousness returned. I could tell she was relieved. For some reason.

The rock hit a couple of trees with thunderous smacks before skidding across the frozen leaves to a stop.

A few more steps and Little Me looked up at the end of the hill up ahead, which had a rickety wooden bench at its apex. As soon as I saw it, my legs had pronounced that it would carry the weight of the world with it. I could even feel my mind not carrying the simulation well. The tendrils of the reconstruction still going strong, though, as if this was necessary. *What was about to happen?*

That same fatigue didn't encroach on Mom's mind. Something else did. Her eyes were glazed, and that intriguing figure in the distance commanded her attention once more, not concerned about me, or whatever roots spawned beneath her. "You know, maybe you shouldn't have gone to sleep that day." She wondered out loud, her hands wandering around with more intensity now.

But Little Me's eyesight was caught by a tree. Its older bark, which stood out in the sea of white, made it much easier to notice. He didn't think much of her words.

I shook my head. "Listen to her."

"You would've knocked some sense in me. Made me realize that I didn't want to take that sip." She continued. Little Me's mind was still focused on the tree and its apparent elegance. He stopped at the tiny wooden bench at the end of the hill and sat. His eyes didn't move from its focal point. Mom brought herself to a standstill too. I stayed standing with her, nervous about what would unfold. Nervousness that not only came from the fact that I didn't exactly remember this, but from whether this actually happened.

"Grandpa was the one. He was the one that kept insisting and insisting. One can't hurt." The last thought of hers was spoken in a ghastly whisper.

"Listen to her." I knelt to Little Me and pleaded. The reality of my presence that wasn't present began to frustrate me. If I was here, in such detail, I knew there had to be a way to change whatever happened.

I started to truly sense what was hiding behind Mom's words. The purest pain without the slightest hint of mercy. I looked at her back and the open spot on the bench she neglected. Her increased heart rate and agitation that fermented her blood kept her upright. *I knew that feeling.* Walking around to untie some colossal invisible knot, she kept uttering to herself. *I knew that too.*

She drifted further and further away like her words did just out of my earshot. Fear started to set deep within me, and I couldn't bring myself to keep quiet. "Hey!" I yelled. No answer, or indication of my younger self even registering me. I waved my hand in front of his face. Now only the lack of hope entertained my brain.

The fear that set in moments ago began to affect Little Me, whose worry began to engulf his eyes. The peculiarity of Mom's behavior perplexed him more by the second as her antics elevated to new levels. "Mom, are you alright?"

"No, Cal I am not." She cursed herself. "Damn it. Why does it taste so good?" She looked me dead in the eyes, and with a quiet - yet booming - intensity continued. "I'm not alright. I'm scared that it's only going to get worse, and that it might affect you."

"Please. I'm scared." She kept looking at Little Me like she was expecting him to say something.

The trees started disappearing. My eyes followed the leaves that flew up into the sun. Except there was no sun. It'd disappeared, even though the light still shone on us three. Then that too started to fade. The tree that held Little Me's obsession started to bend and turn into darkness. The wind that affected only the leaves continued its whirlpool, sweeping the ones on the ground up into the sky.

I reached out to grab his shoulders in a last-last-ditch effort, trying to ignore the collapsing dream. The anger in me wanted to slap him out of the memory, which made the whiff through the air all the more impactful as I almost fell to the ground.

"But it tastes so good." Mom turned into a white haze.

I took a long hard look at Little Me before he left too. His stubborn impatient, immature mind refused to think anything else of those words, even if he could have.

The darkness took over for a couple of seconds before my mind flashed back to the present.

Raged blood pumped through my veins and into my heart at astonishing levels. The car had found itself on the road still. By some miracle. I looked at the sky just in time to see the incoming rain cloud. Ahead of me on the road was a sheet of water I was driving towards. In seconds, the water sprinted towards my car until enveloped me with an explosion of noise and a loss of control over the steering wheel.

I cursed as I swerved around a car wreck that had occurred just moments before, unbeknownst to my vision. I looked back at the torrent of water I splashed on the passengers who'd gotten out to assess the damage, somehow getting them even wetter.

Once I settled back into my comfort zone, my heart rate slowed. I found myself on the edge of the seat. My spine then eased itself back into the seat. The rain subdued itself to a less violent - but still violent -

patter on my windshield. I started the wipers. My hands were white on the steering wheel, but it didn't stop once I noticed it. The grit in my teeth was felt throughout my entire body.

Fucking hell. Another one. I thought all this would be over. I thought I still had some memories that could withstand the endless tainting of my mind. *Guess not.*

Mom always lived in me. But this was the first time I saw her in this light. For the life of me, I still couldn't figure out if it was all real. But what happened after that walk was undoubtedly tangible.

At first, she drank every Saturday. She assured us that it was just a way to release the stress she'd had over the week. She had to assure us more and more. Even though I was barely in the second grade, Greg's absences from his work forced me into the situation.

After a while, it was every Saturday and Sunday. Then, once it bled into the weekdays, it was out of her control. Guilt began to eat at me as I grew older and realized that I could've said something all those times she asked me for a can. I was glad I didn't remember those memories exactly as I did the others, or the guilt would've turned me acidic.

No. My thoughts heaved the blame off of me and onto Greg. All those absences. That was what forced all of Mom's stress onto me.

Poor, kindergarten me. Powerless, as I ever was.

The Beautiful Purgatory

Over the past few days, I'd challenged the fuel gauge, trying to see how far I could go before I had to refuel each time. Inside, I knew the car wouldn't handle any extra pressure. I knew I wouldn't either - my right knee flared up once more - yet I kept pushing anyway.

I had to. I couldn't drive at night anymore. The harsh reminders were too much, even if I sacrificed twelve or so hours. So, I usually pulled over to a rest stop and tried to utilize the break to its full extent. I couldn't do that either, my dawdling memories extending the night until I was too fatigued to think. By then, it'd be two or three. I'd wake up at seven, the opposite of energized. After making a quick stop for breakfast, I'd resume the rubber-burning pace on the highway.

But it wasn't until - out of the corner of my vision - the fuel gauge extended its exhausted orange tendrils in the form of a "Check Engine" light in a desperate effort for my attention that I decided to do something about it all. So, I took the next exit ramp, my eyes gazing at the green signs that popped up for an auto shop nearby. Of course, that other part of me wanted to go another five miles. Make more ground. Save some time. *Get it over with quicker.*

Idling to the traffic light, I was still considering doing so, when the car stopped short of the white line. When it sputtered to life for a few fleeting seconds, I pressed the accelerator as far down as it could and brought it to the shoulder. It then stopped completely. I slammed my hands into the wheel and cuss words flew out.

Now where? I scanned my surroundings, wondering if there was anything that could help me. By some miracle, I caught sight of an auto shop down the road from the exit ramp. *You're so lucky.* The more I thought about it, the more I saw how unlucky I was instead.

It was a push-able distance. Or so I thought until I got out and started to do so. A kind Samaritan pulled over, noticing my quiet struggle and I couldn't help but accept his guidance. A couple more came by and helped, which only embarrassed me more.

No one else occupied the exit, besides some onlookers giving me wicked glares. *Yeah. I hate how I look too.*

We eventually reached the auto shop, which in itself was also empty. Only one garage out of a row of five was filled. A couple of people grabbed the car - and my keys - from me to presumably set it up in one of the empty garages.

Before I could dish out a sheepish "thank you" to those who helped me, a lady appeared and told me to sit in the waiting area. The strangers had already walked off anyway, so I obliged.

Inside, there was a cold blue hue, which was peculiar considering the warm sunset developing outside. Nevertheless, I let the peculiarity leave my mind as it sat empty. For once it didn't wander. I just stared at the small chairs, piles of magazines on little nightstands, and a white desk with no receptionist without any real conviction or emotion. A welcome difference to my usual schedule.

It wasn't long before someone showed up, pushing open the side door from the reception area that entered the workspace. He was short but muscular. The cliche mechanic overalls were what he wore, with the brown blotches on his legs to complete the look. Red hair was all around his face, some going down all over his neck in a shoddy beard.

"Let's see what's going on here." I wasn't sure if he meant to have muttered it to himself, though it was loud enough for me to hear. But the mechanic then motioned with his arms for me to follow him into the workspace.

A smell of gasoline and otherworldly substances hit me as I crossed the doorway into the first garage, which held my car and a splendid view out into the surrounding landscape. With a few presses and maneuvers, he'd pushed the front side of the car off the ground with some webbed yellow mechanism. He then popped the front hood up and took a long hard look at my engine. *Something else I couldn't help but break.*

I didn't know why he brought me out into the garage, so I stood back against the wall and watched as he began to work, occasionally drifting my attention back out to the road. Besides the ramp leading back onto the highway and a scattering of fast-food places, everything was flattened with a layer of wheat that went as far as my eyes could wander.

The man, in just a few more minutes, wiped his hands on his already grimy pants with a conclusive flair. "All done." Soot and other smelly substances were on his face. I made sure to stay a few feet away from him. He listed the price, and my wallet released a ton of weight.

"Yeah, it wasn't too much." He started, as though he'd given me a discount. "Just pushed it too far."

A slight disappointment made its way from the recesses of my mind with the knowledge that my search wouldn't be delayed. I nodded and smiled back, not sure as to what else I was supposed to say. "It seems like you have to be somewhere." He gestured at me with a rag with a chuckle. "I don't see anyone dressed like you often." The rag was then put to rest on his shoulders before he walked off to a workbench.

I looked down. I was still wearing my white dress shirt - sleeves still folded - from the interview days ago. My black dress pants were clinging rather uncomfortably to my side. Nevertheless, I didn't want to change.

The mechanic picked up a wrench, not doing anything with it except examining it in the fading blue light around him. "You alright, bud?" An inquisitive look was on his face as he turned to me. I guessed that I didn't look in the best shape.

Or maybe he saw past my awkwardness. I didn't know how he did or why he wanted to know anything. So, I did what I always did. "Yeah." Sharp. Definite. I didn't want to raise any questions. *It was just easier that way.* The more people knew about me and my life, the more they tended to walk out of it. I didn't want to lose this stranger too, who was the first in a long time to ask me how I was.

The man nodded back. "I get that."

I smiled. Despite our total unfamiliarity, he felt genuine. His eyes sparkled yet didn't show emotion of any kind. A deep emptiness in his corneas. He walked off into the workspace, cleaning various messes here and there. Those hands of his moved in a trancelike state, and he didn't bother to acknowledge my now more awkward-growing presence.

Once everything looked more orderly, he grabbed a small bag and a folding chair off of a rack and set it up a few feet away from the opening of the garage.

The mechanic's gravelly hands disappeared inside the bag to pull none other than a six-pack. His fat fingers pried apart a can from the plastic binding, that crisp opening sound following soon after.

"We close in a couple of minutes." He took a few sips.

I didn't know what else to take that as except a cue to leave. Before I started walking back into the waiting room, however, he called back out to me. "You can stay if you want to. Pull up a chair. I have another six-pack." He turned around and his eyes soared around his garage. "Somewhere in here."

A pause. I didn't know why he invited me to join him and his solemn empty gaze over the stalks of wheat, which eerily chose not to move along with the slight wind. But the solemnity, when I looked at it again, seemed more at peace than empty. I need some peace. I wasn't sure if I had anything to say, but I grabbed the chair and set it up a few feet from him anyway. *Maintain the distance. Don't get closer.*

He fished out a beer and opened it for me. It was a yellow-colored can with a trout on it. I wasn't sure what species it was, but it was stuck on a bait of some sort. My brain racked itself trying to figure out which one I was.

As I took my first few sips, the warm feeling invaded my thoughts, suppressing them until my mind became empty.

But at once, Shannon's presence appeared alongside me, tingling my arm hair. I didn't have to imagine her face to see the inquisitive look that'd turn sour whenever she'd see me with alcohol in my hand. For a second, I almost felt her soft skin again. My mind reached into the nothingness, trying to find her untethered soul. *Bring her back to me. Please.*

The happiness and joy in her smile didn't leave just yet, feeding into my temporary desperation. But the twisted hope disappeared soon enough.

We sat in silence for a while. The awkwardness faded away into obscurity, and it became more familial, more amiable. Like we were two worn friends enjoying the view. I kept looking at our surroundings, trying to find something besides the silent wheat stalks. But he couldn't care less about the world, getting deeper and deeper into his can. To be on the safe side, I took the tiniest sips imaginable, afraid of getting reminded of anything else.

Finally, he asked me. "You worried about something?"

I took a sip. "We're all-"

"A bit louder, friend."

"Right. Sorry." *Has it been that long since I've talked to someone?* "It's just, we're all worried about something."

The mechanic took away the effectiveness of my deflection, choosing instead to stay silent. I had no choice but to speak more. "Everything feels like it's been snatched away from me. And I don't know if it's just me or what, but I can't help but feel like-"

"Shit." He finished my sentence and shook his head. "Yeah, it'll do that to you."

"Well, the way I see it," The mechanic gestured around him. "I don't have anywhere else to be."

It was a while before I realized he wanted me to say something. I still wasn't sure as to what I wanted to say, or what he wanted to hear, or even how much I should say. My mind was almost about to tell my body to get up and get back on the street before I drank anymore. It was, after all, easier that way. *Don't get too attached there, bud. Not again.*

The mechanic began slurping away the final strands of the beer can and threw it away. As he opened another one and took the first sip, he let out a gargantuan burp. "Friend, you gonna stay silent? Besides me, no one else can hear you." He laughed to himself, exaggerated and almost boastful from drunkenness that'd already sowed itself into his speech.

I didn't know what he was laughing at, so I didn't follow suit. But that wasn't what started to turn my gears. His words had an uncanny, eerie, and calming relation to my mother's words. Somehow. Someway.

The relation was too similar to notice. Almost like this man was put here. *For what?*

It was too much of a coincidence to be a coincidence. *Maybe it meant something.* I didn't think he could reach into my life and extract the "Why", but I knew he was here for a reason.

I didn't realize that my mouth was agape while I stared at him. It was only until he raised his hand and waved it in front of me. It was the one holding the beer, which spilled a few drops onto the floor. They sizzled in the concrete despite the dropping temperatures and disappeared after a few seconds of life.

Ok. I guess we're doing it. "Alright." My conscience took a tentative deep breath, similar to how Mom took that breath eons ago. Ready to dive in and spill the depths of its madness.

Before I could reason myself out of anything, I dove. I dove deep, but careful enough to prevent any ties from being formed. I spoke truths that'd never seen the light of day since they happened like something being dug up that was foreign to the present. Some things that were relics of the past. Some were beliefs I didn't even accept myself until I reiterated them. Some were ideas that I thought I'd conquered before.

When I reached the climax, it became harder and harder to even speak. Like I was breaking something I spent years building. The shame made me not want to look him in the eye, worried I'd drive this random stranger away from my life like everyone else once they found out who I was.

My gut kept churning and churning with every word. *Maybe that's just the beer.*

As I talked, he kept drinking. He was on his fourth when I noticed the beer cans rolling around on the ground. I only contributed one more.

Then, as soon as I started, it was over. I didn't even realize it until I had nothing else left to say. My mouth stayed agape, my mind grasping for anything else that needed to come out. When I couldn't find the words, I closed my mouth. My nose flared, taking in the oxygen after being underwater for so long.

The mechanic just nodded. "Well," He didn't seem disgusted by me. *Yet.* He sat back even further into his chair and his eyes began to

38

process what he heard. "And your mom?" *Even that was what he chose to harp on. Way too coincidental.*

"Too much of these." I shook the can in my hand. I nodded and looked at the wheat stalks. "Yeah." The wind had picked up since I started talking, but they still didn't move. The sky had turned so dark, making the world devoid of all warmth. Nightfall seemed imminent. Though the sun still shone, just over the horizon. It was as though we were in the purgatory between the darkness and light. A beautiful purgatory.

The man took another second to reallocate his, no doubt, shattered thoughts. "I get it."

"No, I do." He responded to my skeptical gaze while shifting to face me. "If I was in your position, I don't know if I would've gotten this far, let alone-" He left the thought alone, throwing his current beer down with an empty echo. "I'm guessing you're thinking about turning back?"

"But it's the logical thing to do, right?" I asked. "Visiting him?"

An immediate nod. "Oh, yeah. He's your father. Even if he wasn't perfect, you owe it to him." *No. I fucking don't. Not to anyone, and certainly not him.* "It's important that you be by his side. That part's something that everyone's gonna tell you."

The mechanic paused. "But here's my special two cents. It's gonna be hella painful. And you will regret every minute of it. Thing is, you're making it painful on yourself by not having anyone around to shove into that hole in that heart of yours. You're healing the slow way."

I thought about it for a second. *I guess I was.* "Is that a good thing?"

It was his turn to think about it for a second, while he shuffled through the bag, bringing up and popping open yet another beer can. This one had a purple fish. "Sure." A sip. "We'll go with that."

"Then why doesn't it feel like a good thing?" I knew that I had to force myself to find the "Why" I knew he was right, that I had to go. Yet the turmoiled part of me still asked.

"Cause healing's painful. Some scars are bigger than others, and they hurt the most when you try to let them heal because it takes more time for them to heal. But proper healing is slow." He set down his beer can to emphasize this point with his hands. "It's just common sense if you think about it. A sculptor's not gonna rush their sculpture, because if he does and he takes shortcuts or whatever, the people that'll see it will only notice the differences and the mistakes. And like people do, they'll leave it behind for something that looks better. Something that suits their eyesight instead of hurting it." His voice cracked under the duress of his baritone proclamations.

"But if he takes the time to chisel out any and all the imperfections-" The mechanic burped, reducing the overall weightiness of his words. Still, I let myself be captivated by his words, even though he was drunk enough to get a DUI if he was unlucky. "Then people'll have to think harder on moving onto the next exhibit, don't you think?" The sage-like words clattered around in my head until the weightiness returned, and the syllables sank to the depths of my mind.

He laughed to himself. The drunkenness showed once more. "You can tell I don't know jackshit about sculpting."

"I get what you're saying though." I offered.

A confused smile erupted on his face. "Good, because I don't. Truth be told." He reached over and hit me in the arm with a loud laugh. "I started rambling some time back." I pondered the possibility that he did get what he was saying but the words had the respite of bouncing off the walls of a drunk, empty, and careless mind. *Maybe that's why I started to drink.* To escape. *Even though you ran away.*

"You sound like Shannon." The words were meant to stay in my mind, but they spilled out into the night and fluttered over the wheat stalks which still stubbornly stood, rooted in the ground far past their actual roots.

The mechanic looked over with little to no surprise. I opened my mouth to explain myself but his hand waving in the air interrupted me. "No no, I get it. I talk to myself sometimes too." His eyes returned to the wheat stalks and in the quiet night, I began to see the silent world that took everything away from him, leaving nobody to talk to except himself. I felt that loneliness often in my chest.

The mechanic took another sip. His eyes grew beady and black. Almost sinking in his eye sockets due to its heaviness. The serious tone came back. "You already came all this way. Something inside of you knows that have it in your hands. The opportunity. The chance to make amends." He pointed at himself, then at me. "This doesn't happen a lot, you and I both know that. And when it's not in our hands, you leave it to stuff that's way outta your control to turn it all to -"

"Shit." This was when that full picture began to coalesce, revealing something even I hadn't realized. *A boon. That's what this was.* My mind immediately wrenched the thought away and tried to dive back down into why I couldn't take this chance. That stopped immediately too when I saw this evolutionary response for what it was: the fact that I was somehow on the right track if I rejected the idea like so.

He clapped his free hand on his thigh when he sensed my realization. "And while everyone on this planet takes shit once in a while, we also get those rare opportunities to make our lives better." He licked his lips, and his face echoed a seriousness that I didn't see up until that very moment. "That's up to you to do. I can't do that for you, and no one else can either."

I sighed. The truth in his words was undeniable. *Too much so.* Though there was some hope intertwined in them too, the pill still grew larger in my throat.

Deeper II

The night grew too foreboding to stay out much longer. Plus, the mechanic started to yawn every few seconds. So, he - quite literally - threw the chairs back inside the garage and filled the trashcan with the beer cans that threatened to fly away in the night breeze.

He wriggled my keys in front of me as the trashcan lid see-sawed shut. "Before I forget."

I reached out to grasp it, but I'd only managed to grab at the air. The mechanic waited for me to look confused before he began. "I mean it when I said that opportunities don't come by a lot."

He opened his mouth to say something but then stopped. I looked into his eyes and saw the same hurt eyes that slapped me whenever I was in a mirror. The same hurt eyes with treacherous ravines and canals were split by the red lava that angered the brain, softened the soul, and numbed the pain with its overloading heat. I'd realized over the past few years that the hurt eyes spoke more poems on the pain one felt than the fingers of the greatest scribe to walk our planet. The poems I saw in the mechanic's eyes were too expansive to question. Poems that wanted desperately to be uttered but kept inside with the confirmation that no new answer would be said.

But one of the poems was clear. The words he uttered over the past hour were sparked by a painful experience. The deepest wishes he too had met a random stranger before it all happened. It all swam across his iris for me to see, even if he didn't mean for it to.

I knew he was doing the same, looking into my eyes to find the hurt. Finding the good in someone becomes an alien concept for those who haven't experienced "good" for a long time. They just simply forget what it is. *I miss the good.*

The mechanic snapped us out of our trance by tossing me my keys. It hit me square in the chest before skittering down to my bent palm.

I quickly got into the car and drove it out of the confines of the garage. The mechanic stood watching, with an unfortunate experience only I saw.

Something told me to stop. So I hit the brakes and shot forward in my seat. I looked back as he jumped up and grabbed the garage door. It didn't seem like something you were supposed to do, but I wasn't about to argue.

His feet landed on solid ground, the garage door past his face. It flew down an inch before he let his grip loosen ever-so-slightly until his face was visible. His beady eyes found me again. "A little more advice before you go. You let go of a lot of things in life. And when you get-" He took one of his hands to wave it in the air as he tried to remember where I was heading. "Wherever it is you're going, you may lose some more stuff. Just try not to expect what comes and leaves.

As if that wasn't deep enough, he added. "And the pain you feel, don't overthink it. Stop convincing yourself that it is what it is, 'cause what happens is you try to find comfort and peace in the pain. It's not really peace, no matter how much you try to convince yourself that it is." He then brought the garage door down to the ground. The metal screamed into the night sky until the metal wobbled to a halt.

Something had been lifted. That, I felt intrinsically. The walk across the motel's parking lot was bouncy, with an easier weight on my shoulders. My knee pain even took a break to let the happiness consume me.

But that didn't quell the effects of the clunky small talk with the receptionist drove me into heavy drowsiness. As if that wasn't bad enough, the air in the given room was stale and the white pillows had some brown stains on them that made it a bit too hard to ignore. I resorted to pushing them off the mattress, knowing I'd sleep with more peace without them than with them.

I collapsed on the bed once I deemed there were no other pathogens and plagues that would spend the night with me. At least the ones I had the energy to care about.

My neck was craned in an awkward position, and I hadn't bothered to take off my shoes. But I still slept throughout the night.

As my eyes fluttered open, the exhaustion I'd driven through finally felt free of my body. The sweaty imprint that had emanated from my back into the bed provided a satisfying yet disgusting visual of the feeling. But despite the warm clunky perspiration that still secreted out of every inch of my skin, I realized that no dream haunted me. *Huh.*

With a temporary peace and an itch to smile, I turned towards the windows, not wanting to leave this mental comfort.

The sun. My thoughts stopped. For some reason, the warm light filtering through the blinds was at a peculiar angle. One I never saw unless I was back at my house. One of those morning glows I never saw anymore.

I blinked, and Shannon's face filled up my vision. The glow radiated behind her hair and lit up her shadowy face.

She smiled. *That fucking smile.* "It's okay."

With an easy glimmer, Shannon disappeared. Just like that, the physical pain returned, in the place of the psychological pain that the dreams put me through. Regardless of type, the pain was almost always attached to those memories. Regardless of type, my chest hurt, and my stomach sank even though nothing was weighing it down. Regardless of type, the memories and emotions seemed to hit a bit harder now every single day, with the simplest excuses such as the sunlight.

The hopelessness returned. *If I couldn't wake up with peace how would I ever continue living? How could I even dream with a little less hurt?*

Then it all stopped in a flash. The multisyllabic syntax of my brain abated itself and thoughts that were much easier to decipher returned. My stomach eased up, and I was able to lift myself off the bed. I considered that this was just another evolutionary response, this painful rejection of the healing process that the mechanic mentioned last night. But I still hoped it wouldn't frequent my emotional reserves further.

I thanked the receptionist and dropped my hotel key off. I should've taken the chance to shave take a bath or even just brush my teeth. But I didn't want to, and it seemed like it didn't matter right now.

Once I got into the car, I shoved a random granola bar into my throat. I almost threw it back up, my body having no desire to eat anything. Yet I knew I'd need the energy. As I shoved the bar back down, those neurons firing inside me last night were revitalized. Now, that slump I'd experienced just moments before was gone. For the first time since I identified that there was a "Why" to be found, I found myself wanting to seek it. I almost wanted to go. *Almost.*

The mechanic was outside when I went down the road to the exit ramp. Even though he was well over a hundred yards away, with his head in another car's hood, he turned around and caught sight of me as if he knew I'd cross him then and there. At that very moment, he was my mom. It took me a few moments to register the fact. I just stared back and wondered if he was some kind of divine intervention. Even though I didn't believe in a god, the thought comforted me, almost as if Mom was beside me once more.

The feeling that the divine intervention would spawn worse nightmares sprouted in my brain tissue. Hopeless tears threatened to leave the enclosure of my eyelashes. *Please.* I forced the tears to stop. I couldn't reach this new low. *Not this soon.*

Mom morphed back into the mechanic. I took the exit ramp and sped onto the highway. A jackass almost ran me over when I moved to the middle lane. But the calmness soon returned while my Shoegaze playlist picked up.

My car sped past the "Welcome to South Carolina" sign. The roads immediately began crashing me into the ceiling of my car.

The green sign for Gaines passed me not long after. Immediately, I was hit with a dirty red construction site. A sign for a mall

45

headlined the complex, that had half its parking lot filled to the brim. *That wasn't there before.*

Nevertheless, I lowered the windows to feel the arid warmth that followed the construction dust. The kind of arid warmth that almost made you suffocate after a while. It wasn't ideal. Not in the slightest. But it felt familiar.

The first sign of civilization I saw after miles of empty road was an Italian place. *Italian.* I immediately started looking for something else.

Burgervilles still loomed on many corners, though their cheery designs had been replaced with something more modern. The vibrant purples and yellows now had a dull green and gray finish. The plants lining the outside of the stores had become brown too. A bright brown, bright enough for me to easily imagine the crunch the plants would emit with a simple touch.

Swinging, winding roads lead me past stapled and fabled restaurants hidden in the remotest recesses and roads. I swung past one such sandwich place, one of the most notable for somehow existing through the Burgerville boom. I couldn't pronounce its name, but apparently, you couldn't call yourself a resident of Gaines if you didn't eat there. I never had.

I flew past the lake, which bridged Gaines with Drophead. Everyone hated the Drophead kids. It always seemed like they were richer. More entitled. Unfortunately, they were also better in many ways. Even looking out over the dam the roads seemed cleaner. There was actual traffic on some streets. Here in Gaines the only way we could get traffic was if someone had an accident.

Past the lake, a tiny concrete jungle came into view on Aspen Boulevard and the distant abandoned train tracks. The straighter roads somehow only got more bumpier. Gaines didn't have an established downtown. Rather, there was this quadrant of land next to the high school that connected itself with the only other highway nearby. It seemed like every developer put all their stores in that area. Any other inch of Gaines was off-limits. Tainted with the plague. Of course, that meant that everyone had to crawl out of their homes to get some decent food or entertainment if one would consider a long-abandoned bowling alley entertainment.

46

Tellermen's Plaza scratched its way into my eyesight. Look away. My attention spun around as wildly as my head, latching on to a group of teenagers briefly. All of them had cardboard to-go containers, for some reason.

The concrete jungle soon disappeared, and the roads began twisting around once more. Weird turns. Narrow stretches in the forests with arbitrarily placed houses and dirty driveways that led to them. Random stop signs. Leaves that drooped down and often hit my car. Cones and clay lined some roads, showing signs of road work. Roadwork that would take an eternity to finish. Gaines Middle passed by me at one point, and so did Gaines Elementary (The buildings were too unremarkable, with the memories they provided and the appearance they yielded). Churches were everywhere. *So many churches.*

But it was all so beautiful. Fitting. I hated this place but couldn't bring myself to deny the stunning scenery. There was no possible direction the town could take to somehow look better.

The only way it could look better was if Shannon was beside me.

The familiar cluster of neighborhoods soon came up. Even though the styles of architecture, or levels of poverty varied, they all had that sense of nostalgia, despite the notable absence of Aubrey's peace lilies. The same nostalgia when someone was returning to their childhood home even if they didn't live there before. Of course, I wished all I felt in my head was just this alien nostalgia. The Chicago in me found it hard to believe, after decades of luxury and paradise, that I'd come from such a hellhole and that subsequently I had come back to it with my own will.

One of the neighborhoods ran up to me. Mine, unfortunately. In the distance, I noticed that the brick wall was missing the gold-plated name of the housing establishment. People here were too lazy to commit such acts on purpose. I guessed that age got it. As I got closer, my assumption was proven correct. The gold plate was on the ground, face-down. The rot along its edges and the corroded screws around it told me that it wasn't changed after all this time.

I turned into the neighborhood's straight road. In a few hundred feet, branches upon branches would branch out before that main road would end.

Before that though, was a stop sign. I stopped, even though no one else ever did so. It wasn't because of the sign that I halted either.

It was the fact that I didn't remember where the house was. I didn't get my license until I went to Chicago, so the muscle memory of pulling into the driveway past the "38" mailbox didn't take over my arms. The house numbers rabbited around, mailbox to mailbox, without any real organization to help me even more.

Great.

I found it after a while. A part of me unfortunately wished it'd taken longer.

Both Mom's minivan and Greg's truck were in the driveway, so I had to settle my car next to the mailbox. It took me a couple of tries, the house settled on one of the bigger curves on one of the bigger streets. Eventually, though, I got the car as close as I could to the curb. Of course, that meant it took an ice age to get out of the vehicle. But it worked.

The gargoyle statue placed beside the front door eyed me with curiosity. I considered taking the statue's right eye out to retrieve the key while walking across the lawn. *You're not that welcome here anymore.*

Reminiscent of a stranger, I knocked on the front door, trying not to aggravate the unceremonious fragility it always had.

I looked around, trying to find more fleeting memories on the outside. But all I saw was an alien world. The entire house was smaller than the first floor back in Cherry Hill. The lack of a second floor seemed beyond puzzling to me. *How'd I live like this?* Even the Gargoyle statue looked alongside me with distaste.

I knocked again, trying to be harder without being too hard. A clattering of noises crept through the peach-colored hardy planks. Pots and pans, by its sound. I walked over to the window, which had its blinds closed. Still, I leaned closer, trying to see anything. I couldn't.

Dan opened the door, huffing and puffing. I walked back to the entryway to fully take in his growth after all the years we lost. Sweat glistened around his neck, and there was a slight smile he conjured before it went away. In its place, was a contained stoniness, going along with his light purple dress shirt and khaki pants. It dawned on me, seeing his matured face and puffs of hair clinging to his chin, the amount of time had passed. He looked nothing like what I remembered. It relieved me that he hadn't strayed away from his favorite color purple, but the purple he wore was remarkably subdued. Even his eyes were so much cloudier than before, his true thoughts - previously visible only to me - were now hidden.

Dan held his hands out to initiate an embrace. I leaned forward with surprising awkwardness while he laughed a - very - fake laugh. "How's it going?"

"It's goi-"

"It's good to see you." We both exited the embrace, the cumbersome nature staying throughout. His eyes went up and down, as if in disbelief that I came. I didn't know if it was meant to be taken in the wrong way. *Or if he meant to even show me that.*

I broke the ice that followed. "So am I allowed in, or-" Leaving the question in the air, Dan gave me space to enter.

"Of course, of course." He assured me. "You're always welcome here. But take off your shoes. And socks too. I just finished steaming the floors." I did as he asked without paying too much attention, the words just registering as unneeded fuzz in my mind, which was more focused on what was before me: the living room.

Our house somehow got even shorter. I found myself too claustrophobic to even stay in the living room as I passed through the doorway. The two recliners were almost intruding onto the welcome mat, sifting through who was welcomed into the home. I forced my eyes elsewhere to get rid of the suffocation. The brick fireplace was midnight black. On top of the fireplace's mantle was a flat-screen TV. It's off-center. I looked at the picture frames next to the TV to prevent further annoyance. I looked away from them too once I saw Mom in one of them.

Next to the fireplace was the black couch. *The black couch.* I forced my focus onto something else.

The hardwood no longer creaked as I ventured deeper into the house, past the random bookshelf by the front door that seemed to contain anything but books. Papers and folders, yes, but not books.

The kitchen was in the far corner, away from anyone's view. Mom often hid there, pretending to cook during Greg's tirades. Even when I lived here, it was rarely clean. But now the aged wood on the cabinets and the more-than-dirty countertops made it all a less homely mess.

My eyes spun to the narrow hallway on my right, containing everything else worth remembering in the house. The bathroom. Some other rooms. One of them was mine. Plus, the tiny pantry we spent one summer renovating to house the washing machine and dryer.

I couldn't venture down the hallway, even if I wanted to. The amount of clutter that occupied the walkway was immense. Toys. Some of them were fit for a toddler.

"I apologize." Dan bent down to pick up the toys. "I tried to teach them. It's like they hear me but they also don't." He threw the toys into Greg's old office, which didn't seem like cleaning. However, I never intended to step inside that room, so I was content with it. "Kids these days." Dan saying what the grownups usually generalized us as out of place, at the very least. "Then again, shouldn't have gotten three of them." He laughed to himself as if it was a joke.

The disruptions of peace and symmetry somehow made him seem more organized. This was all just an organized chaos, a dissonant orchestra that only he could conduct. Even being next to him I felt dwarfed, though he was a few inches shorter than me. But as much as I was impressed, it was tough to see that he didn't need me. Some part of me was glad, in the fact that he seemed "together" enough to handle Greg while he died.

But my head still pointed out the pessimism of the situation, as always. *Did anyone need me anymore?* "Where's the wife? Working?"

"No, no. They don't have a mom. They're just mine." He laughed - another fake one - and then sniffled it off. The concept of time didn't seem as stretched as it was in the moment. It seemed like yesterday that

I was helping him with Algebra homework. Now he had kids. While I had trouble agreeing with the fact that he'd adopt two kids for himself, the thought that he'd lie to me flew past my head.

But I digressed. The playfulness that surged through us when me and Dan fought, imagined, and did everything that defined our childhood in this very house. It was painful to think of it now. If our past selves saw us now, the degradation and decomposition would be prevalent even to the blind discarded eyes.

Those feelings were exactly what I didn't want to achieve on this trip. *But here we are.*

"We have the spare bedroom for you to use. Please make yourself comfortable. We installed a shower in there and everything." Dan gestured inside Mom and Greg's old bedroom. "I just cleaned some dishes."

"Dan-"

"Or you can take your old room-"

"Dan-"

"We have everything here. Except beer. Not anymore. Yeah, I'm sober for about-"

No more beating around the bush. "Where's Greg, Dan?" I held my hand up, preventing him from rambling any further.

Dan stuck his thumb outside. "At the hospice." An uncomfortable silence decided to emerge, like I shouldn't have brought Greg up.

"Well, this is all kind of you," I tried to alleviate my lack of social intelligence. "But I'm not staying here that long. Maybe for a day, at the most." Staying at the house would've made everything easier. But I knew that staying in my car would be better than sleeping in all that clutter and trauma. I refused to sleep on my bed here as well. But not because of the nightmares. It was because the nightmare had bought the bed for me for my birthday.

My mind stopped. *"We" have a spare bedroom".* The fact that he refused to elaborate started to make me begin to feel betrayed. Neglected. *He'd done it before. Why wouldn't he do it now?*

Dan sighed, disrupting my thoughts. His hand plummeted to his side, and so did his opinion of me. "Right." He looked around, afraid to see or appreciate these circumstances. *Why didn't he understand?* It was a major feat in and of itself that I came here. At the very least, some gratitude was deserved. But he didn't seem to feel that way. "So, what're you gonna do, now that you're here?"

"Probably just hang out. See how much has changed." *See Greg eventually.* I refused to say it out loud, that tiny part of me still rejecting the thoughts.

Dan nodded, almost still surprised I was here in flesh and blood. It was uncanny seeing him like that. "Nice, nice. My lunch ends at twelve, so I have to get back. Yeah, thought I'd get some cleaning done. Wasn't really hungry anyway." He sighed. "But whatever you want to do, we'll help you." He smiled, and for the first time, it seemed like the Dan I grew up with. The always-smiling kid. *Maybe there was a chance.* I was scared I wasn't going to see him anymore. It didn't seem like he smiled a lot anymore.

Who was "We"? A tiny smile crept up behind me and took my face over. The smile grew bigger, this time for my turn to hide my true thoughts.

The Dense Burdens

I had gone to the car to get something. I didn't know what, but it didn't matter as Dan locked the door behind him and left for work without notice.

The front door's lock was fixed. The key in the gargoyle statue didn't work in the back door either. Calling him would just make things more awkward. Plus, I wasn't sure if I had his number saved, or if he'd gotten a new number. Of course, every second I spent standing outside the front door made me feel out of place too.

So, I trudged back to the car. As the doors closed, the heat of South Carolina provided no relief even though they were still in the spring.

I brought out my phone. I mostly tried to avoid it. I hated the emotional tango that was reading into every text until it became unreadable. That was reassuring people that they were good friends when no one assured me that I was even good.

The emotional tango that was never leaving anyone on read because I knew how overthinking would rot their brain, all while it rotted mine. That was doing chores, so I wasn't too early for an event.

The emotional tango that was balancing my enthusiasm and fake happiness that I'd built at Gilbert drove people away. I was just too excited to talk to people. *Anyone.* Too excited to recommend them to my Shoegaze playlist. When most people had never heard of shoegaze. Or they didn't like me. Even if I'd done nothing to them or if I even actually tolerated them, their days were "ruined" when I walked in the door.

After all the empathy I poured out, I took a step back to realize I got none in return. No one texted me when I fell. *Especially when I fell.* So when the empathic burnout occurred, I didn't stop it.

I never had an interest in mobile games either. Without much else to do, I opened my social media. I regretted it immediately when the first post I saw was some couple happily dancing in the rain. I wasn't too far from putting the phone down, starting up the car, and ramming into our white magnolia at a hundred miles per hour.

The more I scrolled, the worse it got. Everything seemed to remind me of my dilemmas, trying to offer false hopes and misconstrued solutions that didn't work in most situations. *I wish they did.*

Thankfully, the phone ran out of charge. *Too much self-pity. Even for you.* I didn't bother to find the charger.

After a couple more minutes of controlled emptiness, sweat began to perspire from my skin. Some of the sweat accumulated around my eyelids, and I had to close my eyes to prevent it from burning my eyes.

The white magnolia. Greg. The emptiness was snatched away with the closure of my eyelids.

In its place, was another environment. This time, it was my bedroom before the plague of hostility had claimed it for its own. I knew it by my face, aged thirteen.

The pile of pillows holding my right knee above my chest to reduce swelling - though there was still considerable swelling - told me I dislocated my kneecap only a couple of days ago. It happened on the very first sunrise of the summer, while I was playing with my classmates. I didn't call them friends, because when I fell to the ground, they all ran away while I screamed from the torture.

That was when I met Robin. I was fortunate that she decided to walk around that exact morning.

My eyes forced themselves to take it all in before it was all gone. All the naivety. Even the pain. The simple T-shirt and shorts I wore almost every day to prevent any further pain from entering my body. It was a simpler pain. It almost made me want to relive this memory more. *Almost.*

My bed was in the center of the room, with the headboard against the wall - shared with Dan's room - and the three sides of my room almost equidistant to my bed. Blue sheets and some more white pillows joined me on the bed. To my right, the corner contained a basket, strewn with stinking clothes. To my left, a desk with my bookbag perched on top and pieces of paper and pencils spilling out. In front of me, was a double-doored closet with a plethora of clothes, and other miscellaneous items that I was glad to have an excuse not to clean.

But that was it. Those were all the details that bothered to arrive. What happened in a short time would taint my desire to remember this memory drastically.

The window bled some harsh blue light through the closed blinds. Maybe an indicator of the late afternoon. Or early morning. That was the only thing I truly forgot about that day.

I was placed in the far corner, right beside the window, and an entire bookcase containing some educational material that'd never seen actual use. Weirdly enough, the one open textbook was completely blank, even though it was open in the middle.

I looked down, my chin touching my chest. A telescope head went straight through me, but I wasn't surprised at that as much. The expectation overshadowed it.

Meanwhile, he could barely lift his head off of the pillow. A metric ton of lead weighed him, consistent throughout his body. He preferred it, though. The comfort of his sheets welcomed him.

His eyes were red and exhausted, all from a state of incessant tearing. The heavy blanket comfortably trapped his legs. With care, he lifted his arm and opened said blanket, revealing his two legs. He didn't open his eyes until his right knee was up to his face.

It hurt even moving it an inch, and upon the opening of his eyes, it hurt even more. The knee had gotten green - a tiny part around the afflicted area - and everything else was black from the fried blood. Black enough to be seen through the knee wrap. The skin around the knee felt like it was cracking whenever it moved, edging closer and closer to it shattering into pieces. He didn't want that to happen, so he let it fall back down.

I winced at myself, almost for him. The pain shot up his leg and deviated into his thigh. He grabbed the blue sheets and winced. After a few seconds, the pain subsided. He closed his eyes to regain the sleep and the unconsciousness that was so desperately needed. Alas, it didn't return.

After tossing and turning around for a few minutes, he sat up in response to the noise detonation. From the living room. Loud yelling and thumping. He fell back into the bed, the mattress almost sinking him in as one of its own.

I smiled. A childish fear, one I'd developed when I first slept in that very bed. That I'd sink through, leave everything behind. It was a paralyzing fixation. One I hated with vehemence.

The knee was struck with pain once more at the sudden movement, but that wasn't his worry at the moment. His first thought was that a robber had decided to indulge in our non-existent wealth. He almost wished that the bed would sink him in, away from the potential danger.

Then, another burst of noise. He'd heard Mom and Greg's voices at its crux. A slight comfort suddenly paved itself to discomfort.

Before this incident, the yelling had occurred more often for the past few months. It burst out of nowhere, from quiet dinners where neither of them talked to each other until it exploded. Before school had let out, we'd learned about the Cold War, and I couldn't help but think of it as our version of one. Neither talked to each other apart from the meaningless bouts they held, where nothing overtly dangerous occurred. They turned to us to get each other's attention or if they needed to get anything important and involve each other. Of course, the frigidness of the glances they shot each caused most of these, and it seemed to have the impact and penetration of actual ammunition. They seemed like they still cared, but also hated each other's very sight. No matter who won each duel and who triumphed at the end of the day.

A sudden rush. The wind flew past my ears, and my head was now one with my teenage version. My arms were under the folded and unfolded covers, almost twisted undecipherably. I looked straight ahead at the body-length mirror hanging outside my closet. My teenage self's head peeked over my body and bad knee. I couldn't feel the pain I felt back then in said knee, which was the only real reprieve. Because I knew being one with my past like so wouldn't be such a grand welcome. Yet I couldn't argue. It looked like I was destined to view this particular duel up close. The nerves that grew inside my stomach didn't lessen with the realization.

Out of the corner of my eyes, I saw Dan sleeping in front of the desk. The tip of his head, was messy, as was his shirt. He was tasked with watching me that summer, but he spent most of his time sleeping on the mattress at the foot of the bed, which he loved as much as eating.

Was this the same Dan? I couldn't find the answer to my question.

I dropped my head to the pillow and twisted my body until my right ear was as close to the door as possible. Unfortunately, sentences weren't decipherable. But I could make out a few words here and there. Some cuss words. Threats. I hoped they were still like Greg's beer bottles after a long night.

His voice got louder, and this time I could hear words. He sounded angry. "Why would we care if you walked out?" I could imagine the pointy finger directed at the front door. I fumed to myself, even though I'd wasted my energy already in this experience. If anyone should leave, it was him. He already had experience with it.

Mom's voice got louder, but it didn't make sense. It was similar to incoherent babble coming from a monkey.

The shouting suddenly got even louder. The mirror vibrated like it was going to fall off. At the decibel they were yelling, I wasn't going to be surprised if it did.

Dan finally sat up. He looked at the wall, and I knew that he was also speculating as to what was going on. "Did they start?" Dan asked, the permanent smile on him twisted with a slight fear.

He looked at me when I yielded no response, to which I shrugged. "Seems like they've been going through it for the past few hours. Not sure, though." I admitted. Inside, I realized that these were the same words that I'd said that day. I knew because what I really wanted to say didn't come out of my mouth. The horrific realization, that I wasn't in control of my body, overtook my senses.

Dan nodded and sat up straighter, my eyes forced onto him. He turned back to the door as they started yelling at each other again, this time without regard for interrupting each other's incoherent clamors.

The pain shot up even more as I twisted an inch more to the side. I was paranoid the wound wasn't healing well or fast enough, and with each second I started to get worried that it was infected. It probably already was. But the curiosity was too much for me to ignore. *No. Try to ignore it.*

Dan yawned - his yawn was even "smiley" - and stood up in his baggy bright purple tee, which stretched well past his waist. Sweat had congregated around his neck. His face told me he wanted to sleep more. Yet he stood still and looked at the door, an internal debate raging inside on whether to lay down again. The yelling quieted to a close with a few mumbles. Then it erupted once more to a shrill peak.

"I guess I better check it out." He sighed, then looked at me. "Alright, just stay here. I got this round. I'll see if they need anything."

"It's not like I can do anything anyway." I retorted back and gestured down at my knee. I uncovered the blanket more so he could see the situation clearer.

He winced as if he were feeling my pain. "I'd say I feel you, but I don't want to feel all that." He gestured to my wound and started walking towards the door, smiling wider at his joke.

"You need these?" Dan pointed to my crutches, which he must've put by the door when I was asleep. I shook my head because, at the time, it didn't seem like it was necessary. *Maybe if you did have them, you could've stopped them before it happened.*

Dan walked outside and closed the door. His emotional maturity was always praised by Mom. Back then, I didn't see it. But now, it was more present than ever. Those actions of his held similarities to worn soldiers, trudging back into the trenches for the littlest emolument.

In the brief second when the door was open, a cacophony of noise entered the room. I waited for the pandemonium to subside, now that Dan was outside arbitrating in my place, but it didn't. The closed door didn't seem equipped to handle all the noise it was facing.

Seconds passed and mutated into minutes. Yes, I'd already lived through this before, but the dream still made me relive every single moment to reintroduce the importance of the memory into my head.

I didn't like it. As per usual, the restlessness began to consume me while I battled through various exhaustions. I sat up and stood off the bed with my one good leg in one swift motion. My hands waved a symphony in the air as I felt my bad legs' inevitable kiss with the floor, but my balance was eventually gathered. Once I did so, I leaned forward with all my body weight on the good leg and hit the wall with my palms. Gathering the crutches from the wall made my other lithe maneuvers look simple.

Something shattered. My heartbeat stopped, and my mind did a double take. My hands grasped the door as fast as they could, and I swung it open.

My crutches pulled me out into the empty hallway. The pantry space to my left was still covered in plastic draping, even though the renovation had finished a week ago. None of the other lights in the house were on, not even the living room where everyone was congregated. The window right in front of me, adjacent to the front door on the far-side wall, couldn't help but draw my attention at first with its harsh blue light.

Then the gathering before me grasped control of all my other thoughts. The scene was confusing at first. Mom and Greg stood facing each other. He wore his worn jeans and a faded wrinkles brown leather belt. His yellow shirt complemented the gold-rimmed glasses he had seated on his nose. An outfit we'd gotten used to at the time, as I began to recall how late he used to come home after work. Or if he really did, as his pager was still at his hip.

Mom wore a simple set of blue sweats. She never wore sweats. The pieces of the plate were behind her heels. Her eyes were undoubtedly wild. Even though they stayed on Greg, I could feel the rage trembling within her. The pupils were somehow shaking in their place. Her fists couldn't stay still. The veins on her arms almost burst out of her body and attacked me. Mom's hair was also in a tight bun. I always found her hair in a bun when they fought, like she was preparing for an actual brawl. Mom's shirt was drenched with sweat, which would've fooled me as an aftereffect of an actual fistfight.

My eyes found the face that I looked to first on many occasions: Dan's. Dan knew how to forge some pathways to a temporary treatise in these duels. Yet he was sitting on one of the couches, his hands were holding his head up. Dried tears were all over his face. He looked at me, and it was exactly how I remembered it. A sort of bad omen, as he'd never looked that distraught or despaired.

Mom turned to me and most of her rage fell apart. I could see those eyes retreat into its brain and lose the intensity it had held just moments before.

Greg's head swiveled to face me. Though he barely moved, I flinched. "Hey, Cal. How's it going?" I was tempted to say that it was going like I always did. But I hated him too much to even dignify his question with a response. I refused to let his words mean something. *Always.*

His glasses were on the verge of falling off, judging by how far it was down his narrow nose. "How's the knee?" He pushed the loveseat - which wasn't where it was usually - back to its original location.

Sensing that I wouldn't respond he sat down on the black couch and interlocked his fingers. His head was hung low, the chin almost touching the chest. "Well, it's good you're awake. We need to talk." Greg proceeded to gesture to both me and Mom to sit down as if his words mattered that much. We both refused in the beginning, but Mom relented with a grit starting to form in her teeth.

He sighed when I chose to stay on my crutches and began anyway. "We don't want this as much as y'all. And I know all this from us for the past few months is just breaking everyone." A breath. "Because we are. Broken." The facial muscles on his face seemed to contract and wince like his body was trying to stop him from saying these words.

Mom didn't buy it. "We're only broken because of you-"

Greg's quiet gaze drifted to Mom, and she stopped. When he gestured around the space, I realized it looked more like a crime scene. Beer bottles were on the ground, somehow unbroken, and clothes were scattered across various appliances. A manic laughter filled the air, and when I looked at his face, I felt goosebumps form on my shoulders. "Cause we are. And the sooner we can accept that."

His voice choked while my hatred for him rose. All that I saw was someone willing to sacrifice our emotions. The thief of our happiness, to feed his. With all of this happening, my knee started to itch. I knew I did need to sit down, or I'd swell the joint more. But since it was what Greg wanted, I chose to accept the swelling and leaned more onto my crutch with the hopes that the itch would relieve itself.

"Once we accept this, we can grow. Cause no one wants this." His voice got more grave with each syllable that exited his mouth.

"Yeah. We don't. So can y'all stop?" I asked. Tears were threatening to break my vision with that burning tingling feeling. "Like, right now, and fix whatever you guys are going through? Just fix it?" The personality that was in the driver's seat continued for me. The words flew with a freeness, though inside I wanted to say more. But I always felt that I never had the chance to say everything I wanted to.

"Just stop. Is it that hard?" The pleading in my voice jumped out and echoed around the walls. The feelings, the memories we'd been through didn't deserve to be tarnished like this. The sobbing began, though quiet enough for no one else to notice.

Greg nodded in agreeance. He took one glance at Mom, who refused to look at him. "I know, kid. So, your mom and I have come up with a decision. Now, whether she wants to look at me or not, we both still know that this is our only option left. After all that," He gestured out into the air with a hasty hand, and his words bit with a venomous aftertaste on my skin. "This is our last and final solution."

I knew it. In my gut, I knew what was coming. But my brain refused it. I shook my head. I remembered dreaming about this often. The teenager in me begged me that this was some sick nightmare.

Dan's did too. "No fucking way, Dad." After staying silent and avoiding eye contact in a sort of guilty shame - like he could've prevented this - he chose that moment to speak up.

My composure caved. "Yeah, hell no." I found my mouth open, about to fight everyone in this room with my three good limbs.

But before I could even bother, or have my conscience jump in to induce my brain with reason, Greg's hands shot up in the air. His palms were open and facing toward both Dan and I, as though we were unruly cars in traffic. "Now listen. This will help all of us." He tried to reason, injecting his voice with some false authority.

He failed, partly because I wasn't willing to listen to him. Part of it was because the world began to fade into darkness. A numbness - which I assumed was pain - shot up my knee in an instant, and up my arm as my eyes fluttered. The strength in my right leg evaporated, and the feeling in my arms left the house. I fell sideways and hit my head on something. I didn't have time to find out what, as I was unconscious before any contact was made.

I hoped that was the end of this dream. But it wasn't.

Instead, a white room materialized around me. A whiteness that blinded me. Medical instruments beeped everywhere, yet there was an eerie silence.

Dan sat in a corner chair; his knees held close to his chest. He was wearing the same purple shirt, somehow braving through the sweat. Daylight streamed through the mammoth window to my left. Past the curtain that split the room in half to my right, Mom and Greg were discussing outside the door, their heads visible through the small windowpane. In all my maturity, I wasn't concerned about the severity of the situation. I was glad because, in some corner of my brain, I was convinced that they would stay together.

That feeling of security was the first thing that I remembered after falling. Apparently, Dan tried to catch me. He failed. The family dragged me to the car and drove me to the hospital. Mom was the one behind the wheel. They drove fast enough to get a cop's attention. But my head was bleeding enough to garner some sympathy.

We arrived at the hospital, and I was thrown under the care of the nursing staff. They spent a few hours stitching up my forehead and the unexplained infection from my knee that unfortunately started to spread a bit too much.

A nurse appeared from behind the curtain with an abnormally long needle. Before the hesitance could set in, I winced from the meteoric impact. I fell asleep once more without having the chance to think about the pain.

Are we done now?

We weren't. I opened my eyes to the daylight outside. Except there was no daylight. It had given way to the night. A bloodied cast was wrapped around my head. I moved my head and tried to get a feel of the wrapping, but the burden just made me more fatigued.

Greg and Mom weren't outside the door anymore. No nurses occupied the room with me. The only other sign of life was an incessant snoring from behind the curtain. And Dan sitting in the corner.

He saw me awake and got to his feet. With a grinding that shattered my eardrums, he dragged his chair over. Once seated, he grabbed my hand. I expected him to give me some false assurances, but he just stayed quiet. Dan knew that I appreciated the silence better.

I did my best to avoid the overall gravitas of the situation. "That's kinda gay, bro."

He smiled wider, but his face morphed into an aged creature of sorts. I saw that maturity that even Greg didn't contain. A maturity I didn't see Dan have until now.

We sat in silence. Dan's smile didn't waver, and I couldn't see how he could without it physically hurting him. But it comforted me.

I broke the silence a couple of minutes later as I thought out loud. "I'm sorry dude, I didn't mean to react like the world just ended." Dan just nodded.

More silence, but it was a comfortable quiet. "You sound weird when you curse." I laughed.

Dan just shrugged. "Yeah. It just came out."

The TV, which I didn't see was mounted up in the corner of the ceiling and belted out quiet static nonsense. It distracted us both in that moment, but after it was gone, he turned his attention back to me. "Was it cause Dad mentioned-" I nodded quickly enough for him to stop speaking.

Our eyes wandered to the TV, which belted out quiet static nonsense once more. For a couple of seconds, a man clad in a white suit and a blue cowboy hat appeared. Then, it didn't.

"Was it always like this?"

We knew each other enough to the point where "this" didn't have to be elaborated. Still, I pondered it for a good minute. "Kinda. When I was born, I remembered them being happy. No matter what they did, they did it together. The same thing happened when you were born."

"I don't remember that." Dan seemed lost. As if this tumultuous life was all he knew.

"Yeah, you were too young to remember. This was like right after you were born. Whenever you cried late at night, both of 'em would come and get you back to sleep."

He smiled bigger. "Yeah, and how'd you know that?"

"I could hear every single fucking thing." Dan laughed. I waited for him to stop before I continued. "I don't know when they stopped doing the small things together, or how. It doesn't really matter anyway, 'cause now I can't look back on the good without seeing the bad." My tone got a bit more solemn.

Dan's smile changed into a smirk. "In a way, it was kinda like your world ended."

The sentence burrowed itself into my brain. *It did.* Both the personalities within me agreed with that.

Dan buried his face in my arm. I bent my arm back and let my fingers sift through his hair. Coarse and smooth, the curls I knew him by had started to form. I closed my eyes, knowing that such a pure moment was hard to come by.

I felt my shirt getting wet. "Stay alive. Please."

What about now?

My eyes opened, and the interior of my car treated me to its present.

I blinked a few times, making sure this wasn't some other dream. This time, though, my surroundings were more visceral to all my senses. When I tried grabbing the plastic water bottle beside me, I felt the hot plastic kiss my fingertips. I could almost taste the stale overheated water inside.

The talk with Dan comforted the rigid sadness of the dream in a way I never thought was possible. But it was hard to focus on it because the fight lived alongside it in my heart.

The fight. The fight apparently started over a disagreement over Greg's precious truck. A stupid truck would be the ultimatum for years of relationships. The bonds they'd built would always be torn without repair, no matter what happened to me. I didn't know that fact at the time, and for the next day that I spent occupied in the hospital I held onto that belief. Once I got out, however, the divorce proceedings started.

The thought that ate at me was what would've happened if I'd just stayed in the room. Maybe they wouldn't have gone to such lengths. My mind was too angry at Greg, too sympathetic to Mom and Dan. Or maybe if I did come out a few seconds earlier. Before they had the chance to elevate the messiness of their words.

Messy. To say what happened afterward was messy is understating it. Yelling, and a lot of tribulations ensued in the weeks that followed. It seemed that I remembered a lot more than I wanted to. I could count on one hand how many altercations I went to, because neither I nor Dan wanted to see the downfall of our parents, no matter how much it was needed. But I had no trouble remembering.

On the other hand, I wasn't sure if the words I said in that simulation were mine from the present or what I said back then. *Maybe I did have control.* I heard that memories were interlaced with the truth and lies, more so with the older memories. I guess that was objectively true because we only see them from our point of view. What we don't see is filled in by our conscience, which always requires a sense of reason for the reasonless.

Maybe I just knew these memories would come back to haunt them while I was busy making them. Maybe that's why I was lying to myself. *Was I lying to myself? Were these all the lies I was looking back on, while I stumbled headfirst into the truth?*

My hands went through my face and into my hair. Wanting a distraction from the deep self-reflection, I looked over to my right. Through the open curtains, past the slightly grown grass and the slight incline up to the house, I saw Dan cleaning up the couches in the living room. A warm radiance echoed outward onto the street, and even my eyes felt the light. A bunch of bowls were then placed on the center table with steam that bubbled up to kiss the ceiling and lay in wait to be devoured.

I wasn't sure if he saw me, or if he wanted me to come in. My stomach grumbled. Hunger - true hunger - had finally set in. I didn't realize that I hadn't ate all day. Yet I wasn't sure he deemed me worthy enough. There was a certain tone in his words that made me disheartened to even enter my home. I didn't know if I could call it my home either.

Dan briefly exited and then entered my field of view, balancing an array of plates with different sizes. His body contorted and twisted like he was attempting to walk on a tightrope.

More movement appeared. His kids entered the windowpane. All three of them. A baby was among the things he carried in his hand, and that infectious cuteness couldn't help but make me smile.

The smile disappeared afterward. He never told me about them. I didn't expect him to adopt three whole kids, either, considering there was only one income in the house. If there was only one income in the house.

I watched with more agony as the steaming food was wolfed down. The agony increased as I saw them laugh until they clutched their hearts. Dan had his hands full, keeping them in their respective seats on the couch, making sure they all ate, and the food stayed on their respective plates. But he seemed content. The content was what he showed me, at least.

The kids held their stomachs with the newfound heaviness while Dan collected their plates. They'd all gone through two plates - even the baby went through two kiddie bowls - except for Dan, who hadn't finished his first. *The Dan I knew would've been the first to finish.*

This wasn't the Dan you knew. The emotional cushion he gave me in my dream began to grow stiff. Uncomfortable. Painful.

Was it envy, at the perfect life I didn't realize he'd gained? Or that he attained it by leaving me behind? By embracing the thing we used to rebel? The words of the mechanic began to swirl around in my brain again. These hard truths, the ones I never wanted to claim, or even imagine, were beginning to be as tangible as the hot water bottle. Once more, the thought of leaving everything behind was sparked deep within.

Before that spark had any plausibility of growing to a flame, my phone rang. My fingers and limbs tripped over themselves as I struggled to locate it within the mess of my car.

Eventually, I answered the call after finding it under a long-neglected pair of briefs in the back seat.

My eyes sped back to the open window as the phone sped up to my ears. Yet the curtains were fully closed. Nearly. Only one thing was visible, and that was Dan. Standing. Looking at me.

I spoke. "Hey, man. You're gonna need someone with the amount of trouble your kids are giving you. Might help."

In the distance, his lips began to move. "I'm fine." Then silence. A virtual standoff ensued, to see who'd talk first.

"You didn't eat much."

No heed was paid to my comment. "Why'd you even come?"

"And who the hell are you to act all demanding and shit?" Before I could process what he said, it came out. A switch flicked on internally without a moment's notice.

"You don't even want to come inside your own home. Or even sleep." Dan pointed out. "Yet you drove all this way, so I think I'm entitled to be a bit confused. You haven't visited Dad yet, either."

"Oh yeah?" I didn't want to be the first to anger, though I suspected that he beat me to that despite the rarity of his character to be overcome by the emotion. "How'd you know?"

I heard a noise in the background. Dan's voice, in a hushed tone. Through the window, I saw his body turn backward and his hands waved. A flurry of shapes that'd entered the room moments before exited the room. "Well, the ladies at the home like me a lot."

I smiled. The bitterness was apparent. "And lemme guess, they don't like me?"

He turned back around. "I think we both know why." Even from where I was located, I was taken aback. A slight gap in my mouth started to form as I saw my brother turn into someone I'd never seen before. *No. He already turned into this.*

"I'm the one that's entitled? You're the one that was giving me those looks earlier today." I protested. "And you won't even tell me about your children."

He scoffed. "I'll tell you about my children when I think you deserve to know."

The words stung me, and I was tempted to go inside the house to show him what I deserved. But I let the anger go. I didn't want to cause a scene in front of his kids. Not when I was fresh from knowing what damage that did to us.

Dan seemed to share my sentiments. "You know I didn't mean that." His voice was soft like it was when we were kids, and he got caught doing something he shouldn't be doing.

I sighed. I wanted to look at the positives and try and convince myself that it was worthwhile to come here. But I never felt so alone. Neither did I feel so far away from him, despite our eye contact. "Why'd you change? Was it 'cause you believe them? What they say? After everything I've done for you?"

Silence, accompanied by heavy breathing. I could see him open his mouth, but he hesitated before actually saying something through the line. "You did everything for me?"

"Dan," My words were soft, yet a fire raged inside me. The fact that he chose to go down a path of negligence, just like everyone else, and had the gall to confront me with that nonsense. I wanted to prove him wrong, so desperately.

"Come inside." He started before I could get it all out. We can worry about your mistakes later. Besides, I know you haven't eaten all day." I wasn't sure if those words held care or a sense of superiority and overconfidence.

Either way, even if he was right, I wasn't in the mood to entertain his act, especially when it was built on so many falsities. *And that fucking "We"*. He was hiding someone from me. *I knew it.* "I don't have anything to prove or fix. Not to anyone. Not to you." I cut the connection without waiting for a response. I expected so much criticism to hit me, yet I never expected him to be a part of it.

As I started up the car, Dan still stood at the window. I looked away to rob him of his joy. I felt him still watching as I drove off.

But I didn't look back. My ego didn't allow me to admit how starving I was while I exited the neighborhood.

Parasitic Intent

Consciousness reentered my body after a long break. It didn't feel better.

My feet had found itself on top of some white, marbled floor. I looked down. The tiny black and gray specks were clear to the eye. No squinting was necessary to make out their uneven shapes.

The tiles shone with freshness. So did the glass checkout counter. The newest items gleamed in the white light.

Yet my mind traveled back to the first time I visited the gas station when counterfeit items were all over the shelves and the checkout counter was decidedly not glass.

Yes. It started coming to me. This was the place with Robin's coworker who was kind enough to supply me and Robin enough drinks to last a lifetime. It was the middle of the night. I'd popped in for a quick snack after a night of doing jack-shit. Perusing the halls, I saw the guy throw out good beer. I asked him why, but there wasn't an answer. Robin was lucky enough to capitalize on his dejected attitude and sleepy expression. His face almost lit up with a power of a hundred watts when she offered to take the work off his hands. The man left the store in five minutes.

Thinking back on the experience, I could see why he'd gotten bored. No one visited the gas station, let alone come inside, on account of its shadiness. Even now, the monotonous torture tried too hard to hide among the popular labels. All it did was blend in among said popular labels.

I stopped the trainwreck of thoughts, trying not to aggravate the exhaustion further. I scanned the shelves, trying to find something that could alleviate my dopamine addiction. The same one that moaned and berated even though there was plenty of food available, but not the ones it specifically wanted. I continued moaning and berating internally that I should've figured this out earlier.

As I walked down the next aisle, my stomach gurgled more. I could almost feel my ribs pry themselves out of my skin. *Man, do I need coffee.*

I was now in the condiment aisle. At least, I assumed it was the condiment aisle due to the majority of the items being ketchup and mustard.

A row of green jars caught my vision. Pickles. I found it strange, their location. I didn't know why they were with the condiments. *Were they supposed to be in the condiment aisle? What made them a condiment?*

I suggested to myself that they could be used in sandwiches. But all that thought did was make me reconsider what I thought a condiment was. Out of place, my legs walked through the aisle, not knowing what I was looking for. My mind was still stuck on those pickles.

I drifted over to the register, my feet too reminiscent of a cloud just floating without a purpose. Or the pickles in the condiment aisle.

A familiar voice. A voice that probably drew me to this specific gas station in the first place. "You gonna buy something or just wallow in your self-pity for a little longer?" I turned.

Robin. Sitting behind the store's counter, watching someone walk away with their bag of chips. Some blue streaks were in her hair, as per usual. Though they seemed faded, along with the rest of her face. This was the first time I'd seen her without makeup.

Seeing her - at all - this early in the trip wasn't according to plan. But our eyes twinkled when they met. Twinkled, almost lifting me to the stars with their cheeriness. I can almost forget. Of course, when that thought hit my head, I had to let the memories wade back in.

I smiled back, nevertheless. "I didn't know you wanted to see me. What was it, four or five years since we last texted?" My words stung with bitterness even I found surprising.

I got her number just a few years before what happened with Mom. It'd been one-sided, me just talking to her about stuff that was on the news. Nothing else. Nothing more. Her usual response consisted of a couple of words. But at least she responded.

That was until I started fighting with Shannon. More and more arguments would just arise. I'd decided to pin our conversation, waiting for her to hit me with that unique brand of witty wisdom. *So stupid. Desperate.*

The responses devolved until they weren't responses. I was the only one reaching out for anything, too naive to see I was only tripping over myself in the self-induced darkness. Whenever I opened my phone now, I glimpsed at those unread texts from another eon. It never ceases to provide me a complete stop in my day upon the very sight. I hadn't gotten around to unpin it.

All these thoughts did was make me freeze in place. I was in another time and place, while she watched me reject the present in the pursuit of these memories. Of course, I had this slightly open mouth that drooled. When the saliva hit the floor, I closed my mouth and wrenched myself back into the present in a millisecond. An awkward stretched millisecond, yet I laughed. Small, feeble. Something meant to break the ice. Hiding my true emotions. *I hope it did.* "How's it going?"

"Like you always say. It's going." Her lips crept into a smile. "Yeah. I didn't want to be known as that bitch who knows you." Robin's hands did something below the counter with effortless ease.

"Well, it takes one to know one." The comment surprised me. I didn't see myself having the capability to crack a joke - even a terrible one - at that. It was as though her presence pulled it out of my thick defenses." And at least I don't still work for some shitty gas station or mini-mart or whatever this place is now." I gestured around me, which was when one of the lights over the ice cream box flickered off. The temptation to take notice of that was great, but it was a bit too sad to comment on. I couldn't tell if I was still using my bitterness to talk.

"I'll let you know when I figure it out." She sighed with a shake of her head, though I didn't know if it was my joke or the light. "So, what brings you here? Miss me?" Sarcasm was present, but nothing on her face showed it. It was these habits that made her seem like an enigma. I didn't think I'd ever understand her or why she cared about me, and here she was proving me correct. *Maybe that was why I was drawn to her. Maybe that's why I cared so much about what she thought of me, and if she responded.*

"Please. No one needs your ego to be bigger than it is." I shook my head, the gravitas of the situation seeping into my thoughts and words. "No, it's my dad. He's, uh, going through some stuff. I thought that I'd stay here. Do what I can. Maybe."

Robin raised her eyebrows in surprise. "Actually? Well," She clapped. "Looks like I'm getting me some money today."

I opened my mouth to answer, but my confusion got the better of me. She shook her head with a smile. "Everyone knows you're here. Some white ladies came by and talked about you coming back. They acted like they knew you better than me, so I made a bet. "

Robin leaned over, her elbows on the edge of the counter, and her body weight close enough to me that she could've fallen over me with a simple shove. In one hand, a pen from one of her pockets was twirling itself. Her free hand covered her mouth in secrecy. "They weren't fans of you."

She leaned back before she continued. "I just knew you'd come back for something so stupid." The nonchalant nature of her words threw me off, no matter how hateful I was towards my father.
Her smile disappeared, and I couldn't tell if she was joking. "You calling my father stupid?"

But an almost opposite reaction occurred internally. *Did I want to visit Greg? Would the hate resurface?* My mind went back to the words of the mechanic. I could almost feel his wisdom untying its knot on me, releasing the hold it once held. The "Why" seemed to be a dumb pursuit all of a sudden.

I must've worn my emotions on my face because Robin laughed. "Relax. I couldn't care less why you came. All that matters is you're back. Come on, I'll take you to everyone who was either too poor or too dumb to leave."

I couldn't help but laugh at the absurdity of the statement. It felt weird, laughing. My mouth hurt since it hadn't stretched itself so far for a long time. "Oh yeah? Which one are you?" I stared, looking at her and the lack of change. That same sarcasm and snarky attitude. It was refreshing for once. I was - at long last - unable to see the change and the years that happened. If I tried, I knew I could see some of the changes, but I failed to ignite some motivation to do so.

72

She shrugged. "I haven't decided yet." Her hands flew over the counter and without hesitation, her legs jumped in the air. They landed next to me. Robin's hands went back to plug off the computer and grab her stuff. The keys jangled as she continued talking. "Alright. Come on, Cal. Chop Chop. It's like ten. We're no spring chickens anymore."

I looked at the watch. 10:14. It, indeed, was late. And we were, indeed, no spring chickens.

After I slipped through the closing door behind Robin, I took a gander outside. The dark, slightly wet asphalt felt warm, even through my shoes. The rising humidity was almost visible. The only thing that helped me see were the dull gas station floodlights. No activity was occurring, so there wasn't much to illuminate anyway. "Who's gonna close up inside?"

Robin shrugged once more. "Probably one of the guys in the back. I don't think about it too much."

"Even if I didn't close up correctly and got fired, I'd love it." Her head sunk and her mood became more solemn.

Robin kicked a rock over to me while we walked to my car, which was parked at the very last parking space. "I guess you didn't experience that."

I kicked it back without registering the meaning behind what she said. "What do you mean?"

"So, how's your little indie movie plot going? Get through much character development?"

I couldn't help but get sucked into the sudden deflection. It was random enough for anyone with a brain cell left to figure out, yet I let the conversation switch tracks. *She was good at that.* "Not funny."

"Cause it's true."

"Because it wasn't funny."

"Which means it was true, so-"

The comment continued, but I ignored it as bright headlights entered the gas station's parking lot. I put my hand up to cover the piercing blindness. Even through my fingers, the redness I saw in them felt the heat.

The car, a red sedan, parked itself. The bright lights left. The door opened. *The red sedan.*

Robin kept talking, her words drawing me back into her world. "Like when-" This time, she broke her train of thought when she saw who came out.

When I followed her eyes, it all stopped. Time. Feeling. Emotion. Anything that perplexed me before that moment was clear, but my sight was still clouded. Clouded by the sight I saw before me. *What? Why wasn't it just a rumor?*

A pink rain jacket. A highlighted strand of purple in her hair stood out in the high ponytail. Denim pants. My eyes wanted to be drawn to it all.

Yet I forced them into the twilight around us. I didn't want my fears to be confirmed because I knew it was her. This was too spontaneous, even for the strings of our souls.

I found her eyes for a brief moment, which too were somewhere else on vacation. Wrinkled, yet familiar skin. Those same blue eyes and the warm lips I kissed underneath the chapel. The emotions that were hidden in our pupils, the very desires that burn the coal and kindling in our hearts. I sensed it without question.

Yet after all this, my brain didn't want to admit it was happening. *No. It couldn't be. She wouldn't come back.*

Shannon's car chirped as she locked it. The lights flickered on and off with harshness. Her hair bounced as the wind rose and fell, letting me see the weakest and most frayed strands. But she stopped an arm's length away from us, and I couldn't see them anymore. "Hey."

A pause to breathe. "Wanted to see how you were doing. If you were still monologuing. Among other things." A glance off to the side. *Wait. Was that at me?*

I listened in as Robin responded. "I'm good." She nodded to reinforce that.

Her eyes were now a bit darker. No doubt they were heavy with more exhaustion. *Or maybe something else.* Those lips of hers remain pursed in constraint, nevertheless.

The fingers that laid rest on her thighs danced around, performing some sort of exotic ballet that was known only to her. Her family's bracelet she wore danced with elegance, but it was something on her nails that caught my attention.

The same nails that Shannon invited me to paint once. The same nails she cried laughing over as I drew the most horrific jagged shapes in the weirdest colors.

The horrific jagged shapes and weird colors were still there, yet they weren't drawn. As her arms lay to rest, I noticed that her pinky hid behind her hand. Part of me was tempted to step aside and see what she was hiding. *A cut? Something worse?* At that instance, the infatuation that had started to take over me was visible. I controlled those thoughts, but the realization of what those thoughts were made it difficult.

Naive fool. I was worried for her. Back then, too, with all the little habits she used to have. Like the obsession with shades of blue. I was obsessed with it all. It looked like the obsession, that same worry came back with the impetus of her sight.

Shannon hit a conflicted nod back. I didn't know one could be conflicted, but she proved me wrong.

She didn't move after that, resulting in an awkward standoff. During the conversation, she still refused to look at me. Yet I could almost sense a telepathic conversation occurring between her and Robin.

Somewhere in my brain, I wanted to be the bigger one. Make it clear that I moved on, even though there was an opaque clarity over that fact. I looked at her rain jacket.

"Nice jacket. Never noticed you wear it before."

You have. Idiot. Her eyes shot to mine, and for the first time in a long time, they didn't just see, but connected with mine. It was horrifying. The silent strength and independence she held close to her shone through her harsh, blue eyes. They seemed to look at me with cold unfamiliarity. With hate and disgust.

I looked away, feeling alone despite their presence. The darkness around us drew my attention.

Shannon muttered something. The sound of her shoes walking on the gravel faded as she stepped in her car and drove off. It all happened much slower than I wanted it to.

After a good minute of silence, I realized I was holding my breath. I let it out in one big sigh. Even then, the awkwardness clung to me with actual physical weight, not too dissimilar to what I felt in the hotel room. I buckled, my hands on top of my knees and my mouth breathing out into the ground.

Robin patted my back. "Let's get some beer."

Please. I didn't care if Shannon appeared beside me. The maximum alignment our thoughts were at proved stronger, helping me reinforce that we needed to get out of there as fast as possible.

Our Faces

The gas station dissolved into the greater darkness.

I realized some time back that there was no avoiding what I saw. I had to see it even if I didn't believe that the "Why" was hidden somewhere in the depths of the pain, even if I didn't want to experience the pain again.

There was no struggle within me anymore now, for the first time since these dreams started occurring. *When was that?*

The clouds were overcast, yet the humidity seemed to claw at the hair on my arms. I looked to my right. Teenage me appeared, mid-stride in a fast yet meandering walk. Hair was going past my ears. Meaner, scarier eyes. I remember many telling me that I changed a lot. I told them a lot changed me. And those broken eyes told me the very same.

A road materialized underneath both of our feet. Placid Lane. Aspen Boulevard and the high school were off to the right at the Tellermen intersection ahead. Teenaged Me's hands were up in the air, swaying opposite legs. It wasn't until the yellow divider made itself known underneath his toes that the image made sense.

He fell off to the side, losing balance somehow to a nonexistent height.

I'd grown accustomed to walking. Long distances, though dangerous and frightening at first, were welcome in my mind. It gave me enough time to wander the endless halls of my brain.

Then I started loving it. Never did I have to worry about getting lost on these long walks. Of course, getting lost was part of my purpose. The only thing that stopped me was hunger, or the darkness threatening the tops of the trees. The latter was the case at the moment. Besides the silent hue from the sun, which already went below the horizon, there was little to no light.

Oh yeah. Shannon was the reason I took the walk that day. Me and Robin started our lunch block off like any other day. We sat in the corner while I gave her advice on guys and girls. But when it came time for the strategy sessions for Shannon, Robin didn't give me any.

She instead told me that Shannon had gotten a boyfriend. A guy from Drophead she met at church. Her face was solemn as she spoke, which I'd never seen before. When I stormed off without a word, she knew better than to follow me.

As I walked through the near-empty hallways, tears threatened to break through my eyes. I didn't let them, as I'd had a lot of practicing moping around the hallways. The same hallways of the school where I couldn't find respect. I was no outsider anymore, but I still wasn't regarded then. Except when it came to jokes. I did the same stupid stuff everyone did, but I was always singled out when they needed a good chuckle. Everyone knew making fun of me would make everyone laugh. They still did it, because their humor was always above my integrity. But when they showed the smallest bits of kindness, I was just supposed to forgive them all completely. I was just supposed to take the joke as a joke, instead of what it actually was: An insult. It was wrong to think this way, but I still endured the thought that dating Shannon would break the unbreakable cycle and prove them all wrong.

But it didn't. The bitterness inside only grew quieter inside. The fact that even if I didn't do anything to avoid messing everything up it all still got messed up. Now all the insecure dreams of someone else living what was supposed to be my life with Shannon began. I knew it was wrong to think that way. I knew I was supposed to be happy for her. *But how was I supposed to keep the bitterness at bay when she was perfectly fine with me being unhappy?*

It wasn't the end all be all. Their relationship did decay over time. But the only solace I felt then was that I still had Robin by my side. Even that thought - now - didn't contain the same ease it did then.

After I barged out of the school, I walked home with my spare house key. It was the last day of school, so nothing mattered anyway. *Except for her.*

I stayed in my room for the remainder of the school day while my mind fought hard to reframe Shannon as something that wasn't meant to be, even though it was nowhere near prepared to do so. It only spawned an assembly line of existential thoughts I never truly forgot. *Maybe if I wore another face around her. If I didn't say that terrible dad joke. If I was actually funny, or I went to the gym. Maybe if I wasn't so short, or had abs.*

After Dan walked home, Mom started to wake up from her slumber, so I walked out of the home as well with my rain jacket. I didn't want to deal with her or the rain.

The road had very few streetlights, let alone ones that worked. The added darkness added an eerie haziness to the air, similar to this memory. I knew it had importance. But the actual events remained unclear, like I was sitting down to watch a movie I liked but hadn't seen in a long time. The only template or information I had about it was the deep roots its nostalgia buried its way through in my brain.

An insect buzzed out of nowhere and entered my lashes. Usually, when I closed my eyes in these dreamscapes, I couldn't feel my lashes. But this time, I felt them with an additional heaviness, even before I brought up my knuckles to rub my eye sockets into my brain.

The itchiness I thought would bug me had a notable lack of presence. When I opened them, there was no sign of an insect. There was no teenage me to my side as well. My hair felt weightier, and my chin didn't itch from my stubble. The more the transition became known, the more I realized there was no internal power struggle. *Is that a good thing?*

Looking around - besides a flock of birds distracting me shortly - the slight incline in the school's grade made it easy to focus on the bustling baseball stadium above the plaza in my line of sight. *Maybe I wanted to see a bit of the game.*

The game. My teenage conscience moved aside to let me remember. The game generated more buzz than a honeycomb back then, especially since it was the first time we hosted the Lower State Championship in over forty years. The rain, which many saw as an omen and foretold that a suspension would halt what little of the game was played. Either way, everyone was talking about it, especially since it was against Drophead.

I checked my watch. 8:33. Already, the majority of shops had flipped their signs or were still flipping their chairs. The only thing that wasn't was the jolly green Burgerville, which was still flipping burgers. The mouthwatering smell tempted me, but I unfortunately never considered bringing money when I walked.

A crack of a bat sounded out throughout the night. I looked over beyond the trees. The floodlights that lit the school's baseball field shone through the leaves and twigs of the red maples. A tiny white object flew through the air, out of said floodlights. As soon as it appeared, the ball disappeared below the tree line, and a loud cheer ran through the empty streets. Even some of the people sitting outside gave a few cheers.

I never cared much for sports. But this game had managed to induce some care within even me. Of course, the care disappeared over the day when I realized that Shannon's boyfriend was on the baseball team.

I squinted in the distance, turning my attention to the school. I couldn't see the rooftop from my position. I wondered if Robin was at the top, watching the game with the free drinks we'd gotten days before.

My eyes drifted over to the stadium. *Is Shannon over there too? Would she even care if I showed up?*

A breeze hit my back. Forced onto the balls of my feet, my hair almost wrapped around my face.

I reached the front of an electronics store before turning around and looking up. A massive group of clouds pirouetted through the lukewarm air together like a school of fish. Or a group of sharks, hunting prey and intimidating anything near it. The people sitting outside the Burgerville started to shuffle awkwardly inside. Kids were squealing, while their respective parents tried their best to shut them up.

I left behind the noise and commotion, starting a slow jog. In the same corner of the plaza as the electronics store, was a hole leading through the plaza-circling wire fence that led to a path in the trees. It was off the beaten path. Well off. But it would cut through the woods faster than the conventional road home.

A slight downhill propelled me forward. I kept looking around, eyes wild to make sure no cars coming from the game took me off my feet. A few feet from the fence, the wind pushed my back harder. I began to move a bit faster. A few more steps and numerous currents went around at once, including two pushing me back. I started a sprint as the raindrops fell. As I grabbed the fence's opening and tried to widen the mouth to let my backpack in, dismay set in as I saw it wasn't big enough to allow me to pass through at the moment.

My fingers grew numb with the sudden cold that had enveloped me. Most of it was from the rain, which was accelerating exponentially. The now torrents of raindrops prevented me from seeing the opening, and after a few desperate tugs, I relented in official resignation.

I looked around as best as I could shielding my head from the rain with my hood. Panic set in, my swift breathing barely able to be heard even over the thunderous water and treacherous thunder. For a moment, I was blind to all the pathways that led me out of this scenario, like a set of walls closing in in a dark room as I was crumpled to death.

Then, I saw it. A few stores down the plaza's back lane - normally reserved for freight trucks - was a big metal, silver garage. A crack bled out light into the pouring raindrops.

I sprinted, hoping that it was big enough to fit me. It was in the end, though I had to take off my backpack and tuck my chest and stomach in to squeeze through. Once I got through to the dryness, I dragged the bookbag in.

I wheeled away with my hands and knees until I was on my back. My limbs all collapsed to the floor with a wet squelching exuding from my clothes.

Unfortunately, my shoulders touched something in the process. A cacophony of noise erupted above my head. Soil flew onto my hands and face, which closed its eyes to avoid any dirt. Pot shards skittered across the now-slippery floor to meet my eyes. Yet the exhaustion was the only thing that took up my mind. I could almost see one of the shards grow arms and legs. It sat upright, and I felt its nonexistent eyes bore into my skull.

I breathed a heavy sigh of relief. Regardless, I was safe. At least, I thought so. But as I stood up and looked around - doing my best to dry myself with a frenzied pat-down - I couldn't help but wonder where I was. A box was open, and inside were pots. Clay pots, like the ones where you'd put plants into. The boxes I bumped into had clattered into a mess of pot shards, soil, and purple flowers. I would've felt sadder if my heart hadn't threatened to break along with them with the expeditious beat of my blood.

The purple flowers. Now was when the memories hit me. Fear slowly enveloped me, then disappeared. Of all the worries I was weary of here in Gaines, Aubrey was one of the biggest. But I wasn't in danger of facing her - truly facing her - yet.

An open door. Behind piles of soil bags and pallets of pots. I walked through them and an enormous assortment of seeds to a tiny set of stairs, before venturing through the door.

There were a couple of side rooms hidden in darkness, but my attention gravitated to the massive, lengthy main showroom.

Many accessories were decorated on the walls, shaped similarly to alien artifacts. Sharp prongs and other peculiar shapes threatened to fly off the walls and create some more holes in me. They always looked more like murder weapons than the instruments of a gardener.

My eyes then noticed the elephants in the room. The rows upon rows upon rows of plants, seated on long black tables that looked out of place. Big. Small. Pots of all colors. Leaves of all shapes and sizes. Stalks and shapes of all sizes.

They had only one similarity: They were all dead. The stalks had exchanged their attributable greenness for a brittle brown. The leaves not attached to their plants were decayed, brown, and relegated to the soil their very own roots resided in. The few still stuck to their plants held some color, though mostly overcome by the air of degradation. Dirt was all over the floor, and the water dripping from my rain jacket created a nasty mixture of brown sludge.

A door opened to my right. I swiveled and braced for whatever was going to occur. Through the doorway and from the treacherous dismal outside came Aubrey. The head of the door lessened her stature even more, and her black hair was beginning to showcase its grayness. We looked at each other, and the lack of surprise in her face siphoned the surprise over to me.

Aubrey closed the door behind her once she limped inside completely, and the noise from the storm was muted with a magical remote. She closed the umbrella and gave it a few whacks over a table filled with plants before setting it in the corner of the room. More water flew onto the floor, more brown sludge swirling around.

"What's the last you saw the score?" I didn't answer.

Her face started to be injected with worry. Yet there was no question about my intentions and how I got there. She saw something else in me. *I wish Shannon had done that.* "You like you haven't eaten for days." She said, putting the plant in her hands on the table nearby. "Either that or someone beat the food outta you."

I looked down, just now noticing the pain in my right arm. The brown sludge was now tainted by red with the blood seeping by the metric ton.

I felt the urge to smile. I hadn't smiled since the school year started, and it felt weird to break this new norm. But I let the urge overtake me. "Sorry about the mess."

"Don't apologize when you don't need to." She smirked and waved me off. "Let's get it cleaned up."

Aubrey got a towel for me, which I draped over my shoulder. I laid my jacket under one of the lamps. I hoped it'd dry somehow, though common sense yielded that it wouldn't. After a stint standing around, I felt bad for making the mess messier. Especially as Aubrey limped around trying to find the mop she had. Once she found it, I attempted to wipe the red out of the black calcium carbonate flooring. I turned it into a dull pink instead. *Like with everything.*

Afterward, Aubrey brought out a stool, tired of all the limping around. I sat on the opposite side of the main counter and swung my legs into the fragile wood, waiting for the frigid cold to dry off my skin, jacket, and everything else. I felt as though I couldn't move my body more than a few inches from that which I was swinging. I forgot about Greg, Dan, and the time. Even hunger took second precedence over the cold.

In time I lost the ability to sit still even more. I stood around, watching the movements of the woman. With a transfixion, I spotted the cash register. Open, her back turned to it. It would've been easy to take advantage of her kindness. But this face she wore was genuine, and I didn't want to lose that. Not like what Greg did whenever we visited. Because this meant something to me, and he never did.

Aubrey made herself a drink in one of the adjacent tiny rooms. Once she finished, she grabbed the mug and a seat behind the main counter next to the window. She then resorted to watching the rain pitter-patter on the dark-lit streets through the giant windows in the front of the store. I doubted that it was her first time doing so.

The sound of her drinking was the only sound I could hear, besides the soft rain hitting the asphalt. I felt scared to talk, which was contradictory to the way she was treating me. But the obligation I felt to respond to her kindness took over in the end.

"So do you own this place?" I looked around.

All she did was sip her drink. "Yep. Since the eighties." The comment trailed on, her gaze was still fixated outside.

I asked, confounded. I knew every nook, corner, and cranny of Gaines. "Really? I've never seen it before." But as I looked around, I saw the cabinets and other appliances at the end of their wits, torn and bruised like me. The smell emanated all the people and lifetimes it lasted. I could feel the pain it felt, disregarded as it slept.

"Humanity tends to notice only what we want to look for." The sentence hit deeper when I put Shannon back into my thoughts. She didn't want to look for me.

I shook the thought out, not wanting to cry in front of this random stranger. At least, at the time she was just a stranger. "I can't tell you the last time someone came to this place that actually wanted to." She saw my face morph into guilt. "It ain't your fault, kid." A big hearty laugh made its way from the rain outside and followed her words.

"It's what's going wrong with this world. No one seems to want to give some of their care to those who need it. Deserve it." Her thoughts were curious, like someone who's surpassed your run-of-the-mill regrets. Those troubles of hers seemed deeper. "Long story." She chuckled my permutations away.

I felt even more inclined to say something, the wisdom something I didn't expect to receive more of from a stranger. Whoever this was, I didn't want to lose her. "Well, I don't know where I'd be if this weren't here. So, thank you." The storm brewed even stronger outside, as a warning to what I could've faced.

She smiled. "Don't thank me. It's that garage door that to be fixed."

"What's your name?" Aubrey reached across the counter we both sat across and pushed towards me a steaming mug. My teenage brain couldn't tell what it was, but as I cradled it in my hands, and noticed the dark liquid and its sugary smell, the adult version of my soul identified it in an instant. *Coffee.*

I took a sip, both of my souls grateful and energized within the same body. It still wasn't as good as the one Shannon made, but still amazing.

I'd almost forgotten her question, but as I saw her waiting face, I answered. "Cal." I took two more gulps before I set it down, the mug now empty. She smiled once more.

"Remind me not to show you where the rest is." She laughed once more. I didn't find it funny enough to show anything besides a smile. This new experience wasn't enough to bring out my laugh just yet.

Aubrey looked away, the emotion disappearing. "What is this place?"

She looked behind her at the plant life watching her with boredom. "Oh, well, I sell anything that could grow in this ungodly town." She stopped the sentence there and flung her arm off into the air.

Silence again. "What's your name?"

"Aubrey." She seemed glad I asked. "Proud owner of Aubrey's, Your local plant emporium. Featuring the largest collection of plant life since the very dinosaurs walked this very earth." Now it was my turn to smile at the enthusiasm she infected me with.

I looked out and looked closer at a wide variety of plant stalks, pots, soils, and vines. None of them had nametags, which was peculiar. Just prices.

One specific type of flower, a yellow one with five petals and an unusually healthy stalk, caught my sight for a few seconds before returning it to its surroundings.

Some of the pots were broken and were discarded to the side. Trash bags lined the far wall, and the welcome mat was eerily clean like it hadn't been christened.

The lady saw my gaze, and where it was directed. "That mat's three years old, believe it or not."

I drank some more coffee, except as I brought the cup up to my mouth, I realized there was nothing else in there. Drowsiness began to droop my eyelids and calm my brain. If I could've, I would've slept right then and there.

Lucky for both of us a big and yellow poster with black, bolded letters trapped my attention. It almost enveloped the entire top half of the front door, leaving a yellowish-gray tinge with the light filtering in from the doorway. Of course, that wasn't the only reason my eyes were fixated on the poster. The "Hlep Wanted!!" perked me up with delight.

Delight and excitement at this chance for a way out.

If I, with all my wandering, didn't come across this place, then no one else would in a thousand lifetimes even with a big poster. This could be a refuge for me, away from all my plagues. I could also earn some cash while I was at it.

As if that wasn't reason enough, Greg was starting to get agitated with the way I just wandered around. *Not that I cared that much.*

"Well, I'm looking for anyone interested in working for me during the summer. Help me with anything and everything. Manage the front desk when I'm not here." She seemed to follow my gaze and read my mind.

"So basically, a manager." I interpreted.

Aubrey smiled. "I'll take care of the decisions. And even if I wanted to, I couldn't give you anything north of twenty." She scrunched her lips up, as if in deep thought. "Dunno how Burgerville manages."

I scrunched my eyebrows. "How does someone earn more than twenty flipping burgers?"

She shrugged, crossing her arms. "If you're interested, you'll be doing more than just flipping burgers. That's for sure. Now, I know I can't pay you like someone over there." She waved her hand in the general vicinity of the Burgerville. "But, say yes, and you get the job on the spot. No interview, no resume, no nothing."

"No strings attached." I thought out loud. It seemed too good to be true. Besides the pay, a guaranteed job in the town was a big deal if it wasn't for a Burgerville. Even the shitty gas station rejected Robin initially. Maybe the work would be rough. Dirty too, judging by all the soil somehow already on my clothes. But that was no concern of mine. I had gotten my ticket out of the house, to a show where the entire opera sang only to me.

Deep inside, I knew that I'd feel like I was worth something as well. A feeling Shannon had managed to pry away from me.

I couldn't let her win. From that moment, a bitterness associated itself with Shannon in my thoughts. The girl I thought I'd love forever.

"Yeah. I can 'Hlep'." Aubrey laughed.

Aubrey's showroom limped away.

I was now in my dark bedroom, collapsing on the bed while I let my bag slip off my shoulders and hit the ground with a soft thud. The nerves in me were frayed, sending all sorts of electrical impulses to myself. My leg fell asleep, and then woke up just as it dozed off. All the muscle groups I could think of went through waves of relief, pain, soreness, ecstasy, and nausea. I didn't know until now how a literal body part could feel nausea.

My heartbeat began decelerating, even though I sprinted through the back door ten minutes ago. I didn't realize it, but I was holding my breath unwillingly. The red face staring back at me through the mirror told me that.

Dan chose this time to barge in. I shared my room with him now, even though he had his own. In one hand, a bag of chips, half full and crinkling with the simplest movement. On the other hand, a stack of papers and a pencil precariously balanced on top of it. He didn't acknowledge me as he set the materials down. I stared at him while he adjusted his belongings and sat in the chair, ready to work. He didn't smile once.

It was only after he turned the lamp light on that he paused. The chair squeaked as it swiveled to face me. His eyebrows were full of relieved curiosity. "Dude, where were you?"

"Where's Mom?" I strained my ears, trying to hear her footsteps around the house. The sink water wasn't running, which was the norm as she'd preferred this time to wash the dishes before she went to sleep. If she wasn't washing dishes, then she was drunk.

I could tell by looking into his eyes he'd have to wash the dishes before he had to go to school. At that moment, I wanted to unglue my legs and barge into Mom's room. Maybe warn her of these habits, try and force some sense.

Yesterday, she'd broken down in anger with the amount of alcohol she drank. Me and Dan had to talk in our Elementary school voices and explain things like she was five years old before she finally let go of the bottle and slept. She chose the cold tiled bathroom floor to do so. When she woke up, sober enough to realize what happened, she broke down once more. This time in tears.

The entire morning today was spent in tears, both Dan and her as she apologized profusely, swearing that it wouldn't happen again. I stayed quiet until she slept and left for school.

Dan looked back to his homework to avoid any conversation on the topic. He murmured something while he tapped his pencil on his paper with a decidedly un-smiley face. I took a peek over his shoulders while a sweat bead dropped onto his paper. Algebra. He never had trouble with Pre-Algebra, but this year was more difficult at school and home.

For everyone. The difficulties that we were experiencing as one familial unit were astronomical. A recapitulating cycle that sought only to decay and destroy. Not too dissimilar to what I was experiencing now: Pain without mercy.

Greg. My brain found its way to him. I knew it was him. *It was always him.* Mom always assured us that she didn't even think about him anymore, that she was even trying to for a couple of dates. She was sober when she said it, too. But when I saw her drunk, I saw her longing her something. Like a piece of heart had gone missing. I knew Greg would never leave this house, even if he did. The lamentations and wailing the house heard that day was why I'd left in the first place. The walls probably wanted to be demolished, after having to deal with the divorce and what came after. I wouldn't expect otherwise from them.

I looked at Dan and massaged his arm. I wasn't the type to be touchy with someone, but I could see he needed it.

Dan scratched his eyes. "Seriously though, where were you?" Confusion, not helplessness this time. It was almost like he had the younger sibling energy to follow me around like a duck following its mom. Even after his experience, he had time to ask me about my day. *When did all this change?*

I forged into my evening. How I found that lady, and what she offered. As I talked, he continued to display a range of emotions. First, was curiosity. He never ceased to question my actions, like why I even thought about going into a random store, and how I'd be able to manage such a schedule. But some just fell prey to his curious mind, such as the score of the game before it got suspended. I found myself not only answering his questions but also glorifying that potential job.

Looking back, some things I expected out of naivety. There was no way such a job could offer such a perfect salvation. Yet it gave a glimpse into my mind. I needed a perfect escape from everything and was too stubborn to think otherwise. Of course, I didn't care if I was stubborn or naive. *As long as I escaped.*

I wanted to tell Dan about Shannon. I never did. *Who knows what lies and deceit would've spawned from that?*

Soon after, I winded down the rant to a close. Looking at Dan, I found a bit of sadness in his posture. "You good?"

His face was scrunched at the lips and his eyelids dropped a bit. As I gazed, they shuddered a bit. "What're you talking about?" He shook his head, and it went away, a smile in its place. I couldn't see any fakeness. Yet, most likely unbeknownst to him, that was the first time he smiled during that entire exchange.

"You seemed worried." I paused. "Wait, was it something I said?"

Dan was quick to shake his head. "What? No, dude." He shot up and took a few steps toward our closet. I couldn't see his face anymore. "No, I'm fine." After an uncomfortable silence, while I waited for him to turn, he did so. Nothing was on his face anymore. Not even a smile. "Yeah, I'm fine, I was just thinking about stuff."

I patted the space next to me on the bed. "You can talk to me. You know that, right?"

He nodded but declined the seat next to me. "Let me go wash up and get ready for bed."

Leaving his homework behind, Dan took an unusually long time in the shower. Exhaustion overtook me while I waited for him to return and spill what was in his brain. As I drifted off to sleep, I couldn't help but think about that face he wore. Resigned. Battle-torn. Eerily similar to Dan in the present. Somehow even more like a soldier. *Fighting a losing battle.*

Deeper III

I was back at the gas station.

The dream didn't make much sense at that moment, so it was easy for me to pry my feet off the asphalt and get in my car.

Robin held out her middle finger from her own for no real reason. With a jump, she shot out of her parking spot and out of the station, my bumper close behind.

She brought Shannon back into my life. I didn't realize how easily I could blame Robin for all this. It was almost too easy.

We drove for some time. I knew that the gas station wasn't that far away from the school, so we were probably taking the scenic route. Basic navigation had returned to my mind the more time I spent in Gaines, but all the hidden routes one could take on the twisting roads of the town had left. Yet I still welcomed that feeling of being lost, like I did all those years ago.

One of the other good things that spawned out of the scenario was that I wouldn't have to see those landmarks that held so many memories, both good and bad. The night hid it all.

A few more turns, and I saw my neighborhood's street lights in my headlights. I sped up.

Finally, the school entered our sights. The same one that chose to view me for my flaws and stupidity. My mind was a collection of broken records at this point, always finding and preaching nihilism in any place I went. But there was no other choice.

It didn't help that the school was one of the few places that pressed the negatives in my face. All the dirty brown bricks did was take me back to the first days of school, when I met Robin for the first time since her act of bravery. The following days were spent making a friendship ring out of paper. I heard it was possible but never had instructions, and the prospect was too embarrassing to ask for help. Yet I never had seen such a loyal act from a total stranger. I didn't want the act to go unnoticed. I did gain a friend after that, but at the expense of the embarrassment I tried too hard to escape. I hated my classmates from that moment.

We shoved our vehicles into the empty school parking lot. The school's tennis team was finishing up their match. Their facility at the end of the school's boundaries and the floodlights they had turned on helped me see enough. Though there wasn't much to see besides the small neighborhood lining the back of the school and a set of concrete buildings, a less in-depth sight of the expansion I saw when I came into Gaines earlier that day.

Once the cars were parked, we shuffled over to one of the side entrances into the school. I couldn't remember if it was an entrance into the orchestra room or the band room.

But I did remember that it was always unlocked. Someone in my junior year broke the lock during the last days of school when everyone came to hang out and do a whole bunch of nothing. Robin swung open the door - the school never cared enough for an alarm system - and motioned for me to enter. "Look at me. The insufferable female side character bringing the male lead to their secret spot. As if things couldn't get more indie-like."

"Indie-like." I smiled and entered the hallway which opened into a massive room. "That's not a word."

"Sure, it is." Robin fetching a chair was the last thing I saw before the door cut off all light with a metallic thud. "All words are made up."

"I mean, yeah. Obviously. God, now I see where the insufferable part is." Silhouettes of band instruments that were put up on racks were all I could see in the crushing darkness. Yet I knew in the ceiling above it all, a cylindrical hole with a latch and a ladder was waiting for our touch.

I heard the sound of the chair thudding on the soft carpet. "Let's see if you remember." I grasped in the darkness until I felt the rim of the seat. After careful maneuvering, which briefly transported me back to my knee injury, I was standing on the chair. This time, I felt the darkness for the coolness of the ladder, but I didn't have to wave my arms like a maniac for long.

I heard Robin's feet shuffling back. I looked down at her dwarven figure, not confident in my ability to open the lock. But it was too dark to see her facial expression.

Reluctantly, I set to work unlocking the hatch. There was no complicated mechanism, it was the age that made it impossible to open. It didn't help that I had no idea what I was grabbing or twisting.

The metal chill helped me to remember the twist to the left and the slight pull to the ground that yielded the desired result. It didn't feel like I turned the mechanism to the left, yet it finally opened with a satisfying hiss.

The cool, frisk night air came rushing down the pipe and rustled our clothes. The darkness outside was slightly lighter than the one in, so finding and pulling down the ladder to kiss the ground floor wasn't much of an issue. One after the other, we went up to meet the comprehensive sky.

The fact is that besides the comprehensive sky, it wasn't as dazzling as it used to be. I was shocked, to say the least at the feeble, boring sight I was treated to. A smell that stank worse than anything I'd ever experienced before slapped my face a couple of times before moving into the background. I doubted my ability to forget about it.

The trees and the vibrant simplicity they emanated, the small houses adding to a quaint feeling were mostly gone from the surrounding streets. The culture had been entirely removed. I could almost feel the dreariness in the air.

Robin appeared at my side. "Welcome back."

She disappeared once more, this time to walk back behind an outcropping. I ambled over to see her knees on the ground and hand poking around inside a hole that was unceremoniously made with a drunk Robin and a loose brick. If it was daylight, the other holes that Robin punctured into the school's roof would've been visible, in an attempt to find the coldest spot for the beer.

"Got it." She boomed after some struggle. But as she tried to pull it out, her arm got stuck. She stopped moving and looked up at me, her neck contorted in an unorthodox fashion. "A little help here?"

I smiled. "Maybe." I looked around and grabbed an iron rod catching memories nearby.

After kneeling to poke at the drywall for a few minutes - through Robin's stifling laughter at my struggles - I stood, suddenly getting dizzy from standing up too quickly. "Try now." I spluttered out. She replied by taking her hand out without much hassle.

The nausea stopped. I smiled as I saw the object in her hand. A beer can, its logo and details very faded, its structure deformed. But once it was in my hand, I looked back at its label. It was very familiar. It was the same ones me and Robin who hid these up here for the next group of carefree high schoolers to eventually discover.

I knelt and looked inside the hole, glacial air forcing my eyes shut. My legs hobbled back at the freezing surprise. I didn't know exactly what made the spot frigid, yet it was.

"Is everything still in there?"

She nodded. "I wanted to save it for something special."

"Gross. You're making my heart melt." I retorted.

She snickered. "Collins just get the beer and follow me." Robin pointed towards the hole.

My hand reached inside the hole and sifted through the empty cans clinging and clanging against each other until I felt one that was full.

I brought it out of the tundra and popped the tab. The fruity smell wafted up to my nose, and my hand started to bring it up to my lips. Yet I still pushed my hand and the can it held away from my mouth, even though I didn't feel Shannon beside me. Whether it was an improvement was still up in the air like the smoke from the traffic that coalesced beneath us.

A slight smell of gasoline whirled up to us along with the fumes. Robin called me over to the edge of the building, her feet kicking apart the tops of a dead tree. "Hey, let's go slowpoke. You're going to miss it."

It was enough to distract me from the thoughts, though I still kept the can in my hand. "Yeah. Yeah. I know." I walked over to Robin and joined her with my legs swung over the edge. I kept the can to the side. The glow from the streetlights behind us had decided not to illuminate the roof, and the can disappeared in the darkness.

Before I could settle, Robin started, "How does it feel? To be back?" She looked at her watch like she was expecting something important.

"It feels more empty." I pointed over to the gray rectangles, though I also could've pointed inside me. "That was where Mr. Walker and everyone lived." The residential neighborhood was a hotspot due to its low cost. My family thought about moving there too, before the divorce. After that, Greg moved into the neighborhood. *What happened to him once it was demolished?*

Her head was still on her watch, though I suspected her thoughts weren't. She finally looked at the view and sighed. Her shoulders sagged. "Mr. Walker was the last to leave before they completed their move or whatever they called it last year. It wasn't just that neighborhood. It was the homeless shelter as well. You know, the one we got our community service hours at." She gesticulated out to the general area of the massive buildings. It was impossible to ignore.

"I guess they decided that we weren't good enough for ourselves. " I read the comment as a joke. "And none of us were there to say otherwise." Robin looked at me, and the bitterness that saddled her voice was starting to be seen on her face. She looked back at the view, the traffic below beginning to dissipate. "All gone. One by one. Now, the mall expansion. I don't know when it started exactly." She smiled, jaded. "I sure as hell don't know when it's going to stop."

At first, I thought I saw tears in her eyes. I assumed she was faking it, making some large attempt at humor. Yet as I stared deeper into her eyes, I saw the droplets illuminated by the glow below.

"You need some tissues?" I mused, laughing a bit.

She whipped her head around. "Well, at least I feel something." There was no smile on her face, nor twinkle in her eyes. The tears had fallen to her cheeks. All that was left in her eyes was a glowering stare at me like I was an insult.

Yet she bowed her head down. "Sorry. It's just that I don't feel responsible."

"It's fine. At least you still know how to monologue." I retorted. She'd gotten the main lead in a play during high school. Her monologuing became the focus of jokes long after that.

She laughed. "Yeah. I still have the red wig from that." Me and Robin snuck back into the school after the theatre company's last performance of their production for some souvenirs. I stole a plastic trident. I lost mine a couple of days later.

Her laughter subsided, and I veered the conversation back on track. "Like our parents always said, huh? About responsibility? Accountability? How we don't have it?" Greg loved to annoy me with that. I looked over to the can. Still no real sight of it.

Robin disagreed. "I don't think it's like that. When they said that, they always wanted us to be better than them. My shitty brain couldn't handle that back then." She took a swig.

I glanced over. "Probably why they told you." I never knew why they harped on that point. Especially Greg.

She slapped me. Not hard. More playful. It was still jarring. "Hush, Cal. You were one of them, too." Robin looked back out to the cars lining the roads. "With Dad dying and everyone leaving, I had no choice but to come back and take all the responsibility." The tone grew deep once more.

"Sounds terrible."

Robin shook her head. "I kinda liked it. I wanted to be responsible after a while. To have some say, at least. Even though I never had it, I missed it. Didn't realize how much I needed that."
She looked at me. "It sucks. Having something you love just taken from you. Especially if you convince yourself that you could've done something different."

With our eye contact, we knew that she wouldn't have to further explain the feeling. Even though our relationship was in pieces - scattered downstairs with the traffic - I felt she was one of the few who understood what I experienced.

I nodded. "Can't do anything but try and move on."

"Easy for you to say." The glowering stare returned. The words spat out of her lips with a terminal velocity, that voice having an unusual accusatory tone behind it.

I opened my mouth to respond, but my voice stopped, tripping over its limbs. When it recovered, I spoke. "What do you mean?"

She shrugged. "I didn't stutter." Robin looked back out at the traffic, which was nonexistent at this point. In the distance, I saw the lights in the office buildings go off. It wasn't by a lot, just one of two per minute but it was noticeable to the darkness that surrounded it.

Finally, I decided to answer. "No. It isn't. Moving on sucks. It was never easy. Never for one second. All alone over there." I gestured out into the night as I forced myself to not recite the same answer I always gave about whether I moved on. *This is Robin. You trust her.*

I began to speak the truth. "All I could think about was what happened. All that drove me to even live was just fucked beyond anything I could recover." It was my turn to become emotional, my voice cracking slightly. The bitterness I held inside just for her left my grasp. "Because I did everything for her. I kept her fed, I kept her safe, and I kept a roof over her head. I devoted so much for her happiness, and it all went down the drain. Again. I don't know exactly where I went wrong, but it doesn't matter. The energy I gave her is something I can't get back." Something was stopping me from saying her name.

Nevertheless, the words kept flowing, the rapids along the river picking up steam and foam, throwing it out of the water and into the banks. "I still have the house, and I never have to even consider getting a job. But it still feels like she took everything from me."

The river slowed to a meandering crawl. Robin grabbed my shoulder and squeezed it. "I feel for you."

She then joined me on the river, letting the pace consume her. "Have you dated anyone else?" *Shit. Was I supposed to have moved on already?*

"Some girl named Ashley, yeah. We had coffee. It was nice. She was cute. She seemed interested in me. She even convinced me to go to an Italian restaurant, which-"

"Yeah." I liked that I didn't have to elaborate.

"But when I was picking up some flowers, and I was watching it slide over the conveyor belt on the checkout counter, I realized that I bought the pink ones." By the look on Robin's solemnity face, I didn't have to elaborate on that either. "I went back home after that. I told her we shouldn't see each other anymore. Didn't realize until afterwards that their personalities were so similar. Like I was looking for her in someone else."

"What the hell? I've always been stupid like that. I'm too angry. I'm too quick to be mean. Too self-involved. Too selfless. Too hypocritical." My head sunk lower and lower with each word I spoke. "And too volatile, too. Gotten to a point where I can fully convince myself that I'm good."

"I can't burden her with all that. Even if she's a random person, she doesn't deserve all that." I couldn't look at Robin at the moment. *I don't want to burden you with all this either.*

She took another sip and cleared her throat with a meaty slap on her chest. "Bit harsh on yourself. Don't you think?"

I laughed. "You don't know what I think about. If you did, you wouldn't be next to me."

"Cal," She set her drink down. "Everyone has those thoughts." Robin shook her head. "And what if she didn't care how volatile you were? What if she still wanted you?"

I hadn't thought about that. *Was there someone who'd accept me for who I was? Actually?* I never imagined someone else besides Shannon accepting all my flaws. *You burdened too much on Shannon, and she ran away. If that happened to her, it'll happen to anyone.* "Guess we'll never know."

Robin picked her drink back up for an unusually large sip, her throat pulsating with gigantic proportions. Once finished, she wiped away the burp with her sleeve. "Well, while we're talking about this deep shit, can I give you some advice? Seems like you need some."

Where is this going? "I guess."

Robin's solemnity continued. "You take responsibility for everything except what you actually need to take responsibility for. You talk about your regret or mistakes, but I don't think you know what mistakes you should actually regret." Another accusation. *If I popped my kneecap right here, would she help me?*

"Do you have a problem with me?" I questioned her true purpose in bringing me up here. This place of solitude we shared now felt more like a trap she set.

"I mean, you said you were fine with the advice." She looked at me with certainty. "Just hear me out. You might've told yourself for all these years that it was to move on. The reason you left. But we both know that's not it because if you did then you wouldn't jeopardize anyone else's efforts to move on. You'd understand the value in at least believing you can move on." Her voice rose along with the steady sudden influx of traffic, despite the lateness of the night. "I'm not saying that-"

"I think that's exactly what you're saying." My eyes produced a light of their own in the darkness.

Yet she responded to my anger with a calmness. "Listen. I wasn't there, but I know you. I know you dude. I'm willing to bet that she never changed your mind. Once you're set on something you never turn back. Sometimes it's good." Nonchalance. A lack of care in her words. Another swig, and she threw the beer can into the hedges below with all the might in her shoulders. It clattered among the bricks before shuffling among the leaves and settling among the roots of the hedges. It would stay there untouched for some time.

"And that's all I am? Yeah? What else do you think you know about me?

"I think you need to allow people to change, 'cause that's what they're hardwired to do. Change. Evolve."

"But that doesn't change what I'm trying to say." Robin did her best to get the train back on the rails. "Even if they do change, and you don't recognize them, you still have to give more." *Why should I?* Her hands went wild as she attempted to explain her point of view. Robin swung her legs back onto the roof and sauntered over to the outcropping with the beer.

"This's all you think of me?" I repeated myself, hoping she'd understand and stop. Out of all the things Robin said, or could've said, that was something that hurt me the most. She knew the divorce ruined me. *Did she?*

Why was she doing this? Where'd the person who stayed up all night to prepare me for my date with Shannon gone?

Robin shook her head as it went inside the vent to get more beer. Once retrieved, she walked over and stood in a half-stagger. "Okay, I didn't mean it like that. It's just I talked with her a bit after she came back. Still, I agree with you on some things."

"She is a bit strange. Again, I give you that. I don't know why she cares about your family, or family in general, that much. And I get why you don't."

"I get it. Really." For a moment, I saw the pain she never elaborated to me in her eyes. Maybe she wanted to show it. Or maybe I was just that good at isolating even Robin's pain, which even I didn't know fully after so many of these deep conversations at this very spot.

"But even if you don't get what she values, you have to try and respect that." She brought her hand up to her head and pointed at it. "And has it ever occurred to you that she just wanted to help you?"

"I told her to stop asking about my family and she didn't respect that. I told her no, she didn't listen. She never did what I needed her to do." I objected.

Robin laughed at the absurdity. "What you needed her to do."

"Come on. Don't tell me you seriously forgot who left who in the end." Robin opened her mouth, but I cut her off. "If you didn't, you'd never try to say that I didn't do enough. That I had to give more."

"How do you know that you were right? That she didn't know what was correct? Cause you haven't healed anything back here by following your advice of pretending it doesn't exist."

"That is bullshit!" I exploded, but I knew I was wrong.

Robin pounced on my mistake. "Oh yeah, then why do you still call him Greg? You stop to think if you left anyone hurt back here? All alone?" The last words flashed something across her eyes. "If you didn't come back for them, then why'd you even come?"

"I came back for myself." It came out too fast for me to consider the implications.

Robin stuttered as if she wanted to say something but couldn't. Instead, she let laughter escape her mouth. It was haunting. I knew it haunted her too, but the howling stretched thinner and thinner by the second.

Robin sighed the laughter away after a gut-wrenching minute to adopt another serious face. "She cares, dude. That's all. She wanted the chance to care. You owed that to her. Even if the way she cared was wrong, you had to give her the chance."

"But I think you just think it's easier to do what's easier. Once you find that easier option-" She arched her hands all around us, no doubt touching the ghosts of our past selves looking on with consternation. "And god forbid, if there's even one tiny sign of trouble, you disappear. Only you know where you go."

"I don't have to owe anything to anyone, I can't go back and fix anything with Shannon, and I'm here now. So, what's the problem?" My voice was much louder, though there was no real reason. The traffic had gone for the most part.

"The problem is that the damage you could've fixed is already done, and you don't get that it's you who's destroying yourself by paying all your attention to that. Instead of what can be fixed." The face of solemnity, while she refused to agree with me over the past few minutes, stayed the same. It hurt me, considering that she often gave me respites away from the judgments of my life. Robin was now joining in the critique, which I never thought was possible. "Shannon's done. Gone. But what you can learn isn't. And we're all still here. You may think I'm insufferable. Sure, this is just another one of my monologues. Fine. But there's no fucking denying that I'm right."

No. "Yes, there is. You don't get to talk about this." I pointed at her.

She pushed my hand off to the side. "Don't put your finger in my-"

"Who came crawling back when it was her divorce?" Robin pursed her mouth to let me talk. "Who never responded to me when it was mine? Who decided to wait - what - like five months after the fact to decide that I was worth your precious little time? Because that was when I really needed you. That was when I needed this 'care.'" My finger jabbed itself harder at her, and my actions mimicked a knife. Driving it through her flesh. *That sweet flesh.*

I had to relent, the thought scaring me out of that flash of rage.

She threw her hands at me. Robin always started using her hands more the more agitation she accumulated within herself. "Ok. I've made some mistakes. I'll admit that. But I had my shit to deal with here." The deflecting continued, and I knew she would never get it through her thick head. "So-"

"Now who's stuck in the past?"

"This isn't about me, asshole! How would you feel if you were Shannon? When your own husband doesn't care what you worry about?"

"She wasn't supposed to care for me like that. I told her and she did it anyway. That's not my fault." My internal frustration mounted. "You know well and true that I can't just share what happened with someone else that easily. Even you. Because it's my pain. My past. I hate it but it's mine. Mine's." I swung my legs onto the roof to fully focus on her figure. *This wasn't her.* The girl who took my side in a heartbeat. Her loyalty to me had decreased severely.

And I had a clear idea of who corrupted her. I scoffed. "You believe her? After all she's done?"

"Cal-"

I scoffed again. "Is this you talking or her?"

Robin pursed her lips again, holding something great back with the force she exerted. "You know, when you talk with someone you're supposed to let them talk." The sarcasm further opened the wound with its jagged edge.

"Sure, since we're having this very civil conversation."

"Cal, " Robin closed her eyes to rub her head. Once her hands dropped, she opened them once more. "This isn't a contest between who's right or wrong. It's not that black and white, 'cause if it was we'd all lose." Her words oozed with more emphasis. "And again, not everyone prioritizes the same things. That's normal. But you can still respect it."

"Again, I didn't ask her to respect me." My teeth gritted out the words for me.

She groaned. "How many fucking times am I going to have to repeat myself until you get it? You. Didn't. Respect. Her." She started clapping her hands, this manic energy of hers pouring out of her soul in every way it could. "Maybe things could've changed for the better if you were more open with her. Of course, we don't know because you don't know what to do when people care for you."

"And guess what? Sometimes I do believe her because she doesn't let her pride get in the way. Unlike you." A smile. Sick, perverted.

She shook her head as the words strode through the open wound. "That ego controls way too much of you bud."

The numerous times Shannon and I met in court. The times they pushed us out as we resorted to our lowest means: Our voices. I found myself standing on the edge of the ledge, my legs almost shaking with anxious anger as those moments flooded my thoughts.

I wanted to do something. Prove her wrong. *I was right.* I had to be. *I can't be wrong again.*

Instead, I just looked around. In the distance, at the old train tracks covered with moss. It rose with the tiny hills before disappearing into the tree line. A train barreling down the tracks at supersonic speed, and it hit someone right at the edge of the forest.
I saw my limbs fly all over the place, the blood raining with curdling vengeance over the lush green.

"She couldn't have changed anything." I pointed at Robin, this time a little less accusatory. "You know about them. What I've been through." It was all I could say. I wanted this to stop. *Before this bridge is burned too.*

Robin smiled. "No, I haven't heard about your family, or your mom, who died, or your father who remarried. Their marriage is great by the way. No, I don't know about your brother and his kids. He never told you about them, right?" Robin paused as if I'd answer her words. I wasn't going to give her the satisfaction, however, and she continued. "No, I don't know about your father's cancer, and I certainly don't know about the fact that I paid out of pocket for his first chemotherapy session."

Strangely, her words got quieter as she spoke. "My fucking god. You say you hate the past, yet you don't grow up. Pick one! And stop giving me a migraine." Her hands flew up into the air. She swiveled off the outcropping and stood on the roof. The anxiety and restlessness were the sole things turning her wretched gears.

I opened my mouth, trying to come up with some half-assed apology. I knew it was gonna be half-assed because I couldn't think. It was like she froze me to the spot. "I love you, Cal. But let me give you a little lesson, even though I have no right to fix your problem."

"No." I shook my head. "What you faced is nothing compared to what I dealt with. So yeah. You have. No. Right. I'm only here to face

Greg. And I'm not gonna waste my energy to fix the past or their shit because it's their shit to fix." My finger jabbed itself off into the buildings twice.

"If they want to, fine. But me? No ma'am. It's fucked me enough." I murmured the last part. A meek attempt to reinforce the idea in my mind. The mind that wanted to identify with Robin so badly.

The occasion seemed well enough before this argument started. I'd stopped regretting the decision to come back here. Well, that feeling disappeared very quickly. I jumped down from the outcropping. My hands grabbed my can and threw it, letting it hit the metal and clang in the abyss, devoid of any other presence.

Robin's eyes followed the noise. Once it settled, unable to hit any other obstacle, she continued staring out. Then she looked down. I almost saw emotion in her face, yet the gentle wind blew hair into her eyes, almost like a shield to her true self. I doubt she'd clear her face of the strands.

My breath inflated my chest with tiring peaks and valleys, but I still wasn't done. The volcano inside me rumbled and thundered. Growled and roared. Magma threatened to seep out of my eyes and mouth. "And all this isn't too harsh for you? Wow." I thought out loud.

"You know I love you too. But I know what I need to do." I was growing tired of the deep conversations, the ones whose answers I already knew. "You don't get to comment on marriage and responsibility, especially when you were the one responsible for your wife growing tired of fucking you and decided she needed someone-"

Before I could finish, a right hook. It came faster than I could think, and it was after I doubled back in pain that I realized that Robin punched me. The agony stopped me from charging after her, the only thing I was able to do was massage the wound. She'd somehow managed to hit me just above my right eyebrow. Nothing major up there. Maybe that was on purpose. *Or maybe she missed her target.*

After a glance into each other's pained eyes, we looked over the roof at the familiar quiet.

A quiet, more than just a description. A feeling. An aura. The few cars left on the road were everywhere below us but without a mind, going in every which direction. Scattered, like seeds in an endless farm. Hoping to reap what can never be sown.

The quiet continued. Yet down the ladder, we both went. Robin was in a hurry to get out of there and away from my very sight. I felt her sentiments dearly for the second time in a few hours. I wasn't happy about that this time around.

My feet found themselves by my car. I fished my keys out of my pocket and inspected them in the straining moonlight, trying not to exhibit how much Robin's punch hurt.

I looked up and saw her approach her car. With immense speed and intensity, her driver-side door slammed shut. For a few moments, the car sat. Almost quieter than the night. The car then jumped to a start and bounded across the parking lot.

Robin hit a curb as she jumped across the exit to the school's parking lot into her driveway just a few meters away. The noise reminded me of just how close her house was. Nevertheless, she was late more times than the school could count, a side effect of the lack of responsibility she had. Before she changed. *Why did she have to change?*

She jumped out and bounded to her front door. The door opened, and it was still silent. Yet an abundance of light escaped her doors and spilled out onto the road. Inside, dozens of shapes milled around.

My confusion joined my curiousness, which shoved my keys back into my pocket. As if she read my mind, her figure stopped herself from closing the door, and she disappeared into a side room.

I drifted over the lengthy parking lot. The distance between us lessened until I found herself on her welcome mat. Trodden, and dirty. It was also a bit lopsided. I was too mentally spent to want to adjust it, so I just cleaned my shoes on the "Welcome" and walked inside.

A warm smell hit me. Food. Both are being cooked and sitting with finality. I could almost taste the love that it expelled. Off to my left, was a morning room with a dining table. Trays of aluminum held a variety of foods, spices, and tastes galore. Yet they were simple. Potatoes. Brussels sprouts, even. The mac and cheese had three trays, with one of them already empty and the other halfway there.

The people in front of me lined the food layout with paper-to-go containers and plastic utensils. I recognized some of them. A couple of classmates who always treated me with hate that'd never make me call them friends. Some were friends, though never as much as Robin. All were sitting as one, with tattered clothes and faces that seemed too big for them. Their faces looked earnest at my clothes, which despite its cross-country trek, were leagues more than they could imagine.

Robin came out of the morning room, having covered and handled some empty trays into the trashcan. A woman was with her, to which Robin was talking. "I'm sorry. Maybe you can come back tomorrow." The lady, with a tear-strewn face, walked past me with a brush on my shoulders.

Robins's gaze caught onto mine as the lady walked past me. I didn't realize the shock I still wore. I didn't know where it came from either. The fact that they chose Robin's house to claim as a haven. The fact that Robin had the resources to manage such an enormous population. Or that she still had enough room in her heart for these people.

"I told you I was going to show you who was too poor and dumb to leave." A small smile. No indication of our fight just moments before. Like it was all gone.

She stormed off further inside. "At least like this, I'm more responsible. I like fast-track my character development." I followed her trailing voice, wondrous as to what other secrets she'd contained for these years. As we walked further inside, there were many other people, with various backgrounds. Men. Women. Kids, even. Everyone.

The house itself seemed to have been wholly repurposed for this exact purpose. No life, no identity was on the walls. No carpets, no artwork, and no furniture, except for a bunch of white plastic foldable chairs in seemingly endless supply everywhere. Everything I could see had to be there to support the people.

"You should stay." She blurted out. "I mean technically I don't have any room, but I can make an exception." Robin's voice sunk beneath her breath. "Plus, we make a mean mac and cheese." Her voice rose again.

No. She doesn't get to try and be above it all. I let my ego grab Robin's arm to pull her off to the side. We were barely secluded, yet I asked. "So we're just going to pretend that nothing happened?"

She pursed her lips, clearly wanting to say something else. "What do you want me to say bud?"

"How about sorry?" Her words hurt me as much as her right hook.

"Sorry?" She looked away. A pause, as she carefully considered what she was about to say.

Robin looked back at me. "I will apologize for how I said it, but I will never apologize for what I said. I wanted to enjoy that view with the one person left I could enjoy it with. The one person I can talk with about that random fucking blizzard from god knows how long." *She remembers?*

"I understand that you may not be all for fixing mistakes and responsibility as much as me. But I will never be sorry for what I said. I need your life to be the best it can be. I need it. And if it's wrong to try and need it for someone hard enough so that they see how much they need it, then call me guilty." Her hands flew up in the air like she was being arrested.

I stayed silent. I knew she had more to say, and I knew better than to interrupt her anymore. "What you faced is nothing compared to what I dealt with, right?" Robin's voice entered a threatening growl. "You have no idea how lonely I was. You think you're the special case. You don't get how all the loneliest people always help those around them the most. Even if those around them don't deserve it. Like her." I noticed she couldn't say her wife's name too. "So, I'm kinda glad I decided to come home early that day."

She didn't stop. Her feet got closer to mine. Even though there were already so many watching this taking place, I managed to feel even more vulnerable. "You know those questions at the doctor about how you're feeling mentally?" She didn't wait for me to answer. "I want to answer those questions truthfully. But I can't, because what does that tell them? I'm not alright? But I think they'd put me under surveillance twenty-four seven if I did answer them honestly. That and they'll give me the solution, and I hate it when that happens."

107

"Exactly. You understand why I'm frustrated? I know my solution-"

"No. You don't." She smiled in response, and I realized I'd dug my grave a bit deeper. "And even if I don't either, I still know your pain. When we do a lot of things that don't make sense, like sleep on the floor even though we have a bed. Or when you go out and buy some dresses or clothes even though you know you have way too many at home that you don't wear. Plus, you don't have enough money." The words stung with a soft personal touch. "The ones that're hurt want that tiny bit of control when they do this. That small chance of a high. They want to prove to life that it hasn't won, that they can control whatever comes at them." *She's right. Down to a tee.*

"That they can feel responsible." Her voice constricted itself. "That all that went wrong in the past was because they were just stupid and naive and it all could've been solved if they were just a bit more responsible. They want to prove that that's the answer, that they have the only answer."

"They can't prove it though, no matter how hard they try, 'cause life rarely gives you one answer." Robin's voice reached the ground. "But you still go on trying to do the things you love to see if you can feel better. Or you try something random or follow some weird instinct to see if that changes anything."

"It doesn't."

Her breath was getting more ragged. My grave kept getting deeper as well. "The pain is so much more than what people think." Robin didn't want to let up just yet. "Even what I think, like you said." She laughed, and her hand amiably touched my shoulders. But her words oozed anything but friendliness. "The pain makes everyone around you feel more mature. The pain makes me think I think that's my destiny. To always reach out to everyone, only to feed their egos." She shrugged her shoulders again and again as if she couldn't explain or define her words further. "Somehow leave emptier inside. They don't reach out to me because they know I'm too unstable to help them." She laughed again. This time, tears were in her eyes.

"But wait, there's more. I know much more." Comically, like she was on TV trying to get someone's attention about their product. "I know the pain makes it difficult, after being lonely and broken and in pain for so long, to convince yourself that you deserve better. That you can feel something else. The happy ones say that the pain is there to make the joy feel better, but the broken ones will feel like the joy is there only to make the pain hurt more." Robin smiled wider than I'd ever seen her.

"Ok. Ok. You got your point across. Calm down." More and more people kept circling us, pretending not to pay attention even though their ears were glued onto our mouths.

"To be completely honest, I didn't think you were a priority those years ago. That's why I didn't answer. I couldn't answer all your questions. And I'll regret that, even if you think I'm some heartless bitch."

The rage and resentment I felt flew away, out of the rupture in time and space me and a broken Robin were in. "No, you're better."

"No, you're right. When I want to try to put myself first, I end up a heartless bitch."

Another pause. Another deep breath. Not like one someone would take when wading into the depths, but it held gravitas, nevertheless. The conversation had evolved from a spat about who knew more about pain to what we knew about pain. From whom won the argument to why we were arguing in the first place. Our deflections almost worked too well.

"I thought I didn't have to prove all this to you. To you, of all people." Her voice was shameful. Shameful of both of us.

"I thought you didn't have anything left to say after that up there." I gestured over to the school.

She ignored my weak attempt at a truce. "Shut the fuck up, dude. I know I got off track there, but I'm still trying to help you." Don't fight that."

"Well, how do you magically know all the answers that can help me?" *I don't know if you even know my problems anymore.*

"I don't, but I know which answer you'll keep. I know when you're hurt you're confident that it's the worst you'll ever feel. So, you'll settle for an easy answer, the one that takes less pain to find. But if you let the hurt control you, I guarantee you'll find out what it feels like to hurt even more."

"It'll do that somehow. Get worse. Whatever can fall apart will find a way to fall apart. And I don't want to see you go through that like I did."

"Don't fight this Cal. I fought it, and I had to dig my answers out of the ground with my bare hands." Robin bared her hands in my face, which looked in worse condition to tell me she might've physically done so.

The increased passage of tears stopped the flow of her words. She looked around at the people, who pretended their eyes were elsewhere with heightened virtuosity. "You got everything out?"

"Almost. I know I've been monologuing for a decade." Another laugh, her hand also shooting up to point at the school. This laugh was less bitter and sarcastic, which was a lens I couldn't view Robin. The tone was almost accepting of her joke forever attached to her. "I know you can't just change because change is hard. Hating yourself a bit less every day is hard." She leaned closer, her words accompanying her teary desperation with ease. "Trying to be happy with what I have is hard."

"Yes, I still should've checked on you. Yeah, it was probably me who destroyed our relationship. But for what it's worth, we can try to fix what we had."

I nodded. "Ok. I can help."

Robin shook her head. "No. Accept the responsibility for all of us."

"What?"

"You hurt all of us." The accusation felt too big for my head to handle. Too grandiose. "Fix us, and then you could fix everything else." We both knew it sounded selfish, but she didn't care about that or the desperation that somehow grew past her eyes.

It was my turn to shake my head. "That's stupid. That's y'all's problem. Just 'cause I played a part in it doesn't mean it's mine to fix. Why is that my fault?"

Robin stared dead straight at me. "Could we do that? Can we still do that?"

She knew the implausibility. Her words screamed at me, but not as much as her face. The impassioned hurt she had in her eyes had the fragility of a newborn baby. She needed someone to carry that hurt as much as I did.

But I knew I couldn't carry it. All the change. *It'd be too heavy to even try.* I shook my head. "You're right. I do think it's easier to do the easier thing."

The silence that birthed itself afterward permeated, and those who were sitting around our feet began to dissipate as our souls landed back on Earth. Robin's intensity drew back inside her to a close, and an awkwardness lifted it into the air. Our eyes were stuck to our toes in a painful trance, one we both wished would never come to fruition.

The day was getting full, almost too much for me to contain. Tenets I'd grown up on had been destroyed. Ripped apart. Chewed.

Someone had accidentally tripped over a cord, and the light in the room was snuffed in an instant. Shuffling and slight mumbles ensued before light returned to the world. Robin, in the corner with her hand on the tripped-over cord. It was now plugged in. *I wish it was that simple.*

I looked at Robin, into those green eyes of hers.

Guilt started to run its course in the form of confusion. A confusion that ran over me like the train did minutes before. *Am I the only one who can fix everyone? Why can't I fix myself first?*

Why can't anyone fix me?

Why do I have to fix myself?

The thoughts kept swimming deeper and deeper. I walked outside in the meantime. I had a feeling Robin was at the door, staring at me. Wanting to call me back. I didn't turn around to confirm my suspicions.

Deeper and deeper.

On the trek back to the school's parking lot, I brought up my phone and summoned the courage to unpin our text conversation. *Too much.* I couldn't delete it yet. Instead, I jumped into my car, and the sadness that'd accumulated had made my heart heavy. A heaviness I thought I'd left back at with the mechanic. But it was different this time around. *Maybe Robin gave me some of her burdens.*

The car rumbled, waiting for me to command it onto the now-empty roads. Yet I didn't want to. I didn't want to discover or dig up anything else.

111

There was no contentment or relief in my heart, nevertheless, when I turned the ignition off and leaned back into my seat.

Deeper and deeper.

As my eyes closed, I went even further. The heaviness pulled me into the depths. A heaviness that I was starting to think would never truly leave me behind.

ACT II

The (Assistant) Manager

Even in my sleep, it didn't leave me behind. *I was right.*

Now I was on the black couch that belonged in my home. Except I wasn't in my home.

I was in the void again, blackness all around as far as the eye could see. The ground was invisible as well, yet I knew it was there by the fact that I wasn't spiraling through the air.

Nothing was forcing me to sit down. Yet I remained seated while I waited for something to happen. My heart ached for something else I could do. But the ache was all my heart could do in the end. *What was the end? Where does this end? Where am I at the end? And what's left of me?*

All around me, like tiny minuscule screens, the darkness exploded with light. A piece of paper was the darkness's focus. Words upon words upon words. Lines with filled signatures. All were filled. Except for one.

I looked up. More light lay in wait. *No. Not this. Anything but this.* I pleaded to the darkness. Instead, the pressure that glued me to the couch became apparent. I closed my eyes, hoping I'd yield myself to a different environment. But the images and memories followed me into my enclosure. The few I successfully hid. Until now.

A truck with bags of soil.

There were countless more waiting to be transported as well. This was a couple of days after our first meeting, at six. I was supposed to report at 5:30 that day. I woke up at seven, my body still conditioned to waking up for school. I'd made the mistake of skipping breakfast to account for my tardiness. Half an hour in, I would've traded anything for food, even if it were spoiled beyond recognition or had spent years in the sewer alongside a murderous clown.

A faded green hose in my hands, spewing dirty water.

Next, I had to water everything to give the plants the nutrients they needed, plus the gleam they so desperately desired for the eight o'clock opening. I spent an hour making sure each leaf was sparkling with life.

The dirty empty counter.

I stood behind the counter on my naive toes, hoping for the bell to ring over the door with a customer eager to give this store a simple chance. I sat down after the first thirty minutes. Soon, I didn't even bother to be at the counter, as I moved to the back to help Aubrey out with some of her duties. After a couple of minutes, a burst of red rage was let loose as she barked about her customer base.

The dirty smelly underbelly of the library, with bookcases behind bookcases of discarded texts, a small oak table, and a brick-thick computer.

So, I went to work on a solution. I had to use the computer in the library's basement to make them (which was as close to hell as I'd gotten up to that point in my life), but after a good hour's worth of hard work, I had over a hundred printed and ready to go.

The hot South Carolinian sun that I was saved from by Aubrey's shade sail. I stood outside the store's entrance and gave them to whoever wanted the flyers. No one did. Aubrey herself didn't like that I went out and did so without consulting her. But my strategy was seen to induce some change over the next few weeks.

The glass of champagne, with a grapevine running along its side.

It almost worked too well. We were able to get more products to sell, even if it was just a couple of weeks. We even got someone to fix the sign outside, which just said "A". It was a wonder that the handyman came to the right spot. But our luck would run out when a woman came back into the store claiming that we sold her a dead plant. I did, but Aubrey didn't appreciate her directness. Even with her limp, the fight that ensued had caused the cops to come and moderate. The guilt that I was the one who sold the plant ate at me, and I almost cried. Almost. So, Aubrey chose that moment to give me my first paycheck. The gleam of the words and numbers on the check drove away all my worries. After that, she opened a bottle of champagne that she always said was reserved for the perfect moment. When I told her I wasn't legally of age, she shoved a glass in my hand and chuckled. It didn't taste like I expected it and was immediately repulsed. I ran to the trashcan, vomit ready to come out with thunderous force. Behind my coughing, wheezing, and ringing ears, I heard her laughing hysterically. The laughing was a stark contrast to the heavyweight bout she almost started earlier that day.

My first purchase.

Either way, I made sure to go out and use the money to buy something to hide my copy of our back door key, in case I couldn't discreetly shimmy the front door open without Mom noticing. There were many statues I could've chosen, but the one I chose was the Gargoyle one on sale. On the outside, the elongated tongue, sharp teeth, small ears, and gravelly gray outside seemed perfect. Its right eye, however, had broken off and was put back in an attempt to still seem normal. That was my first-ever purchase.

A girl carrying a Peace Lily up to the main counter during my lunch break.

I was sad that I didn't get to take that all-important first bite into my Burgerville burger. But I was elated to see my hard work paying off, nevertheless.

My body sprawled on the tepid floor behind the counter.

But I knew it wasn't enough. The next day, I went down the stores on the street - one by one - and asked them if they wouldn't mind my putting some flyers up. No one objected, and some helped me out. The only obstacle I encountered was when I entered the adjacent Burgerville, as the manager pushed me out emphatically, yelling stuff that probably wouldn't abide in one of the million churches in the town. The closest of which was glad to accept some flyers. Aubrey, despite seeing the positive effects of my work, got angrier. After the colossal distance I walked and a quick squabble with Aubrey, I could only lie on the ground in a state of never-ending hyperventilation while my legs did their best to wear off the soreness in my quads.

The hot sweaty evenings I spent behind the counter.

After school started again, I had to do my homework while working. I didn't mind. There was enough space for my worksheets, at least the ones the teachers bothered to give me since it was my senior year. There weren't many customers either. Yet there were a few. Joseph came to buy a plant for Shannon. I guided him to the near-empty crate of peace lilies, which I knew she loved. He was surprisingly nice to me. Greg, as a part of his renewed craze in gardening, also came in to buy white magnolias. He tried to make conversation with me, but I kept it to a minimum.

My first smile in a couple of months.

Despite our difficulties, we became something more after a while. Even the adjacent Burgerville warmed up to my constant appearance for lunch and put up one of our flyers. In the growing expansion of the world, we - apparently - offered some relief. Plants had disappeared from the everyday garden people tend to in their backyards. The ones that used to have a random assortment of flora and fauna, were mostly based on convenience and aesthetics, not practicality. The messy ones, with no real organization or arrangement. We gave all those who wandered - willingly or otherwise - into our store with this elusive service (plus a whole bunch of our desired Peace Lilies). A door into better days, the ones deeply seated in the past. I don't know why they sought that door back then, or if they even truly knew what was behind it. But I got more money every week, so I wasn't arguing. By then, she barely had to come in anymore. The arguments she'd begun picking up with the customers helped in convincing her to finally give me control. Of course, she still had to come in to help with all the carrying and closing shop, which she insisted had to be done by her despite the worsening limp. But everything else was me. Me. Before she closed, Aubrey crossed her big arms to watch me handle a customer. It was the last of the day. A long day. My legs felt heavy behind the counter. Yet I was patient with the customer. Ecstasy filled them as they walked out of the store into the November chill. I walked out to say goodbye, and then I turned the sign to the black and white cuckoo bird before coming in. That was when I chose to smile. Just to myself. My mouth ached, having not been stretched that way for a long time. When I came back to the counter, the joy on her face couldn't have

119

been louder. I thought it was her pride, the fact that her business was finally thriving. So, it was unexpected when she pulled me into an embrace.

The hug.

Her inflated ego seemed to be brought down to the floor. The confrontational nature and fear of aggravating that side of her were put in the background of my mind. Plus, it felt right to hug her. We embraced for some time. It was nice.

The alleyway and the hole in the fence.

Like everything else, it was the same every day. I'd opened the fence with a wire cutter so I could comfortably squeeze through without much thought. The only thing that changed was the abundance of clothes the dirt had collected on to keep my skin from burning off in the wintry air. Other than that, the walk home became another movement in the hand of a clock. But something about it felt wrong that specific day. The guiltiness of that hug came back. The gentle hug I'd never gotten from my Mom. The night she spent teaching me how to cook. Aubrey was smiling more like a proud mother witnessing their son do something great. In that second, I preferred Aubrey's smile over Mom's.

Me and Dan, sitting on our bed at night.

For some reason, that comforting hug caused utter discomfort. More questions arose that I didn't want answered. I confided in Dan as if his conscience had stolen the glue that held my spirit together. He didn't understand what the hell I was saying. Of course, I couldn't form a coherent sentence. My words were slurred and nonsensical like someone who'd woken from a long nap and had a big dream they could remember, but at the same time couldn't. He dismissed it as though it was nothing but a stray thought that I was taking too deeply.

The morning after.

I couldn't face Aubrey the same after that. Even looking at her felt wrong. Because that feeling of replacing my Mom was something I never wanted to feel.

The flu that razed the town.

One of the drawbacks of such a small town was the fact that if one person got the flu everybody got the flu. Aubrey became one of its victims. I was glad when she didn't come in. The nicety, even with the bursts of ego, seemed too far ahead of Mom. I struggled more every day to reign it back, to feel that pain again, but the guilt just walked off into the night when I slept. I'd gotten the flu around that same time, yet I didn't want to face Mom either, so I kept trudging every day to work. No customers came, upon fear of the sickness. It was nice and quiet, so I didn't mind the lack of a paycheck for once. I hoped the guilt would leave all the while. It didn't.

Dan's permission slip, missing one signature.

He had a field trip he was going to. Unfortunately, it was the day before, and he had forgotten to get Mom to sign it. Of course, Mom was dead drunk, so a simple matter became inflated. The narrative shifted to the 'fact' that he didn't care about her. One thing led to another, and I admitted it openly to her. That I preferred Aubrey over her. Luckily, Mom was almost dead drunk, so she couldn't understand any reason. Once she passed out, I had to forge her signature for him.

My butt was on the black couch once more. Everything around me had resumed into its darkness.
Aubrey never found out about my feelings. She fired me before I could even think about it.

Her words were short. Decisive. They left me wanting a deeper explanation than the scraps I got. Yet they killed me all the same.

I'd never told myself about those feelings again either, choosing to hide this memory where I thought I'd never see it again. The feelings that were so strong because of the belief they instilled, were made so weak for all the same reason and stupid naivety I had back then. The stupid selflessness. *Look where that fucking got me.*

The bitch even got me in trouble for putting up flyers without a permit.

I hid it all in the darkness. The depths of mind I thought I'd escape. I couldn't. They were too deep. Too steep. Now I was forcing myself to marinate in it, to make sure whatever creature would soon swallow me up could taste all the lies that I filled my stomach with.

Truthful Murder

The light turned red before I could enter the intersection. I slammed on the brakes and stopped the car's momentum. Panting slightly at the twenty G-forces I experienced in about two seconds, I let my head hit the steering wheel while a new round of stomach cramps started.

I forgot my main objective when I went last night to the supermarket. I didn't know how I slept without something in my stomach, but I was grateful for the deferment from the pangs of hunger.

That wasn't exactly the case now. I had to take a hand off the steering wheel to press into my stomach every few seconds. Not that it helped much, but it was better than doing nothing. In addition, the bandage I placed this morning above my right eyebrow had some hairs stuck under it, affecting the overall adhesion. So now and then I had to take my hand off again to force it down. The sweat from the heat didn't help with my exertions.

The sporadic sleep and the dream didn't either. I slept once more at three but woke up at six this time. I thought it wasn't going to get worse.

Robin's words then came to mind. *Why the hell's she right?*

My eyes spun wild around Tellermen's for something. Anything. The Burgerville didn't appeal to my senses. Nothing else I passed that day did either.

I had spun by Dan's house with an early-morning surge of courage. He was cooking breakfast for his kids when I arrived. It seemed he liked cooking. I was a bit proud of him to see such growth. But the image of those delicious pancakes only made my stomach grumble with jealousy. It seemed like that was my only way of eating now. I was fated to look at those delectables from a distance but never destined to experience them. I was tempted to take that analogy to other aspects of my life, but my pessimism faded when the signal turned green.

I thought my luck would change the more I drove. But all I saw was the consequences of a directionless town. At every single turn, there was a soul just walking the sidewalks. Young ones. One of them held up the middle finger when I didn't stop in time, even though he had no right to sprint onto the crosswalk right then and there.

When I went into my senior year, it always felt like the incoming freshmen were more entitled and demeaning than the ones before them. Especially in high school. That was another conception that decided to stay the same, by the looks of things. *If that could stay the same, why couldn't anything else?*

I drove some more before - unfortunately - my brain deemed I was long due to having another reminder of the pain. This time, it wasn't in the form of one of those hyper-realistic dreams. But rather, it was right in front of me. Unavoidable to no extent.

I had completed the loop back to the intersection at Tellermen's, within eyesight of the row of abandoned shops. The only difference was I was somehow hungrier.

I looked closer at the plaza. One of the stores showed signs of life, with figures moving and shifting around inside. Aubrey's.

A black sign with a cuckoo bird etched in white hung on the door. *No. Never this early.*

A loud honk rearranged all the organs in my body, and my instinct forced the brake pedal down. When I regained my senses, I saw a violent red car right in front of me, at the center of the intersection. Another car - a blue truck - had spun off to the side, staying upright only through sheer luck. In the madness and the barrage of honking, the man in the red car caught sight of me and waved a dismissive hand before he ran off. This time, it was my turn to extend my middle finger.

No response. At least one I couldn't see. He flew into the Burgerville and parked with oozing haste. *Why the hell does he need a burger so badly?* Rage boiled in me at another obstacle that tripped me at the wrong time.

Another honk behind me. I jerked the wheel off to the side and missed the curb leading into the Burgerville with an almost meaningless margin. At least, I thought so until I jumped up in surprising fervor. It didn't matter, and as my head returned from the ceiling, I flew into the parking spot next to that same car.

I jumped outside, my fists ready to taste the man's flesh. Luckily for him, no one was in the car at that moment.

A rage-fueled intensity filled me as I strode inside, the bell above the door dinging as I entered and settled in the back of the line - around the fourth stanchion or so - that twisted and turned on its way to the main counter. My eyes returned to that same wild spinning but with an additional angry starvation.

I looked past all the heads, into the order station. Now and again the door leading from the kitchen into the main lounge area would open and provide me a glimpse of what was happening inside, though it was tough to see through the chaos. From what I could see, people walked by in a hurry, yelling the names of different items on the menu and different ingredients. Chili. Beans, Peppers, Burgers. Fries. Shake.

In the five minutes I spent inside, I'd barely taken more than two steps. Those in front of me let their eyes sag and shoulders drop from the weight of the air. The children that joined them by their side grew antsy, tugging on the rope that laid out the lines and kicking the stanchions. Some of them were crying.

The person who flipped me off disappeared from my mind, and the emotions subsided. The people sitting in the booths wore a weariness even greater than mine. Like the food wasn't even worth the wait. I saw more than one person go and throw out their half-eaten sandwiches. The boxes containing the nuggets and the fries were discarded too. Some of the boxes weren't even opened.

Still, most of those in the line stayed put. Burgerville was the town. The town owed many things to Burgerville. It was too hard for both parties to give each other up.

An odorous smell became more apparent the more I inched forward. I winced at the disgust and the epic proportions of it that didn't lessen no matter how much time passed. *I didn't know a Burgerville could smell bad.*

Finally, I reached the end of the line. I took one more glance at my lemon, which was visible through the window. A scratch was on its side, engorged past the ability to dismiss it. Inside, there was no confirmation that it was the red car's driver who caused the damage, yet the anger still returned.

"You have anything in mind?" Just like that, my anger was interrupted by a heavy Southern accent. The lady seemed exhausted, her uniform disheveled. Her eyes contained almost no emotions, and the forgettable face they belonged to was stuck in a permanent scowl that grew hard to look at after a few seconds.

I'd already decided that I wasn't going to get anything - despite my starvation - and the smell getting even worse proved it. "No, not really." Something must've been on my face, souring my words. She looked down at her computer, feigning something while raising her eyebrows in disgust even though she wasn't looking in a mirror.

I turned to the window once more. Someone was blocking my view, throwing yet another food item away. But once they did the deed, I was able to see Aubrey's with a clear line of sight.

A van bounded past the corner of the electronics store. It then slowed down. A shadowy hand from inside the vehicle waved at the old lady who stood outside to see it pass by. She waved back. The van then rocketed into the back alleyway. Before it left my view, I took notice of the white color and the multitude of boxes painted on it.

The old lady went back inside Aubrey's store with a familiar limp.

I pointed at the plaza. "What happened to Aubrey's?"

Somehow, life and color reentered her eyes, almost as if she was grateful for the distraction from her duties. "I don't know. She put it up for sale a few days ago. I think it's all these new things coming through, like that mall they're building. You must've seen it when you came in yesterday."

"I did." *How did she know I came in yesterday?*

She spluttered her lips before I could enlarge the plot hole and see what was hidden inside. "Plus, property taxes went through the roof last year."

She realized her pun and a wry smile entered the margins of her face. She had to turn around to address it to her coworkers.

I looked down to the plaza once more. My eyes began jumping on and off the "For Sale" signs on the storefronts. Most were already emptied, some of their doors opening and papers flying.

My mind just couldn't see Aubrey's that deserted. Left behind. The thought created a panic that swelled up throughout me. *She kicked you out. Why do you still care?*

I set off regardless.

I flew past the people who looked at my craziness and shuffled their kids away from me, the balls and toes of my feet flying over the ground.

I was out of the store without a second thought. My white shirt began flailing in the wind. The only thing that seemed fast enough to catch me was my thoughts, but even that had the grace to leave me alone for the time being.

I reached the sidewalk, cutting across the Burgerville's parking lot and ignoring the honks I received. Then I sprinted over to the plaza, jumping across a car that threatened to have me meet Mom. My dress shoes somehow got caught behind my body, and the concrete teased its rough surface, inviting my head to split itself open and my kneecap to pop out once more. Luckily, I managed to regather my manic balance.

Finally, I reached the front door. My breath was still a few blocks away, back at the Burgerville. I could've sworn my kneecap popped out more than once on the way. Even if they didn't, my thighs still burned through my pants. In a jolt, I realized that I still hadn't changed my clothes since the job interview.

I brought my shirt up and took a quick sniff. It wasn't too bad. *Don't notice it. Please.*

The main outside window pane still contained a hefty quantity of flyers. The special challenges, like finding a sticker under the pot that would get the finder a free lemonade, were advertised on big pink letters that I knew Aubrey didn't know how to create. I did that for her. Other signs, marketing slogans, and business practices I had a hand in creating were present alongside a sense of euphoria, nostalgia, and bitterness.

Before my mind could think itself - as well as my body - out of walking through the door, a man opened it with his back. Big. Burly, with a brown beard. His hands seemed to be built specially to carry stuff, the fingers themselves almost engrossing the entire box in said hands.

Another man followed the burly man. Lean. Various skull tattoos sat comfortably across his neck. He had another box.

The lean man kicked open the door before giving me a small nod and walking off. He just kicked open the door for you. *Are you going to go in?*

The door began to close. *The doors closing. Are you going to go in?*

The other brain answered for me when my hands shot out to catch the door just as it was about to close, and pulled it. Not too hard, though. I knew how flimsy the door was even back then. I didn't want to venture a guess as to how close it was to breaking after all the eons it lived, so I opened it just enough to let me squeeze through the entryway.

Aubrey had her back turned to me, her hands in a box fighting and tumbling over each other. "I told them three times that the garage door was broken." She muttered. My body weight was on the back of my heels, my left hand holding the door open a crack. *You can still leave.*

For the first time that day, my argument with Robin came up. *Leaving was the easy thing to do.* I let the door close.

The door dinged behind me, and Aubrey stood up straighter. At least, as much as she could. Her hair, gray like ash from a fire burned long ago, was run through with her arm. The skin she wore on her arm was more worn than what I'd grown used to. The white apron was harder to describe as white up close, even though I was with her when she got it straight out of the package.

How would she react? What face would she wear? The angry one? Or the disappointed one? The sudden realization that I didn't process all the possibilities, all the ways this reality would branch out from here ticked off all my alarm bells. I knew this was the right thing to do. For the first time in a long time. I knew that once, I was wholly welcome in this place. But I still hesitated.

Aubrey hobbled around to face me. That mouth of hers was still curled into a permanent, distasteful look. Her first look had little to no reaction. Like she was looking at an unknown specimen from an alien world, but didn't know how to react. The specimen who knew he wasn't truly welcome, even though he'd learned behaviors of the human race for years. The specimen, who knew he was forever alienated. Even here.

I imagined how I looked. My beard growing ragged far past its normal length. The lean figure that I boasted. My pants weren't ripped yet - somehow - but the dark black cloth had sweat dripping onto her floor. Even imagining myself made me disgusted.

She continued looking at me, yet I suspected that she knew who I was, even though I had grown far from the awkward face and long hair I wore just after hitting puberty. Maybe she was trying to see that Cal. *Where'd it go?*

I looked down at the puddle of sweat I created. "Seems like I'm always making a mess."

You always were a mess. I wanted her to say that. To throw me out like she did for so many people at my behest. Yet, she just put the purple-flowered plant that she carried in her hand into a brimming box. The table in front of her had been cleaned (A now-black rag sat on the table, and dull white streaks showed themselves being pushed into the table), with nothing left except for those purple-flowered plants, which occupied the space inside another box over to the side as well.

She just took a deep breath. I waited for the argument to begin. "Coffee?" *Can't argue with that.*

I finished mine too quickly in the excitement. We both sat in silence while her empty mug joined mine on the counter. The same counter we sat at when we met all those nights ago, my legs dangling on the same stool.

It was a weird feeling, the environment around us. The time we've shared, and the numerous thoughts and words that went along with it, had gone. Like we were just two strangers once more. I tried finding her eyes, but she slipped them out of my grasp.

I didn't know where to begin, often losing track of the times I opened my mouth and couldn't speak as the frog found it snug in my throat.

Thankfully, Aubrey initiated the conversation. "I heard you went to Boston."

"Chicago." I nodded. Almost excited. *Maybe she'd be happy with the life I created over there. Maybe she'd forget her anger. Maybe she wouldn't.* "The crime rates have gone up over the past few years, but it's still a good place. Of course, I have enough to live where I don't have to worry about all that." I looked at her, measuring her facial expression and body language, to see if her reactions to my words were filled with anger.

My words didn't appear to blow her nerves, so I continued. "Got married for a bit. Grew that beard that I always wanted." I chuckled, though her stone-cold face caused me to stomp on the brakes. She refused to give away a single emotion, a single morsel for me to begin nibbling on.

I cleared my throat. "The town's grown. More buildings, more roads."

I waited for her to say something. When she didn't, the awkwardness in me forced the silence to break. "Yeah." Of course, the silence only got worse after that.

"I talked to Robin-" It was at this point that I realized the words were coming out without any control. "You know Robin, my friend." I slapped my thighs, wondering if I was making everything worse. "Let's see, what else? Mom's dead. Greg's on his way to meet her."

I winced inside. *Too insensitive.* Plus, I hadn't told her about the argument I had, after which I'd left. Probably because I was too busy stealing Greg's truck. My feet were on thin ice, and my mind racked the possibility of getting off it. I was afraid of what depths I'd sink to if I didn't in time.

"Some stuff happened at Greg's house." I started, looking for a way out of my grave. "And I left. I couldn't handle it right then and there."

"Oh, and you're mature enough to handle it now? Is that right?" With the venomous words I became aware that the pit was too deep for me to dig out of. My brain was stopped in front of the car's headlights, afraid to move aside as I crashed through the windshield and to my death.

It was my greatest fear. To have her act that way towards me. The woman who held such unabridged generosity was now forced to throw it away.

She already threw it away. Yet you still came back like the idiot that you are. I wanted to believe otherwise. But there was nothing else I could do, except take whatever she was prepared to give me. The wavy expression that spun all over the place on her face told me she had a lot to say.

She sighed and rubbed her fingers on her head. "The pain you have caused everyone here, even to me-" Her hands flew up in exasperation. "I just don't see it in you." Aubrey clasped back her eye contact with me.

"I've already been through this with Robin." I felt my voice raise. I would never reveal this anger in front of Aubrey. But the archetypes I was desperately hoping to avoid just kept coming back. "I don't need to be told that I'm the failed son or friend again. You can save all that, 'cause I've heard it already.

She scoffed. "Well, you need to hear it again. You keep making those same half-assed mistakes again and you're gonna keep ruining everyone around you." Aubrey brought her hands up and wiped her tears. I focused on her words. *There's something behind the anger.*

The eye contact we held made it unbearable, an infinite torture, draining all emotion out of me except sadness. Tears never came out though, as I looked away. I saw the yellow-colored flower that caught my attention all those years back. The long stalk and the five bright petals. In all the time I spent around them, I only just noticed their faded yellow insides.

I waited a bit before starting again, hoping it would alleviate her anger. "For what it's worth, I'm going to meet Greg after this. Fix what I can of his pain." Maybe I'd take some of the heat off me. Maybe she'd forget my past and cut me some much-needed slack. Slack I needed before I met Greg.

Aubrey continued, not even concerned with what I had to say. "You proved everyone around here right. All those bitches who were betting on what you'd do." She shook her head. In a disappointed-mother way. She paused for a moment to lift her shirt and wipe the tears in her eyes again. Soon, her face regained her usual composure. "You didn't even stop by Lonely Pines and meet your own father first, who's on his deathbed? Do you have any idea how much he has sacrificed for you?" Aubrey shook her head, and I felt my heart twinge.

I nodded. The door dinged behind me. I was thankful for the hurried steps away and the door dinging once more. "Yeah. Thank you. Really need this right now." A glance upstairs, trying not to let the tears come out. *Not now.*

"So when do you need it? When will you let these lessons help you like they're supposed to?" Aubrey's voice shot up to the ceiling amidst the exasperation. "When are you going to learn?" She pointed at her. "You think life spared me when I messed up?" Her voice quieted. Aubrey pointed to the ground. "That's why I'm here. Cause of my proudness. I don't like admitting that. But it's true." She grew silent.

This is not your store. The same thing she said when she saw that I wasn't worthy enough to grace her presence for the rest of my time in high school.

I started. "Aubrey, I can give you some money or-"

She waved me off again. "Like there was nothing left here anyway. It's too late for me. Anything I could've fixed died years ago. And I've got some dang good mac and cheese waiting to hold me over until I die."

"But it's not about me right now. You let them win. And you don't seem to care. You seem like you don't want to prove them wrong. You want them to see you for your mistakes. You still don't care." Aubrey's anger left the building, and the last word was emphasized with worry.

She scoffed still. "You let your mistakes kill your mom here in the meantime, but you don't care about that either. As long as you're fine, am I right?"

Before I could snap back at her egregious statement, she continued. "Whatever. No use bending something if it refuses to bend, right?" She smiled. Even though I could deduce whether Shannon's Robin's or Dan's smiles were fake, I didn't have to do it with Aubrey. She didn't hide her contempt when she was angry enough. Anger I didn't want to create. But here we are.

"He hasn't walked for months now." Aubrey leaned in close, her eyes bloodshot red, of which I was able to note every minute detail. I was able to see many more wrinkles on her face by the passing seconds, and the frayed tips of her hair, which was aging along with her face, it seemed.

What was I supposed to say to that? "Yeah."

Aubrey leaned back in her chair and crossed her big arms. "Of course, you still call him Greg. Through that thick head of yours, you still can't call him Dad, can't you?" Robin's conversation from the night before, which I had managed to keep out of my head, clawed its way back. As if my head wasn't assaulted enough, out of nowhere a stick appeared in her hand. It whacked my head and shot into the air, almost vibrating fast enough to turn into nothingness. I groaned, the pain increasing once I realized that it managed to hit the wound above my eyebrow.

I rubbed the place, which started to throb. *At least the bandage didn't fall off.* "Bitch." I mumbled through clenched teeth.

"You'll live." She struggled to get up and out of her chair, giving a good five seconds of effort before being able to stand. After that, I realized that the stick she had was a walking stick. *How did I not see that before?* Sure enough, she leaned on it every other step. Her stride had gotten smaller and slower. Even small and slower. It took her a longer time than usual to get around the table, grab the yellow plants, and put them in the box.

I wasn't there to help plant them. Was I that self-involved?

It was tough to see her like this, even through all her words. My guilt walked outside for a smoke break. I let my hand drop from my head, knowing inside that I put her through much more pain than what I was experiencing.

Yet, I still felt the need to defend myself. "You don't know, Aubrey. You don't know what they've done." I repeated the same phrase that I had uttered too many times over the past few days. Inside and out. "Yet everyone just wants to make me feel more guilty." I let my exasperation command my arm's nervous movements. "Like I'm not allowed to feel what I feel."

"I'm going to pretend you didn't say that." She summoned a roll of tape and taped up the box in a couple of smooth, breezy motions. "Cause I know you ain't that stupid."

She laughed a bit more, this time bleeding bitterness rather than contempt. "What am I kidding? You cause way too much trouble for someone who needs to change." Aubrey continued before I could get a word out of my tongue. "Especially to your poor mother."

The box she'd just finished up was shoved off to the side. "You heard that?" The words picked my attention up out of the box.

But it was too late. She sighed when she saw my lack of attention. Even the sigh sounds disappointed. Aubrey let the only noise in the room for the time being was the air conditioning.

Appropriate to the situation, it turned itself out. "You need to realize that you're also hurting yourself with this immature garbage." She gestured all around me.

"Wow, so I'm immature and garbage? Is there a prize for being both?" I joked. The sick smile I'd been receiving the past few days was now being flung back into the world.

"Yeah. Dying like your mom."

The sarcastic jokes my hurt had invented in that second fell apart, and a raging darkness spoke for me. "Aubrey, teach me all you want but never go there."

"Why? Mr. Collins is afraid of the truth?" A mocking tone made its way out of her throat, the condescension behind every syllable not helping her words about maturity. "Afraid of dying like your mom did? Ruining herself with everything she could drink or snort?" The stun was too great for me to respond. "And that's something I think you're too afraid to accept. You think she was some angel. Well, let me tell you, son. She was not. She may have hidden her flaws from you, but not from your dad. I bet if he was able to decide to divorce again, he'd do it."

My mind just couldn't hear the truth she thought she was saying. *No. Mom would never resort to drugs.* The memories my common sense went to only showed her fuzzy smile and huggable skin. *She couldn't have.* "Just 'cause she drank doesn't make her a bad person."

"But I thought you hated Greg because he drank." Aubrey wore an inquisitive tone.

"No, it was what he did while he was drunk-"

"And your mom was a perfect woman while she drank?"

I couldn't find any response. "You're wrong."

She chuckled once more, the condescension making its way into her laughter.

"You know, for someone who says they have a lot of flaws, you sure act like you don't have any."

Aubrey didn't care enough to even respond to my reasoning once more. "I don't know where you got this stubborn selfish little act. Probably from playing that little grown-up in Detroit, or wherever you were."

I shook my head. "You cannot talk about being selfish." A renewed violence overtook my head. "Where was that kind little act you put on when you got me inside this wretched place? Or is it back there, gathering dust like the rest of this hellhole? You just brought it out to get me in here and be your slave for months and months?"

I stopped to gather my breath. "This is too much. Even for you. If you know and care so much, fine." I gestured around us. "But you think you can care someone into listening to you?" *Shannon.* My voice broke. "You can't do that to me." Tears almost broke through.

Despite that, I was tempted to grab her throat and swing her to the ground. The feeling of the sweet flesh just writhing. *Writhing.* "How dare you talk to me like that. After I came here to check if you were okay. You're lucky someone in this place knows - and I mean really knows - about you and still cares enough to do that."

She opened her mouth, her eyes glowering like she wanted to chew into me more. I was ready to wrangle, the emotions running through the vines lining my body, my legs swinging fast with a preparedness to jump the stool. My grip on the edge of the countertop was ice white. Like it would be when I held her throat. Thoughts that I normally wouldn't even dare to consider. Soon, I was enveloped by it, as Aubrey continued to stay silent. In the softest voice she could muster, after a good moment, she started talking.

"My ego's not going to change the truth. And I don't know if you knew this, but your presence before you left was the only thing sort of keeping your family together. I don't know how. But it did."

"And he needed you. He was a bitch sometimes, but at least he knows that. Your mother was too cruel to admit it." A sigh in which she looked away. "I never imagined I'd defend her anyway, but." Aubrey looked back. "She still needed you. And her son decided to leave while she was going through that phase in her life. You know what? There was no overdose. It was murder. And you know damn well who murdered her."

Aubrey waited a bit before she continued. No thoughts were in my head. I figured they went on the lam with her breath as well. Just silence remained in my mind as I replayed those words again. Murder. Truth. "Sorry child. Shouldn't have said that. I can tell what you've been through. What you've seen. Even back then. Now, it's worse. Somehow. And I know we never talked about it and it's not my place-"

"If I told you everything, would you have still fired me?" I'd thought about the question for so long that I couldn't resist staying inside any longer. *No more beating around the bush.*

"Yes. And that's the unfortunate truth." She finished as if she deserved an award for being honest. As if our relationship wasn't anything more. *Now you look even more stupid for looking at her like Mom.*

As I thought the inevitable thoughts, Aubrey limped off and worked on packing up another box.

I turned around, sensing someone looking at me. Sure enough, the two movers were stationed outside. The big burly one was pointing at me and saying something. Once they saw my eyes, both looked away and walked off to the side of the building.

I stared at her back. She didn't turn around. I flung myself off the stool and began walking to the door, my gut churning and my head hurting as I realized that in our last encounter, we wouldn't face each other.

Walking out the door, snippets of the two mover's conversation entered my ear. "Yeah, dude. He just ran off-"

They stopped once more, their eyes looking up and down my body. My hand shot out and grabbed the door before it closed. Out of the corner of my eyes, I saw Aubrey limp around with another box in her hand. She realized it was too big to carry with only one free hand when it fell. But I knew whoever came to help would be berated away.

She was right. The stubbornness forced the thought off, but I still couldn't bear to see her like this.

I opened the door as wide as it could go. "Take care of her." That's all I said to them. *That's all I ever wanted.*

But she'd never understand that. *No one would.* The movers hurried through the door. Before it closed completely, Aubrey started yelling at me. "You better-" The door shut, and her thought would never come to fruition.

I trekked back to my car, rubbing the bandage. The pain I felt ventured as fat as the secluded hiding place of my soul, however.

I knew one thing. One solitary thought stuck in my mind as I embarked across the road and got in my car. I was going to visit Greg. Get it over with. I wasn't going to talk about, or even think about, what was said either. *No. Never.*

Resumptions of Solace

Of course, my mind - still - had other plans while I drifted along the curvy Gaines roads.

There was no dramatic transition to the darkness. I was about to contemplate whether that was a good thing when the darkness disappeared and her hands - hers - were in my hair. The touch of her fingers burst my mind into remembrance, and I felt content. This was one of the other memories I wanted to remember always.

We were in our bed. It was soft. The blazing yet forgiving sunlight lay with me and Shannon. The warmth her smile radiated overtook the sun that desperately tried to compete through the window behind her head. I kept staring into her eyes, not wanting to lose the blue gaze. *Not yet.*

In one effortless motion, she swung over onto my lap with her family's bracelet hitting my eyes. Shannon sat up straight to move it up her arms so that she could kiss my eyes without any hindrance.

It was a deep kiss. Like she was waiting for time to stop. I was willing to wait as long as I needed to, as long as it was with her. Her stature, at least compared to mine, suffocated my breath. My only response was riotous laughter.

The expectations I held in high school, the dreams I was too scared to admit even to Robin. Surprisingly, the fears and insecurities themselves moved aside to fully appreciate the best way I'd ever woken up.

Yesterday evening was one of the few instances that threatened to upstage the perfection of this moment. We'd decided to take a long walk - hand in hand - as the sun drifted below the horizon with the orange glow providing a feast for our eyes even though our stomachs were ripe from the dinners we hungrily wolfed down. The scenery always excelled at Cherry Hill and the adjacent neighborhoods, yet it pulled at my heartstrings a bit harder when I saw the same gorgeous sights with her. I hoped she felt the same with me. *It's a nice feeling. I'd want her to feel it every day.*

The thing was this was every day. The beautiful introductions to the day. The evening walks that the birds chirped endlessly through, which we sometimes skipped dinner for, just to have that chance to experience the beauty with each other. We even stumbled on the end of a rainbow one evening.

Whatever we did, we did it together. It was all part of the ritual or trance that always felt spontaneous, yet simultaneously served as a good break from the schedule I'd prematurely gotten used to with Aubrey. *I couldn't get tired of it.* Even if I did, this was the perfection I needed. There was no choice but to maintain perfection in an imperfect ever-changing world. Even if the perfection was motionless, without much definition. We didn't need the definition for these perfect moments.

I sat up, and she drifted off to my side. She still held my arm though. Her presence here at the house, despite her firm opening in just an hour, surprised me. "You ought to get to work. Beat the morning rush."

She flipped around and turned on the lamp, despite the sun shining through the window. "Are you trying to get me out of the house?" Her arms reached into the air, and she leaned back with a quiet yawn. Somehow, she looked more beautiful even with the dried drool on the corners of her mouth.

"Well, then you're gonna hate seeing my mistress." Her hair whipped around her head as soon as I said that. Her face and eyes were a mixture of curiosity and annoyance. Shannon then tilted her head and looked at me as if I was crazy. I just shrugged in response. "Just being honest." It was my turn to yawn, yet I didn't feel tired. If anything, I felt energized, ready to leap out and conquer the day.

She stood up and closed the blinds, turning off the blazing light to completely envelop the room in slight darkness. "Ah yes. Your mistress. I'll believe it when I see it."

"What?" I laughed at the absurdity of her comment and then dodged the white pillow she chucked at me. "I'll get one just for that."

"No, you couldn't. You barely got me."

"Wow." I raised my eyebrow. "You doubt my charisma?"

"Sure. If you wanna call it that."

I threw the white pillow back at her. In between laughs, she continued her teasing. "You could barely talk to me in high school. How're you gonna talk to her? Or do I need to teach you how to flirt?"

I jumped across and wrestled her back onto the pillows. "I could be your wingman-" Her words grew more halted, and the laughter took over most of her sentences until the infectious laughter was all that remained.

The feel of her skin and hair felt visceral enough to fool my brain. At least, until I was transported downstairs in the blink of an eye. The slap in my face succeeded, and the reality of this simulation returned. *Right.*

As I stared across the long granite countertop, I could barely see a speck of dust or other foreign substances. I remembered that I couldn't sleep the night before, and in my late-night inspiration, I went downstairs to clean the kitchen.

The coffee maker at the end of the counter stopped making its syrupy racket, pulling me out of yesterday. Even the noisy racket it made supplemented its mysterious hunger-defying, mind-clearing powers that attracted me to it ever since its first sip. Especially in the coffee maker that Shannon brought. It tasted differently, as if every cup the machine made was made by her sweet touch.

I poured the coffee into my mug. A tiny spot of liquid permeated down the mug's handle - taking its own milky time - and across the granite, while creating a small circle, perfectly rounded around the mug's bottom. A seamless mistake.

I walked around, opening the blinds and letting the sun's glow embrace the living and dining room. There was no entrance or exit to either, the entire space growing a few more feet with that mere feeling.

The white couch we placed in the center of the room looked ever-so-appealing. Shannon spent her afternoon naps in it. I slept in the adjacent white loveseat. We'd bought one too small to use, except for said naps. Even though I was tinier than most, I still had to bring my feet up to my chest to get some comfort. But I had a good view of her beautiful face, even while her lips drooled away her dreams. *I wish I still could.*

Shannon's footsteps coming down the stairs distracted me from my thoughts. The thoughts that wanted to keep believing that this union could never be interrupted were forced to realize that it could. *And did.* "Oh yeah. Your phone kept ringing last night after you came back to bed."

I opened the blinds of the last window and walked back into the kitchen. Everyone at Gilbert who had the courtesy of having my number - I tried to limit my number to those only at Gilbert - knew that anything after work would be picked up under the rarest circumstances. "It was around two. Or three."

My thoughts centered on Dan, my only non-Gilbert number. I figured he drank a bit too much last night. I'd come to expect it over the past month when we first bridged a tenuous schedule of contact. So much so that I stopped picking up his calls in the past week to prevent any ideological argument from ensuing.

Out of her pocket, Shannon fished out my phone out of her sweatpants' pocket and set it on the countertop. "You gonna do anything about it?" With the milk suddenly appearing in her hand, she grabbed my coffee mug and poured some in. Then, she took a sip, followed by a slight nod as she put the milk carton down.

I looked at the phone, grabbed the mug from her, and took a sip. I shook the bitterness out of my system. "Needs sugar." She remained silent, staring almost with full intent at the phone. I indulged in her curiosity and brought up the call history. A number had, indeed, called me last night. *Greg's.*

Not now. Just a bit more. Setting the phone down, my hands and thoughts rose to the shelves above. One by one I searched them, looking for anything to add that could sweeten my coffee, which was already growing cold. On the third shelf, behind some plastic boxes lay a big glass jar of sugar, half full with a white spoon already inside. I got it down on the counter and undid the lock before adding the six scoops of sugar into the mug.

"I still don't know what it is with you and sugar," Shannon smirked. I smiled with ease in reply. My mouth muscles were used to it back then. She knew too much of me to not know the truth. I was never a fan of the raw bitterness of the drink and preferred it softened down a lot. She was the opposite, like in many other aspects of life. The thing was, she didn't have to know why, because I was the same in her eyes.

"You ever have one of those gut feelings?" Out of nowhere, Shannon's question permeated through the perfect atmosphere. A thick cloud of doubt began to form.

I didn't want to acknowledge it. *Not yet. Just a little bit more time together. Please. Until it all goes belly up.* "Depends. Are we still talking about the sugar?"

Proud of my joke, I turned to face her, my arms swirling the sugar around my coffee. A wry smile was on her face, a little disappointed and annoyed at me.

It disappeared, however, and seriousness took over her consciousness. "Cal, why don't you answer your brother's calls anymore?"

My smile disappeared as well. *She does know me too well.* I never bothered to tell her, afraid to let her into my troubles like my ungrateful family did so often to me and ruin her life. It was my justification, to save Shannon from a fate similar to mine, that she'd suffer with for almost decades at this point. She wouldn't be able to handle all that. I don't know how I did all this while.

Some blackened, weathered writing on the side of the sugar container caught my eye. It'd expired a year ago. I poured the coffee out, not even attempting to deduce what this new concoction would kindle my taste buds like.

"I think I deserve an answer at least. You don't even mention your family. You never took me to meet them, and you never answer when I ask about them. Why?" She seemed less curious. More agitated and desperate.

I proceeded to grab a mug from the dishwasher. Dishwasher water swiveled inside and raced around the cup. I poured it out. Except for an ounce that stuck to the bottom. I grabbed a towel that was draped over the Oven's handle. I looked inside, yet the water didn't lessen. At that point, the frustration amounting to was starting to prove too much. I put the mug aside, my hands split wide on the kitchen countertop and my shoulders kissing my cold ears.

"Do you think I'm not good enough?" A bitter statement, but again no anger. I've never seen her get truly angry. "I am, Cal." Her voice was softer. Like our bed. I wanted to sweep her up off her legs and carry her back upstairs. *Just to lay down.* Forget this conversation even existed. The office itself didn't look as attractive now. "I know how much you hate-"

"Exactly." *Snap.* "You never thought that there'd be a reason?" Shannon stepped back. I almost thought I saw fear in her eyes. The tangent in me that had laid dormant for quite a while threatened to come back up again, yet I realized there was actual fear in her eyes.

I sighed and relented. I still didn't think it was enough to say sorry. "I'm only trying to protect you."

She nodded, then reached out and touched my arm. "The reason I'm asking you is 'cause something's not right. I see that, even if you don't want to admit it to me. Could you at least just make sure I'm wrong?"

She got closer to me. "Make sure I'm wrong." I could feel her voice breaking. Like she'd these words before but to deaf ears.

I looked into her eyes. *Why are they so blue?* I sighed. "I'll see what's going on."

There was no extreme reaction to this from Shannon, but there was a slight look of happiness and relief across her face. She must've been truly troubled. *Why was she feeling so strongly about this?*

Shannon went upstairs, probably to get ready to take her red sedan to work. I had to take the day off today. Just a small break from the enormous amount of pressure I dealt with. Yes, I had power in this company, but the toll it came with was just something that was starting to get too much to handle. *I think I deserve that much.*

I picked my phone up off the counter. The nights I'd spent just wishing hard enough that Greg's number would relieve itself from my memories, were for naught at that moment. My thumb moved across the phone's dial pad without a second thought or hesitation. Before I realized it, I'd pressed the call button.

Whatever was going to happen, whatever I wanted to stop, wouldn't matter. I almost cut the call, nevertheless. The reality of my senses gambled with my thoughts, and for a second, I had hope again that it wasn't meant to be this way. *It could change. I could set it down right now. Go back to sleep.* Even though I already got my answer as to the extent of my influence in these dreams, it didn't stop the insatiable desire within me.

"Hey." Dan's voice. I waited. I couldn't find any drunkenness in his voice. Instead, all our shared images over the years resurfaced and became visible like oil in water. *I was the oil.* A rejection of my surroundings.

"Why'd you borrow his phone?" No hello, no greeting. My coldness determined he didn't deserve it.

No noise came from the other end, except for Dan's quiet voice. "Cause I knew you'd pick up." *Not wrong there.* His voice, though meager, was starting to mature. He must've just gotten out of college and couldn't be more than a few years younger than me. Though it wasn't as deep as mine, I could sense his age all of a sudden. It was a strange feeling, like seeing someone after a long time and not seeing anything but the differences.

He sniffled. "How's it going over there?"

I shrugged in real life, as though he was there in front of me. "I don't know."

"It's going." It wasn't. "What about over there?"

"It's going." For the first time, he talked to me with no familiarity. Like he was talking to a stranger. The awkwardness was palpable. I didn't want to continue the conversation.

My fingers tapped the countertop, full of the anxiety that overflowed from my heart and brain. "Why'd you need me to pick up?"

"I'm sorry for the drunk calls. I know it seems random. Just-" He sighed. "You'll understand if you come back. At least for a bit." He

144

started; his words slow. Patient. Calculated, like he was negotiating with me. "I know, and we all know." There was no specification, but we had enough of a relationship to the point where no specification was needed. It didn't provide me much comfort though.

"But just for a bit. Not more than a few days." His words didn't seem trustworthy, no matter how much I secretly wanted them to back them. His words didn't seem to originate from a brotherly love, either, but rather out of necessity.

I followed up on my instincts, which were still unanswered. "Why?"

There was no answer over the phone, but I sensed a pause in his thoughts while the two demons inside him came face to face. "I've wanted to tell you for the past month now. But it's not something you should hear over the phone. It's best if you come here. See for yourself."

He paused once more, no doubt hoping I'd agree. I stood in silence, trying to decipher the code he gave me. Intentional or otherwise, I stood staring in the distance. The coffee mug gained my interest, and I twirled it with my free hand.

With each word, the pacing of his dialogue got speedier. "I can pay for a hotel. If you want. Or I've got some rooms open at the house. Well, no. Sorry. Just yours. No one touched anything—"

"Stop." My mind latched itself on the choice of words that he used. "Who's in the other rooms, Dan?"

Silence. *Got him.* "What have you been hiding from me?" I rubbed my eyes, discomfort in my stomach growing. "Dan, answer my question."

"Some family." He relented.

The comment was vague enough to stop my mind from conjuring up any thoughts, yet it troubled me even more, the fact that he didn't want to validate that statement anymore. We did have an extended family, but they were too big to visit for any reason.

I paused. The thought grew in my brain. *No. It couldn't be.* My mind refused to believe it. I tried to stem the thought, but my attempts were in vain.

I started. "Tell me what happened to Mom." The decibels shot up in the air in a controlled rage, and I refused to let them come back down.

I didn't expect that to be true, the hope that I'd get him to talk motivating me. The hope made me wish what I was considering was the truth, was indeed false.

Yet he didn't argue. He stayed silent, yet it was the loudest noise he'd ever made. My breath started to waver, becoming uneven. My heart raced ahead of my brain, which took its milky time to process what was going on. It didn't want to, but it was slowly dragged into the hints of the terrible realization.

"Dan. What happened to her?" My wavered breath started to influence my words, which were choppy and inconsistent. The words floated down from the ceiling and nestled themselves next to the growing coffee stain.

He still didn't answer. It wasn't out of anger, impatience, or frustration. I didn't know what else it would be, however. *Mom would've never gone that far.*

Silence still deafened the line. I was tempted to cut the call, to delay the inevitable.

He sniffled. Once, then twice. Then thrice. His voice reached me, incoherent and broken up. He was sobbing. Silently, maybe hoping I wouldn't hear him. But I did. It grew louder and louder, becoming more emphasized before he abandoned trying to hide it.

At that point, I knew. *She's been dead for a month?* The tears calcified in my brain, refusing to leave yet wanting to all the while. It was alien, feeling such sadness yet not finding the tears to let out. I struggled to find the energy to follow my promise and keep the tears in. Even if I did in the end, the loneliness weighed me down like an elephant putting its foot down on me and pushing me down to the floor. It would only be a matter of time before my heart exploded.

My voice broke with each passing second. "You knew what she meant to me and you still hid this for a month." *You know what? No. Just stop. I cut the call.* There was no need for him to clarify, but not because of our relationship this time around.

But because my heart confirmed it.

I woke up. The sun I drove under was cold and distant. Covered by the clouds. I no longer considered it a miracle that I was still on the road. The dents had already created themselves inside me like cancerous ulcers.

Clawing at my skin was the need to feel her hair. *Stop being so weak. You hate her. And what she's done.* The need and naivety went away.

No dream was necessary to relive what happened after that phone call. I didn't go to the funeral. It was a tough choice to make. Very tough. Dan called me three more times that day. I picked up once, only for him to spout some nonsense about how Mom wouldn't like to see our family like this. He talked about my lack of care, but I just cut the call before he got further.

The amount of care I had for Mom was monumental, which made his words more frustrating to hear. If the funeral was for Greg, I wouldn't have even considered coming. But it was the attachment she had to me that would've torn me. Walking through her house again would've broken me, to see that place devoid of her presence, yet filled with the memories she brought to the table.

Shannon and I started entering into more fights than I could count after that. That smile of hers had scheduled often disappearances as well. I was surprised, to say the least, to see her fight for a family that didn't know she existed, or one that she didn't know.

Of course, she had the perfect family, so it was easy to put them on a pedestal. Her dad was a Wall Street investor, and her mom was a housewife. A four-bedroom, three-bathroom house was what they called home. Their neighborhood was gleaming in white, with tall pillars and columns lining all the front porches. Their house was mostly white too. White picket fences, neatly trimmed hedges, and bushes. White poppies and roses too.

At least they had a black cat to combat the whiteness. But even his name was a stereotypical "Jack". *Why do you still remember that? She doesn't remember anything about you.*

147

Every time I visited them, it was during Christmas, Thanksgiving, or their birthday (Her Mom and Dad had the same birthday). The food was plentiful. Their maid always made sure the house was clean, and the pool was always pristine. Fitting considering their environment. They finished the mystery surrounding Shannon's bracelet one day by showing me identical ones that only the ones in their family had - White, Purple, and Blue - which they insisted were all three of their favorite colors. Pink wasn't on there.

Shannon did mention some family issues to help me. She was the one who first planted the idea of fixing my issues with them. I didn't listen. She didn't understand enough. She had security. If I went, the security I'd fought hard to get, and the memories I ran away from would be for nothing. Even the sacrifice that I'd need to make for Mom's funeral, though honorable, would cause me to lose myself and what I'd built. *She just didn't understand.*

But as I thought more about that sacrifice, I wished that the only thing I lost was myself.

The Futile Impossibility

It took me a while before I found out that Dan didn't tell me where Greg was.

I brought out my phone once I stopped at an intersection (I made sure it wasn't the one at Tellermen's again). I considered texting Dan yet finding an excuse not to all the while.

Luckily for me, the day that had already sprinted past twelve provided enough of a reason. Unluckily for me, the day had already sprinted past twelve. *How the fuck is it already twelve?* I looked deeper into the big white letters of my clock, trying to figure out if it got some lessons from Dan about lying.

Satisfied that it didn't, I left the white line and left the honks behind me.

I forged down Gaines for the next few hours - passing the mall construction site a few times - trying not to let the lack of breakfast and lunch deter me. It seemed that the pain in my stomach stopped for the most part. Of course, like with anything, that only made me wonder what greater pain was going to be thrown at me next.

"Lonely Pines." I was here.

The dirt road leading up to the front of the hospice was longer than was possible by nature, by physics, and by the very laws that defined us. It was evident that I was going somewhere where it was all up in the air. A zone where whatever could happen probably would happen.

I'd never been more fearful in my life.

As if that view wasn't already metaphorical enough, the white magnolias lining the road caressed my windshield with their blooming flowers. Green, fresh grass went as far as the eye could see. Like flesh, the grass rose up and down - just a tiny bit - with the tree's roots in a seamless harmony. The hospice, upon entering clearer view, was stocked from top to bottom with a white finish that exuded flawless grace. The white chandelier on the front porch and Roman-like columns greeting me helped with that. I couldn't deny that it was a beautiful scene. Despite the omens it yielded.

Luxurious cars lined the front. No brands that screamed luxury, but it came from the peace it emanated. Some of them happened to have those family stickers with the stick figures and the smiley faces. I assumed that it was a personal dig at my current un-smiley face.

I parked my wreck beside a minivan that looked identical to Mom's and walked up the front steps into my doom.

Shannon. *What?* Complete with her denim pants and pink rain jacket. People strolled and sat in the waiting room; with many faces I could've focused on. Yet my eyes tunneled in on hers. She seemed even worse for wear, like a wet and discarded baseball mitt. The wrinkles on her face seemed more noticeable, each a crevice splitting open wider and wider. She was talking in hushed tones to the lady at the front desk but stopped when she glanced in my direction.

The receptionist ducked to bring out her phone. "Good." Shannon peeled my attention back to her. "I didn't know if he would stay awake any longer." The worry she had in her face for Greg was surprising, the care someone would have for their family and not for their divorcee's father. *Why was she here?*

She pointed up the stairs. Her other hand brought itself up to her mouth, but it flew back down and struggled to find a pocket with her eyes blinking furiously.

I followed the outstretched hand, letting impending darkness from the shadows scatter my brain from its confusion of Shannon. Even so, I caught sight of the steps' aura that told me - begged me - not to go upstairs. But I didn't want to stand staring at the stairs for much longer and give the people in the room more grounds to keep staring at my soul. *Here goes.*

Each step was short. I was up to the second landing in no time.

The second floor came soon after. It was much barer than the first. At least the first floor had more people milling about, some furniture in the basic leather chairs, and some personality with half-dead peace lilies. This time, besides a nurse going from one room to another, there was no one. Just rooms, and a couple of stock photographs of black and white images lining the pale-yellow walls.

I looked inside the first one, to my immediate left. *No.* The bed was empty.

The next one wasn't him either. An elderly man did indeed inhabit the bed, but there was a family already inside, standing with their backs turned to me; One of those perfect families, the one with the husband and wife around the average height. The man was slightly taller than the wife, which I knew would cause no trouble when they wanted to kiss. *Unlike me and Shannon.* Two children, one boy, and one girl stood at their sides. Their outfits were almost matching, and the loving glances no doubt exchanged beyond my eyesight caused me to avert my attention. Yet I wanted to be in that room.

Alas, it wasn't my destination. The third room was up next. *Feels like he's in here.*

The door was open. I stepped into the opening, and a beeping noise grew louder to attract me further inside. It worked, my legs dragging me into the magnetic field that was in the room.
I saw the face on the bed. My guess was correct.

Greg's gaze was focused up. He didn't seem awake. He seemed like a glass sculpture, just left on the curb.

The birds chirping through the open window soothed my angsty hands, which trembled with agitation. *In a way, you did leave him on the curb.*

Fuck off. My thoughts were thrown out of the window.

I focused back on him. He'd gotten older, that much was exceedingly obvious. But the amount of strength - or lack thereof - surprised me still. Combined with the frailty of his skin, the amount of visible veins, and the seemingly oversized bed, it wouldn't have surprised me if his age was strong enough to shrink him. The AC flowing through the old vent on the ceiling would've ripped him to shreds at any minute if

151

I didn't know any better. Either that or it was going to carry him far away from this desolate isolation.

The tubes in his skin fed numerous liquids that I could only look at in fascination. I couldn't count them all.

The initial shock left my mind, deciding it had enough. I looked at Greg's eyes. Sea green. Lacking any signs of life. His hair was in puffs, reduced to his sides, and almost overshadowed by his ears. His mouth had its lower lip curled inside of it upon closer inspection.

I walked closer. Step by step. When I kept my hand next to his, those sea-green eyes burst to life. They drifted like lily pads on a pond to my hand.

Despite my grumbling and protesting stomach, I forced myself to look deeper into his eyes and find anything salvageable.

He forced himself to open his mouth.

Departure

My thoughts flew back in from the window. *Of course.* They couldn't leave me alone that easily.

I was on the black couch once more.

Looking around in the enduring darkness, I couldn't help but laugh. "You got something else for me now?"

Instead of the levity winning over and plunging me back into the realm of reality - I assumed it would - I was plunged straight into a new location. This time in Mom's dirty secondhand minivan. The one every family had at one point, with the random plastic straws and dirty stains on the carpeted floors and seat covers.

Mom was driving. I was in the front seat. Dan was in the back. I looked outside. The high school passed my view, leading my stare right into the cold evening sun. I spun away in pain.

The cold evening sun. I realized when this was. *I dreamed this a week ago. Could I have something else?* The feeling of dread was still strewn across the worn windshield. Impossible to ignore. Her time with us for the week was still over. It remained Greg's turn.

There wasn't much difference between the two households then. Brawls and tussles had evolved long past a simple norm. Especially the last one. *Why didn't you get her to sign it earlier, Dan?*

The minivan rolled into view of Greg's house, which was copy-pasted into existence like the rest of the community. Yet, it was wholly different from the others on the street. In the front were an assortment of White Magnolias, planted without any organization or care. Me and Dan were forced to help during our weekends with him, even though he listened to none of our help. It was torture, to say the least. Dan and I mostly just held stuff that didn't need to be held for hours on end while Greg played around. Dan at least played along. I didn't bother. I spent the time chastising myself on why I sold him all those White Magnolias. He still had a couple that needed to be planted, almost a year later.

We'd mostly be doing that tomorrow. *Great.*

I tried not to look at his "garden" as we bumped into his driveway. Mom slowed down a bit too late, a mower recoiling in agony. She threw the gear into reverse, and we stumbled out of the open garage. Once back in his driveway, we grabbed our bookbags and shuffled out. Except Mom. She was extra quiet that day. I didn't know if it was because of what I said about Aubrey, but no throwaway comment about Greg was made while she drove. Not even a simple attempt to learn about our days.

"You got your stuff?" I asked Dan. His curly hair was much better defined than the Dan of the present.

"Yeah." He responded, holding up his bag to reinforce it.

Part of my attention latched onto his voice. This was around the time his vocal cords decided to grow up.

The other, bigger half of my attention latched onto Mom. *This was the last time you saw Mom alive.* The last memory. At that moment, both of the souls in me were aligned in purpose, to say something to Mom. One saying goodnight. The other saying goodbye.

The door opened before either one of us could actually say it. Dan and I turned around, and Mom sped off into the evening.

Greg emerged. Ruining my experiences as per usual. Everything about him seemed new. New tie. He seemed to wear a suit now. This one was a villainous white and red. He also smiled a whole lot more.

A lady was holding a bottle of wine and looking out from behind him—expensive wine, which I judged from looking at the engravings and designs on the bottle.

I was disgusted. Not just by the brand-new wealth, but the smile on his face. My jaded thoughts wanted to slap it out of his face. Those same thoughts deemed he didn't deserve such happiness while Mom suffered in silence.

Mom's suffering had grown easy to sympathize with over the years. Aubrey relieved me of my job only a couple of days ago. I followed the grieving process to a tee, even convincing myself that she didn't care about me. Of course, that just got me angrier at myself for the naivety and care I tore out of my heart and kept with her. It didn't help matters that I found out that day. That Shannon would be going to college in Michigan of all places. I didn't where exactly, but it didn't matter. I'd be away in Chicago. I guess there was still that part of me that wanted us to randomly choose the same college together. It was going to be perfect, given the fact that she broke up with her boyfriend a couple of weeks back. Irretrievable in every which way. But it seemed that even the universe was driving us apart.

Greg smiled even more as we entered his doorway. "How are you boys doing?" I wanted to walk back out and scream into the night.

I tried not to look at any details of the house around us, knowing that I had a hand in creating even these evils when we helped Greg (mostly) move in. I just sat down with Dan on one of the black couches, my dirty shoes too loud for the quiet red carpet everywhere.

The Peace Lilies were the only thing I bothered to look at, my head down otherwise. They were everywhere. On top of cabinets, and books. There was one in the sink.

Horrifyingly, there was even a Peace Lily inside a Peace Lily. A tired mistake. *A glitch.*

The mandated conversations began after a few minutes of maladroit silence. Dan didn't, but I knew how to avoid them. It was the same ritual every single weekend. I'd just sit down and bury myself in the textbooks that were shoved into my bookbags along with some extra clothes and a toothbrush. My senior year was over, and even though graduation was still left, there was no content left that the teachers bothered to care about. But I needed escape, a way through Greg's monstrosities, even if it meant putting Dan under his wicked spells.

One of my textbooks was for World History. The section I had to be interested in tonight was the Roman Empire. But the interest soon appeared of its own accord. The viscosity of their aggressiveness, their unyielding will to stand. To not bend to some other's will. The same weak me who lost himself to Aubrey and Shannon wouldn't have survived, provided his will existed around their time.

Meanwhile, Dan and Greg's girlfriend seemed to hit it off. They both were interested in engineering. Greg's girlfriend was apparently an expert on that topic. After a few minutes, they were already talking about him shadowing her at her plant up in Columbia.

As the painstaking moments crawled along, the memory sped up when it reached the stuff I didn't remember enough to matter. Dan's mouth moved at a speed that was a godsend to the cops who roamed the night like hungry ants. Hungry to get their next catch, their next meal. Greg went often into the kitchen. He sprung up like a spring chicken every couple of milliseconds and flew out of my view. I had to focus my eyes on his feet to make sure he wasn't flying.

Greg's girlfriend - I hadn't bothered to remember her name - went through a carousel of emotions. Contemplative thought. Happiness. Mostly, though, just quiet pondering. With her big mouth, I was surprised she could keep it shut.

Even the candles flickered at light speed, their lights waving their arms left and right to get my attention. The Italian-restaurant-esque music in the background skipped from song to song, record to record, singer to singer, beat to beat in a decidedly ugly manner. I wanted to close my ears. *Make it all stop.* I pleaded to my brain. Yes, I wanted the night to be over. Back then and now. *But not like this.*

Greg's torturous loop became more apparent. Going to the kitchen. Coming back into the living room and unbuttoning his jacket before shooting a slight apologetic smile to the crowd. *Sorry.* The anger I had only repeated as he slid back into the kitchen. He unbuttoned his jacket again before sitting down. That same smile came back too. *Sorry.*

The noise elevated itself to another extreme. The lights flickered faster and faster, so fast it almost slowed down. The last thought I could still hear in my brain was a wish. That no one should experience this time of pain, mental illness, or whatever this elaborated maltreatment was.

After some time, it slowed to a halt. Everything. The candles resumed their normal flickering pace. The music returned to its easy-going speed. Greg was deep in his couch, with no urge to get up visible. Even his girlfriend had chosen an emotion to keep on her fake face. I was glad.

Then they had to turn their attention to me.

Greg started by asking about school. Even now, his words were mumbled and indecipherable. I still remember how I felt, an anger that added to the rage that only grew with each passing second.

I'd decided that the simpler and quicker the answers were the better. My mouth opened, and my voice didn't have to come out for me to count how many times I said no or yes to questions that weren't yes or no. I could tell my vagueness got under his skin, and words couldn't say how satisfied I felt.

His girlfriend then started talking, asking me the most elevator-esque queries. Her mumbling was high-pitched. Very high-pitched. Already, her makeup-filled face crept and irritated me. I felt as though I was undergoing abuse just interacting with her.

I also felt no desire to look up from my textbook as we "spoke", choosing instead to wait for my words between each of her questions through my gritted teeth.

The prodding and poking of my decaying body continued as she expanded on her list of never-ending inquiries. I had to say something.

Noise entered the room with knife-edged definition. "Look, just stop," I said, looking up from my textbook to glare into her eyes. They were innocent. It made me hate her even more.

Greg's girlfriend still was smiling - which puzzled me - though it seemed even more forced, fake, and insincere. Joining us in the living room was a fireplace stoked with coal, comfort, and a side of sinisterness. The warm glow had been flickering ceaselessly along with the candles, yet now was when I noticed it by the way it touched the fake smile of the lady and permeated it across the room. But it dimmed down in an instant. It was as though the fire had stopped. The flames almost stood still for a moment. So did the candles, both watching how the scene would unfold.

I looked around said scene. Dan had looked up, not in surprise but in curiousness, like he was also interested in this encounter playing out. Greg, on the other hand, was someone who was showing emotion for the first time in his life. His always downplayed face had adopted a slight reddish tinge, and his pupils were unusually beady.

He took a deep breath. "Cal, she's just trying to get to know you." He looked down as if he couldn't even stand the sight of me.

Greg's girlfriend sneezed. Everyone said "Bless you" except for me The fire in the room had plummeted, yet it still fueled the anger flaming within me. *I don't know you, and I don't want to because I hate you.* "Ok. Sure. I just have more important stuff to worry about without her distracting me." I buried my head back in the textbook.

Greg saw my unyielding temper. "That's enough. Whatever it is, we'll talk about it later." He protested.

I shook my head. "Yeah. It is enough." The room was more silent after I finished talking. The record player stopped itself now, wanting to see how far we'd get before one of us was getting beaten up.

"Stop. We don't need this right now." Dan's voice. A voice filled with expertise and the perfect weightage of care and authority. This was the first time - at least that I remembered - that Dan disagreed with me. The hate rose within me before I could reason with myself. *Who was he to disagree? Who was he to act all mature? Who was he to act above me?* Dan had started to drift away, which I first noticed when he did nothing while I sulked from Friede firing me. *He doesn't care about me.*

"Yeah. We don't. Cause we know he's gonna have another one next week." Greg looked up and saw my eyes dart towards his girlfriend. He gave me a long hard glare. I could feel him trying to control himself and the environment. His girlfriend looked at him with contention, clearly not happy with my words. *Good.*

"Alright, that's it." The leather couch crinkled and squeaked as he got up. The glass he held clinked as he put it on the table next to his girlfriend's wine glass. His hands scraped my skin as he grabbed my collar and dragged me off the couch.

I was surprised, to say the least, at this response. The textbook slipped out of my hand, my attention now on trying to pry Greg's grip away from my shirt. He was stronger than I thought. Cursing, as I was led into the deep recesses of the house. My body hit the walls and doors of the house as he dragged me into a room, before throwing me on an empty bed. Judging by the room's empty bookshelf and the opened empty closet, I guessed it was the guest bedroom, waiting for me and Dan to finish decorating it.

The bed bounced me into the air. "Dude, what the fuck?"

As he closed the door, a look came across his face. A look of pure rage. "You need to keep your mouth shut. You are not messing this up for me." Greg snapped his fingers. "Hey. Look at me when I'm talking to you."

"I'm good." I laid my head back and let my legs dangle off the side of the bed. I felt vicious, like one of those Roman warriors. Invincible. I didn't care what Greg thought about my words, because I couldn't care less about what I said either. It was exciting, the feeling. The fearlessness.

"First of all, no. I'm not gonna take back anything I said about you, or that bitch out there either. So don't waste your time." At this point, the words came out freely.

Greg buried his head in his palm. "Cal, stop here. Please. I want this. Can't you understand?" Sweat glimmered under his dress shirt and down his neck. He raised his head and raised both his arms to the sky. "How did you expect me to live like that? With her?" He was cowardly enough to avoid saying her name.

Mom's outbursts always paled in comparison to Greg's. No one else figured as much, but I knew. "You know nothing about her." As soon as he mentioned Mom, I got up, unable to take the spiteful word against her. *Did you really know her?*

"Yeah?" He nodded, almost a genuine curiosity on his face. He put one hand on his hip and used his other to gesture out towards me. "Educate me."

"No. I don't need to say anything to you and I never needed to say anything to you, so quit it." I spat out. My eyes were on the verge of tearing up, and I tried my best to stop it, but there was little I could do. While Greg silently deliberated, it all came out. As angry tears, not ones of sadness. *No, never.* Not since that day, when Greg decided that he was prepared to let us go. I promised myself that, and I was ready to do anything to uphold it.

"No, you never knew what she went through. And don't try to pretend like you do. No one does. Not even fucking Dan. Except me. I know. I. Know." I said with a forceful bombastic jab of my thumb into my chest. It hurt. The words stung my mouth as I said it, but it was true.

Greg sighed. "Well, that's good for you Cal, but when you get out there, you treat her with respect." He motioned out towards the living room as if I still cared.

I laughed. "Oh yeah? What are you going to try and do, fight me?"

The look on his face told me something. A gleam, specifically. A gleam I knew all too well now, as the years passed. I laughed. "You do. You hate me." With a fake sense of disbelief. *I always knew he hated me.* "So, now's the right time, you think? To get rid of that fake-ass shell you've always had?" I walked towards him, my grin getting bigger and his face getting redder.

I raised my hands and gestured at my body, my first-ever flash of violent need. "Well, go ahead. Come at me." I stopped a few inches from his face. Even though the feelings I had had been festering for years and centuries up until that point, that was when I truly stopped seeing him as worthy enough to call himself my father.

"Yes."

"What?" A chirp. *What?*

"I hate you. The man you've become." His eyes were level with mine, as were the words he told me. "I'm tired of you."

"And if I had the chance to travel back to that day," The gleam in his eyes was no longer hidden. "I'd let go of you all over again. All of you."

Greg's words were still level, yet with a newfound venomous tone. It was clear that he stopped seeing me as worthy enough to call me his son. But I wasn't relieved. I was . . . sad. *You didn't see him as worthy, so why do you care what he sees you as?*

His eyes told a different story as if matters weren't convoluted more. Teary, but no tears resulting from it. Red, but not bloodstained. The words he uttered had killed him.

I didn't think much about it at the moment. I simply waited for him to walk back outside. A conversation resumed, but their hushed mutters weren't the highest on my list of priorities. I couldn't even wrap my head around the humiliation I'd witnessed. Against me, against Mom.

The lava erupted, and a sea of red oozed out of my brain. I punched the nearest photo. After the snap and the slow cascading fall of all the glass to the floor, the living room quieted down again.

At that moment, I decided I was done. Done with whatever bullshit they gave me. If I wasn't worthy, not to Dan or Shannon or even Greg - of all people - then there was no reason to stay anymore.

Shannon. Shannon's presence in my mind hurt the most at that moment. I knew deep down she could have been a beacon of sorts. A rope to lift me away from everyone. Now, I needed to be lifted away from her.

No. You're angry. The sensitivity walked out of the room's open door. All the insults and embarrassments over my lifetime flashed through both of our eyes. My mind gave no discrimination to anyone. Greg. Dan. Shannon. Even Aubrey and Robin. Even Mom. Enough to make me run away twice. *Why did I come back?*

These thoughts - and more - shattered and clattered around my head as I ran outside on the front steps, stopping only briefly to gather my bookbag. No one noticed. Either that, or they didn't care about me.

I tried to run off fast enough to avoid the possibility of my thoughts becoming true. But halfway out the door, I stopped. Through a path of brushes and roses off to the right, was a windowpane. I walked through them, wanting to look at them for the last time. See if I was wrong. See if they gave me a reason to stay.

The thorns made it difficult, but with some maneuvering and twisting, I managed to find myself next to the windowsill.

Luckily for me, the shades were drawn. Unluckily for me, the shades were drawn. I couldn't refute the clear sight. The three were smiling, the fireplace lit up. Their shadows were leaping with joy across the foyer. The wide, emphasized grins plastered on their faces - which didn't look humanly possible - caught my eyes. I knew the memory wanted this image. To reinforce the hate.

Even if it was a lie, I no longer wanted to witness nor participate in the treachery.

I wandered over to the opened garage looking for the keys to his truck. I knew it was the car he loved the most, which made me want to steal it even more. To my luck, whatever was above shared my disdain and bent their moonlit light onto the key, which I scooped up with a raged promptness.

I cared naught about the world outside the truck, as I hopped in, threw my bookbag in the back, and drove off into the darkness. No nosy neighbor or cop who tried to stop me would change or dissuade my purpose. My chance at vengeance. It wasn't just from rage. It was their association with my struggles and the subtle, yet present parts they played in them. Everything was lost, that I knew, loved, and cherished before. *So why stay?*

The blame lathered them all up in a honey. *All of them.* I watched them in my head as they tried to escape its slow viscosity, its stickiness. In the past and the present. *But they'd never do it.*

I was catapulted into traffic. Highway traffic. There was nothing around me except for a wall of trees and an endless line of cars. But I knew every detail of that fateful drive away from Gaines.

Great. I stopped trying to find a system of rules or patterns that governed these mini universes.

All my college professors said that I had a creative and imaginative mind. That was one of the bigger reasons that got me the job at Gilbert. If it did that, it wasn't a far stretch to assume that my mind could just as easily bend shape and logic in whatever way it saw fit to fuck me over.

It wasn't even teenage me in the driver's seat of Greg's truck. Looking in the rearview mirror, it was Normal Me who stared back, even though I was far from normal. *This is new.* My presence in the truck felt wrong. *Probably because it is wrong.*

The traffic was wrong as well. There were too many cars for a normal traffic jam, all bumper-to-bumper with zero movement. Zero ripples were made across the metal ocean. Zero cars were honking. Zero noise was being made. Zero cars were running too. Upon closer inspection, zero people were in any of the cars. The wall of trees even began to look suspicious. Everything was a side detail to me. I didn't like that.

I stayed seated, nevertheless, waiting for the dream to change or whatever was driving all this to input some external force into the simulation.

Nothing happened. I tried opening the door, but it fought back. Welded shut. With me in my prison. A prison I'd gotten into willingly.

My thoughts began to wander, with no other alternative. This was the drive that started my love for driving. Mostly because I was in control and had gotten good enough to shut my brain off. But also, because that tiny part of myself was allowed to truly wander without any ramifications. The ramifications I was desperately trying to escape. I began to hate it while I lived in the Chicago traffic. But the love came back.

The sun, abusing my back with its heat, made me turn around.

I drove for a long time that day. Miracle or not, no one noticed me, or my half-baked driving. No cops, no one. Two states over, with roughly the same sunlight hitting my back, the car stopped. The accelerator refused to fuel my rage fantasy.

I found a gas station a couple of hours later and convinced a truck driver to give me some food. Luckily, he was also going to Illinois.

The homeless shelter. The bureaucracy, the paperwork, and the technicalities I had to work out with my college for months. The gradual finding of my grooves, and that confidence I never had the privilege of having. With all that came after, not once did the guilt successfully catch me or haunt me.

Maybe all this is the penance.

163

Currents of Time

The adhesion of my bandage succumbing to the chill air currents transported me back home. Greg closed his mouth while we both watched it drift onto the floor. I didn't imagine it could fall slowly, but it did. The bandage seemed to grow arms and legs to hop onto the dust specks happily illuminated in the sunlight, trying to climb into the atmosphere. It failed. *I need to leave.*

Once it finally laid to rest on the ground, my eyes went to Greg's glasses that sat on the nightstand, reflecting more sunlight into the empty, lifeless room. The gold had flaked off a long time ago.

No. Stop. He was happy without you. Like everyone else.

I couldn't see that same malicious character who dragged me from that living room. *I just couldn't.* No matter how hard I tried.

No. Stop. Please.

Greg's hands flew into motion. He pushed his body up off the bed, into an upright position. I put my arms around him, yet they didn't do anything out of cluelessness on what he was doing, and what I was supposed to be doing to help him. The words trying to fly out of his mouth were stuck inside his teeth, emitting a low growl.

One of the tubes snapped out of his skin, and a beeping noise made a shiver crawl down my neck. "HEY! Hey. Lay back down."

Greg listened to my instructions, his back falling to meet the bed again. "Alright, what do you want? Tell me and I'll get it for you."

Greg wheezed to the office chair in the corner while he sniffled his nose into his white - but yellowing - shirt. The chair was a beaten leather one, with most of the skin peeled off as if it was attacked by a hundred birds all at once. For a moment, I didn't know what he wanted me to do. But once I heard the nurse creak the floorboards behind me, it hit me. I took the chair and rolled it over.

The nurse came over and rested her hand on Greg's shoulder. She did something with the wires going into his skin. I didn't process what or how, but the shrill beeping stopped. I gave her a subtle nod and a slight smile to indicate everything was going alright. She didn't seem enthusiastic about my presence, making it a point to roll her eyes and not look directly into mine while she walked away.

I wasn't too enthusiastic about this ordeal either. I didn't want this conversation to last more than five minutes. I hoped we didn't talk long enough for me to sit down. *They were the same person. He hasn't changed. You're not that weak.*

I made use of the chair and put my elbows on the bed next to his arms. The chair was with my back in the sunlight at first. But the heat hit my back with the force of a sledgehammer, so I fervently pushed it to the other side.

After I was done shimmying around the bed, I sat down and stared into his eyes as he continued to try and convey whatever it was that was so urgent.

Greg sighed with finality. "I told Dan to get you here. It's my fault, I'm sorry." With each sentence, he took a longer breath. It seemed that he was speaking as fast as he could, but it still took ages for him to finish. "I just wanted to talk."

I continued to stare. "Ok. What did you want to talk about?"

Silence. "What's going on with you?" With all the gravitas surrounding the situation, and the barren and desolate nature at hand, I was surprised that he smiled. "How are you?" *I've never asked him that.*

I shrugged. "It's going." Greg continued to smile.

He waited as if I had something else to say. "Well? You gotta job?"

"I have enough money to last me the rest of this life. And then some." The hate I felt in my memories resurfaced at that moment, angry at the weakness I decided to feel upon his condition. I did my best to make my smile richer. *I succeeded, asshole.*

Greg nodded. "Wife? Kids?"

I paused, the smile struggling to hold. Part of it wanted to endure, the thought of Shannon inducing glee in me. But the other part let the thought of Shannon suck the glee right out.

My eyes twitched. "No." Before Shannon and I could decide on the formalities and details of the kid debacle, it all ended. I wasn't going to tell him that. I didn't think he deserved to know. *Is this how Dan sees me?* I eased myself with the fact that it wasn't possible. *I wasn't like Greg.*

He nodded again. "Are you happy with that?"

I thought about the question again for a minute and shrugged once more. "I don't know." *That doesn't sound right.* "I guess. I lost the job sometime back. Again, it's not like I need it. But it keeps me entertained. And like I said I have the money. Plus, I did really try to find someone else." *I didn't.* "I think so."

"But yeah. No wife-" My voice stuttered. I looked away from his gaze, glancing around the walls, trying to bounce my mind off my pitiful existence. "No kids. No job."

"Well," He cleared his throat and sat up the tiniest bit. The bed creaked and groaned like his voice did with every word. "Honestly, I don't know what to say to that."

You never did. I looked at him while he reached over to his nightstand and grabbed his cup of water. It boasted a greasy exterior, the plastic smudged with random brown fingerprints. I doubted that even if that was the last cup on Earth, I wouldn't drink from it. Yet Greg swallowed it without any seizure befalling him.

"What do you think I've done to you?"

"Think?" I echoed the preposterous notion before he even finished talking. I knew too much about him to know where it was going. I shook my head, letting my head drop. "Let's stop this here. I don't want these long conversations about soul and morality and shit. No. Now is not the time." My voice was quiet.

"So, when is it?" His inquisitive eyes, as hard as it was to admit it, made it tough to see him like this. No hidden agenda was there to force me to change. No hidden malice. Just a question without any emotional baggage.

At least on the surface. *You know better than to be blinded by him.* "All I'm trying to get is some answers. After that, you can do whatever you want with me. But I need to know."

His words only made me feel worse about my reluctance and anger. *Don't.* But his determined face told me he wouldn't shy away from

166

the topic. I let my eyes drift to the sky. The clear sky had started to attract clouds, much like the whispers of white fuzz that were stuck on Greg's head.

I sniffled and let him seize the attention of my eyes. "You want me to be honest?"

He didn't answer, but his stare told me yes.

"I hate you. For what you did to Mom. What you did to me. All the time I spent with you, in that stupid garden, I regret." I clapped my hands together and then rubbed them. Holding them in each of my palms, I looked at his gaze.

The words that I wanted to say all my life, words that took so long to fester and rise in my tumultuous oven, were finally out. After all, he wanted me to tell the truth. But the way his expression broke, and the way I saw his soul almost leave his eyes, made me think twice about what I said. "I never liked gardening. I just didn't know how to talk to you." He reached over and took another sip. It was more hurried.

Once the cup was back on the table, he opened his mouth to speak but it closed. Greg forced it open. "I've never forgiven myself for the way I acted. What I said. It must've hurt you-"

"It did."

Greg's eyes glanced over. I tried to see something else besides the apologetic light in them, but I couldn't. He pursed his lips, almost as if he knew my despair. "I broke you. I see that now." *He doesn't.*

"Really. I do. And I get your anger. I'd be angry too. I am angry." His words didn't sound angry, but they still had a degree of insistence. "You were never taught that losing people is okay. Even the ones you cared about. I mean, what childhood did we give you? What lessons did you get from both of us? We gave you nothing. And what hurt it the most was in the end it didn't matter who was right or wrong or who won the argument that day. We were both wrong to put you two under that. But we were dumb enough not to change. And here we all are."

"Me. You. The little boy I walked in the woods with all those years ago." He smiled.

I shook my head. *Wait.* I refused to acknowledge his words. *No. That was Mom.* I played through the memory, in a rapid-fire row of stills like a projector did. A projector projecting only to my conscience. His face didn't appear. Just to be sure, I did it again. Nothing. *No.*

The thought of putting Greg's presence in Mom's came up. To confirm that the memory would feel out of place. I didn't let the thought develop for fear the memory would click into place like a piece in a discarded puzzle.

"Either way," He brushed aside the thought as if it meant nothing to him. If he was truly there that day he couldn't. "I shouldn't have shown you that that night."

Greg sighed. "In a life where every choice, for some reason, felt wrong, making you feel like you were easy to let go of was the one I regretted the most."

I don't want to let her go. I don't want to regret her. I don't want her to stay a memory. My thoughts cut through the devious self-made mazes in my heart to find Shannon.

"After that, I've always wanted a chance to go back home." Greg flung his hand at me. "Fix everything I messed up." A wry smile. "I've accepted the fact that I can't."

"Even though I'm your dad-" The sentence joined the dust in the air. He extended his bony, wrinkly pointer finger and let me stare at it for some time.

Then, he let his hand drop. The words sputtered out of him with great struggle, yet they didn't. His mouth was open, with no audible noise. When the noise eventually came out, my heart began to drop. "No. You stopped calling me Dad a long time ago, right?" He nodded while his head shuddered at light speed.

Before I could consider the confusion of how he knew that a noise erupted in my gut. Our eyes locked and my mind disappeared into the currents of time.

The walk in the woods came up first. My kid self was in front of me. I watched in horror as a set of fingers inched up to my face to wipe that tear off my eye. Fingers from a male hand.

Unfortunately for me, it got easier to remember. Easier to picture. Easier to feel that touch. *No. He couldn't have remembered. He's old. Too old.*

Nothing changed the course that the train went on. The more the memory went on, I became forced to admit Mom's emotional confession was nonexistent, a product of my guilt. My mind contended with the possibility of the fact that everything was the product of my guilt. *If that was fake, then what was real?*

That fateful night was the next one on the list. The last night. In Gaines, at least. I never knew who searched for me after I ran away. Now, I was forced to find out.

My head shook as I assumed a panicked run into the street. I could feel the earth-shattering wailing that would've escaped Greg's throat as he frantically strode down, trying to close the distance between me and the twin red lights of the truck. Dan was by my side, a sense of confusion and pure worry on his face.

The truck sped up. Pretty soon, I was all alone on the road. Panting. Regretting. Crying.

The road disappeared. An assortment of neighbors, cops, and nosy Southern figures surrounded me in Greg's living room. I could sense their insistence for him to sit inside his home while they searched for me, even though he wanted to jump up and keep running. The vision almost shook with the restlessness he felt.

My stomach started churning. Turning over and over and over and over again. It liked none of this.

But there was nothing else to do except lay witness. To the false assurances that they gave me. To their promised search efforts that I knew wouldn't yield my presence. To Greg's mind that had already begun churning out ideas. That ranged from crazy to insane.

To the hurt that I left Mom with. Dan with. Most of all, Greg. He'd probably assume it was because of him.

Because it was. It had to be.

I was back in the leather chair. At this point, I was crying uncontrollably. Groaning. Moaning. Mucus filled up my nose. "Don't do this to me. I hate you. Don't make me change that too." Through shuddering breaths, I spit it out.

Somewhere in my head, I was attempting to take his words out of my brain. But the pure pain, and regret he oozed throughout his remarks was unbearable.

Tear after tear after tear. It only grew in intensity. Some of the drops dribbled down to my mouth. I was able to taste the salt in them.

I stood up and walked to the window, my hands over my face. In it, a disgusting mixture of snot and regret. I put my hands down and used my hands to wipe whatever was on my face. Straight ahead, I saw my car gleaming in the afternoon sunlight. The South Carolinian evening sunlight was peaceful enough to make my wreck look worthwhile.

The thought arose in my head. Once more, I felt immensely ashamed. Yet now, more than ever, I wanted to leave it all behind.

Stop it. Now. The tempestuous medley was hurting my brain, overwhelming me. I turned around. The intent in Greg's eyes was unknown. It was cloudy yet gazing through me. I ascertained that it was trying to conjure up an explanation for what I was thinking. I almost saw the worry-twitch at the corners of his mouth. That I'd leave again. We were both thinking that. But it was nearly like he was scared I'd leave. Scared for me.

His smile was the easiest one so far yet carried a greater tonnage than the world itself. "It's okay. You don't have to call me Dad if you don't feel like I was your dad. It'll all be fine."

I took a breath, the air freezing my lungs with its sharpness. The tears stopped but resumed once the comment took over enough of my thoughts.

"No one's told you that?" I shook my head. "Then you're stronger than you think."

My sniffling stopped. "Huh?" I looked down for the first time in a long time. I'd never had abs before. I never went to the gym in my life. I'd grown overweight over the past few years too. At least, overweight for a lean person. *Does he need his eyes checked too?*

Greg laughed, though it was frail enough to be disguised as a cough. I tried to find the villainous undercurrent in it, but there wasn't any. "I don't mean physically. I mean in here." He brought his finger up to his forehead. "It takes a lot to keep living without anyone helping you. Or someone to live for."

The optimism did its best to fight off the hordes of pessimism, but it was for naught in the end. *Now you just look stupid.*

"You aren't stupid." *How does he know what I'm thinking?* "It's easy to think that way. I get that. But you aren't. You may hate me, but never allow you to hate yourself."

"Oh, and it's that simple?" The anger returned, my hands doing a jumping jack even though my feet stayed put. The hatred felt right. "Really pal? You think you get me? What do you know about me?"

"I know that you're scared." *What the fuck's he on about?* I almost laughed. I resorted to a small smile.

"I am scared." My smile disappeared. *What? Why'd you say that?* Neither half of me could answer that question, yet the third soul inside continued speaking. "I'm scared because I can't control my thoughts and they say the absolute worst stuff. The worst stuff."

You're going too far now. I stopped myself, forcing my lips shut. But Greg shook his head. "You're not done."

I wasn't. "I'm scared I'll leave behind the people I care about. I'm scared they'll feel as lonely as me. I'm scared that I chose the wrong people to care about. I'm scared that I care too much and I tell everyone I do stupidly care too much about me and I just drive them all away. I'm scared I chose the wrong people to let go of. And of all those people I let go of, I still stupidly carry parts of them with me while they all carry the worst of me. And I'm scared that it hurts them. Like it hurt me." My hands went up to my hair, pulling at the roots. The pain did its best to distract my thoughts from this unknown cycle of emotions. Yet I knew the emotions too well for it to be ignored that easily.

Don't stop. "I'm scared that I'll just have to keep struggling with moving on and that I'll have to move on from everything eventually. Everyone. Like nothing's actually permanent. And I know life doesn't normally do that to people. But I seem like the exception." I laughed, pulling harder at my hair.

Stop there. I looked at Greg. He shook his head as if he knew the battle I was fighting. "I'm scared that I hate myself." *Why? You should.* "I'm scared I feel this way. I'm scared that I'm scared I feel this way. I'm scared that I can't prove myself wrong and if I can't prove myself wrong I'll never prove anyone else wrong." I declined to breathe, the words coming out faster than I'd ever spoken. I could feel my brain rewiring itself, reexamining the hatred for everyone I desired to punch in the face.

"I'm scared that I can't control how I feel. I'm scared that the dreams will get worse." *They will if you don't leave right now. You're talking too much.* "I'm sorry. I know I'm saying too much-"

"Don't say sorry when you don't need to. You're not-"

"You don't understand." *Don't agree with me. It's harder that way.* "I have so much to say. We'll be here for hours-"

"That's fine."

"You'll get bored. You won't understand-"

"That's fine too."

I guess I should keep going. "Alright. Don't say I didn't warn you."

A deep breath filled my lungs up sufficiently before I waded in. "I'm scared that I'll always be wrong, no matter how much I try to be a good person. I'm scared that no one will really know what goes on inside me, and how terrible it feels." My voice grew in decibels until I was sure they were sprinting out the open door into the hospice. I didn't care.

"I'm scared that I'll keep regretting every decision I make, and that life will go by too fast for me to fix them. I'm scared that I don't regret some decisions, even though others do. I'm scared that I have to prove to the ones I care about that I should be loved. While they don't have to fight for love. And I can't help but look at them and be jealous." A terrible jealousy.

"I'm sorry. I know I'm talking too much-"

"You're not. Be strong. Keep going." Greg nodded again. It couldn't help but reassure me immensely.

I guess I will. "I'm scared I'm not as good as I think I am. I'm scared that I don't actually know what I want."

Strangely enough, the tears slowed to a halt. "I'm scared that I'm capable of being stupid enough to want everything. To even think I deserve it. Of course, I lost everything because of this. But I'm scared that

I'm still stupid enough to want something. And I'm scared that every second I spend here-"

"You risk losing everything all over again." For the first time in my life, he finished my sentence.

Our eyes caught themselves. For the first time in an eternity, we smiled at each other. We smiled at the pain. *He did know.*

Greg saw the need for silence and granted it. The silence took the invitation and walked into the room. It made itself comfortable. Very comfortable. Yet we didn't bother. I just sat back down and waited for the silence to live. Amid my nerves calming down, he reached over and grabbed his glasses. Once he put them on, I could see the Greg I hated so viciously. *Why did you hate him?*

"Jeez." Finally, Greg spoke. "That is a lot." I laughed. *Greg never made me laugh before. Right?*

"That's fine. We'll figure it out still. Let's take it step by step." *Really? Can we? Please? I'd like that.* "I have all the time in the world." We both knew he didn't, but the statement wasn't corrected. His calming ease took over my senses. I loved this break from the confrontational nature of the past two days.

"I don't know everything about your problems. And no one can answer every single one of your questions." Greg cleared his throat. "Just don't overthink it."

"First, let's get that business out the way that you're a terrible person." *He said it so easily. Why? How could I do that?* "You are who you are. People will evolve, but who they are really will never change. That's the beautiful thing about life, kid."

"How is that beautiful?"

"It is."

"And if I'm not a good person?

"You are. Doesn't mean you're always right. You're also flawed. But you are good. No matter what you've done."

"Huh." Silence. A headache I didn't realize I had released itself. *That feels nice. Did I just decide to live with it? For how long?* "And what about for moving on? You got any wise words for that?"

Greg didn't react to my joke, taking it as a challenge instead. "If moving on was so easy, no one would talk about it. It's painful. Slow. Can't do anything except sit with your feelings until you come to terms with it."

"But?" I leaned forward with expectation. *Please. Let there be a "But".*

"But there's no schedule for it. No timeline. It's different for each person. Each relationship. As long as you wanna move on, you're moving forward." Greg finished the thought with a simple wave of his hand.

No. It couldn't be. "It's that simple?"

"Just because it's simple doesn't mean it's easy. But yeah. It's that simple. It's just the human tendency is to complicate it in our heads. Overthink. It's hard to consider that it'll be alright. That it can be alright." *When was the last time you went into a situation expecting everything to be alright?*

"Huh." We sat in silence for a few more minutes while the wisdom rattled around my head. The more it did, the more it made sense.

"Ok. Wow. I already feel much better." I did.

Greg's smile was the proudest I'd ever seen it. "Good." He didn't seem to doubt it. *I thought he would. Please doubt it. Then I can doubt it.*

"Yeah." Almost as if I couldn't believe it myself. "Ok. Everyone wants me to change? Ok. I'll accept that. I'll figure something out." All this time, I was worried about how other people wanted me to change. Worried enough to ignore how things could be if I started to want to change. But now, my words were no longer frustrated, nor were they secretly looking for a way to prove me wrong.

"You're right." I never imagined I'd say those words.

I rolled my chair even closer to his side with a newfound determination. I put my hands on his head. He almost leaned over, like an eager baby waiting for a human touch. I patted his head. The ratio of my hand size and his head was alarming. Like I was cradling a baby.

Greg closed his eyes. He seemed at peace with my touch. "Anyone can give you advice. Some of it will be right. Some of it will be wrong. You choose what's best for you to grow. Not the right answer. The best answer."

I shook my head, still trying to reject the water. *No. He can't be correct.* "Then what happens to the right answers? The stuff you're supposed to do? The potential you're supposed to reach? The person you're supposed to be? What about that?" *Surely he doesn't have an answer now.*

Greg didn't seem fazed. "Well, life denies you the beautiful gifts in order to give you the right ones anyway. You just gotta accept it, champ."

He took another sip from his doomsday cup as if this was nothing. "What next? I want to talk about everything that we can, 'cause I don't know if we can talk again truth be told." *I hope we do.*

You do? "Ah yes." He started before I could consider a response. "You being terrible in everyone else's head."

"It's inevitable to become a villain in someone's story. Even worse, to become a no-one. Even if they were heroes in yours. Even if you wanted to be more than a villain in theirs. But it's not about what you mean for them. It's about the role you serve in your own story and the stories of those who love you. No one else."

I laughed, though there was nothing humorous in the room with us. "How do you come up with this stuff?"

"Why do you think time's the greatest teacher?" He still couldn't take the joke. *He knew I was deflecting.* "Because with recontextualization, you get contextualization. Everyone makes more sense out of the senseless in retrospect. That's all." The ease was gone in his words. Even the bigger ones. It seemed like something to boast about to me, the retrospect, but Greg seemed to regret it.

"I can't believe you." Half the meaning was drowned in levity, and half of it was drowned in truth. *What happens to it all if you believe him?*

Greg scrunched his lips, the ease returning. "Don't stop believing in the change, because most of the time you'll be the only one who can believe in it."

"You'll be tempted to stop changing. A lot. But don't stop. Don't. No matter how easy it is. Please. Not for me. For you." His eyes spoke with bitterness and regret. "Make sure you aren't too late to change. Please."

I don't have to end up like this.

That means you're admitting that you were him.

That's fine.

That means that all that anger towards him was for nothing.

That's fine too.

Are you sure?

The opportunity that the mechanic imbedded in my memory resurfaced. *Yes.* I can be better than Greg. *I can succeed.*

Greg nodded. *He wanted it too. Every step of the way.*

My words were quiet. Tentative. "I'm sorry for everything. I'll be back tomorrow. I'll get you somewhere else, somewhere better. I'll be better." My arm still held his head, but now it was at a weirder angle. I didn't have the heart to move it. "I passed a couple of other homes on the way here, closer to the house. Dan could visit you a bit easier if he isn't already. I'll stay and do what I can. Whatever's best. Sound good?"

The words came out faster by the end. Fast enough for my brain to question my conscience and the logistics behind this proposed arrangement. A civil war ensued inside me. My voice wavered the more I spoke, and vomit threatened to escape my throat, this sudden change in my mentality not sitting well with my stomach. I continued still. "I actually want to do this. Don't worry."

You do. I laughed. Quietly, my throat still adjusting to the weird sensation. *You do.*

I paused. Greg's eyes weren't open. "Dad?"

He still didn't open his eyes, but he nodded.

I didn't mean to call him "Dad" - I wasn't that reformed just yet - but unfortunately to my stomach, I couldn't take it back. The heart rate monitor beside me skipped a beat right after I said the word. I took a glance at it, then back to him. His smile was bigger. Almost louder.

Finally, Greg decided to leave our embrace. He swiveled his head to face up at the ceiling. He didn't open his eyes yet.

Downstairs in the main lobby, I began conversing with the receptionist. Greg's healthcare plan. Whether he was in a good enough state to even be transferred. What they were giving him.

Knowledge became immediately ingested. Some of it was the pure adult nonsense my ears had acclimatized to. I knew I just had to endure this little bit. I was - finally - heading in the right direction after a lifetime of figuring out where I needed to go.

After she walked away, my eyes became stuck to the stack of papers she left on the counter. I signed what I could, and initialed where it told me to. The only other signature I needed was Greg's spouse.

Crap. I hadn't thought about his new wife. I didn't know if this was the one I met all those years ago. Either way, a tiny sigh entered my lungs. Greg may have accepted me for who I was, but everyone else didn't. Especially if she knew what I did to him.

My eyes peeled around to the various people. Everyone had different emotions that they chose to wear. Disappointment. Regret. Exhaustion, internally and externally. *When would I be able to see something else in people?*

Finally, I saw her. I didn't know how she was here. But she was.

She wore a dull brown jacket over a yellow and red plaid shirt. Jeans and some boots completed the outfit. It was the only thing about her that was together. Her hair had woken up on the wrong side of her pillow, and the bags under her eyes were visible from the receptionist's desk. I dove through my memory - which was easy enough now that I had such rigorous practice - and found her face. It was different now. Not just from age. But I knew it was her by how she used her pupils to stare at me. Everyone else shifted uncomfortably when I looked at them. Yet her posture was incredibly still. *She seems nice. Why was I so mean to her?*

I walked over, my shoes feeling heavier. As I got closer, her gaze and presence seemed to intensify. My eyes went searching for something else to look at until they saw the coffee table right next to her. I reached down and set both the pen and paper on it.

We exchanged a heaty glance. Her pursed lips turned her whiter somehow while she exhaled. A big, meaty exhale that only went through her nostrils. Yet she reached over and signed the paper. *Easy as that.*

That was until the color returned to her lips. "What's your plan?"

"See what I can do. Move him somewhere closer to our house. Keep him alive for as long as I can." My sentences were short. To the point. Like I was being interrogated.

"As long as you can? Is that right?" The words stopped my flow, and her hook put itself deep in my tongue. "Who kept him alive up until now? Who got him here after his home got destroyed? Who made sure you didn't get another phone call from him?"

Before my thoughts could formulate a response to the question, she continued. "Exactly." I must've worn a stupid face to earn such a remark.

"I'm sorry. Look, I know I've done bad things-"

"Don't talk to me." She buried herself in her phone. *Fuck. I shouldn't have forgotten her name.*

I left before she could wound me further. I kept all the signed documents on the receptionist's desk. The receptionist sifted through the stack, a wired phone in between her head and shoulders in the ultimate test of mettle - and handed me back something that I needed to get notarized. I didn't have the energy to question it.

I didn't have the energy to start the car either. Once I got inside, I took a moment to get off the rollercoaster and let my legs stop shaking. The paper I needed to get notarized felt so heavy that I had to toss it into the driver seat's pile of fuck-all.

Out of all my considerations and expeditious thoughts, I'd forgotten to account for how hard all this would be. Truly. I'd be fighting a town and a population who wholly despised me. Although time had brought something new to everything else - threatening even my stubborn convictions - my notoriety wouldn't succumb to such delights.

ACT III

Enigmatic Misfortune

The long driveway that led into the hospice flew by faster than when I came in.

Waiting at the intersection leading back onto the road, I put on my indicator. Right. I knew the road well enough. It'd lead out into the highway, and out of South Carolina after a couple of hundred miles. I'd get my stuff from Cherry Hill and deal with the notary business on the way back. Then come back and use the newfound hope for good.

The only thing that was stopping me was the constant flow of traffic. Every so often, I thought there was a gap to leap into the gridlock. But just as I was about to rev up my engine, the openings closed.

Pretty soon, I stopped looking for openings. My attention drifted elsewhere.

The words Greg said began to haunt me. The clarity he offered me disappeared, and the gaping holes in my thinking returned. I couldn't help but look at the years past, at the house, with a different lens. An entirely different microscope.

My stomach churned again. My chest grew an entire ecosystem that fluttered and metamorphosized within my very being. Something was starting to happen.

Images began to form in my mind's eye. *No. I thought this was over.* I tried to fight them off, but the memories still washed over me with ease, as they flew past my windshield in a blur. They were thankfully unlike the more in-depth psychosomatic recollections. Still, they were unwelcome.

When I realized what I wanted to do, I blew out the biggest flurry of curses onto my steering wheel, which then endured a beating. But whatever I did in my anger, the thoughts remained. *Stop trying to prove yourself wrong.* A gap opened. Yet the loose ends I was happy to leave grabbed my legs, almost pulling my foot off the accelerator. *There are no loose ends. Don't fall for that.*

The right turn was now emptier. *But so was the left.* My fingers, unbeknownst to me, had started a jazz melody while I weighed the options. The car waiting behind me decided that I'd had enough time to wallow in my self-pity and spew out a flurry of honks.

I sighed at myself, still waiting a bit before I moved to take the time and muster up enough courage to leap. The traffic on the road bunched up once more. I doubted whoever was behind me would appreciate that, but the chasm I was about to jump off was growing deeper by the second. *Are we doing this?*

As if on cue, the gaps between the cars lessened enough for me to leap. I made sure to take a deep breath before I switched my indicator signal.

The ride was tumultuous, at best. Combatting thoughts still did their best to ruin Greg's insight.

Relief washed over me when I opened the car door, almost taking out the "38" mailbox stopped right by my window. Dad's truck was missing, but I still didn't feel my jalopy deserved to be next to Mom's minivan and Shannon's red sedan.

I closed the door. *Get back in the car.*

My footsteps, almost at a snail-like pace, guided me to the front door. *Stick to the plan.*

It wasn't locked. *This will just ruin things.*

I took off my shoes before I entered the doorway and held my breath in case anyone was there. Shannon's pink jacket was on one of the recliners. The sun had dipped way below the four o'clock point, yet Dan's kids weren't home. All the doors were closed and there was peace around the house. I took that as a good omen.

The first sight that stopped me was the black couch. Or rather, the broken glass that was littered around it that day. The hand that threw it was always as rough as Greg's inside my mind, yet now it imagined Mom's hand had thrown it.

"How dare you?!" The words rang loud behind my ears. I turned. Mom towered above me in her blue sweats. Crazed, maniacal. For the first time, it was me - not her - taking those fearful few steps back. My calves hit the recliner, and I tumbled down into it. My hair still felt the cooling sensation of Shannon's jacket, its freezing zipper. Yet Mom remained.

Now Greg appeared, bent near the black couch.

No. Dad.

He wore the same yellow shirt. But this time I saw his elbows were above his face, forearms bleeding with glass shards lodged in them.

Leaving his body behind, Dad's eyes wandered up to Mom, fearful without any other creeping emotion.

Dad then rose to join his eyes and began talking. Yet, his words were muffled. My mind had registered the movement of his lips, the shaking of his head and his hands and his eyes, but no words came out still. I chose not to let it ruin my mind and did the only thing I could still do, that I had the freedom to do: Watch.

Mom snarled like an animal before she got into Dad's face. The way her head spun and berated his very existence was frightening. Yet I had no trouble deciphering what I saw.

It continued. On and on. Dad's movements were simple. Up and down. Off and on the couch with tepid hesitation. Either that or a skewed sense as to what he possibly could do. Sighs of deep breaths were all he dared to do, the only response that he could justify with the onslaught he was receiving with his mouth agape. The tension he gave made me stand up as well.

I smiled and looked up. At the ceiling, yet my attention was set on the lump of mass in my skull. *Ok. Nothing got fucked up yet. Anything else you want to revisit?*

The smile disappeared when I looked down. Mom filled my face, an inch away from my nose. The wild eyes I saw all the while back, back in our - my - walk in the woods, returned. I didn't have to hear a word she said to know that no remorse lined it while it flew out her mouth with deadly accuracy. I dodged my way out of the warpaths of the two, even though there was no tangible threat.

Then a gasp escaped my pursed lips, and it all vanished. In a misty haze that shot up into the ceiling and left no trace behind.

I fell into the black couch. I was too tired to get up once I realized it was said black couch. Tired from the emotional rollercoaster I was on. Tired from the fact that I'd forgotten to put in the harness. Tired of making sure that I didn't fly off into the depths of my mind by holding myself to my seat. Tired of pretending that I wanted to. Tired of these harsh realizations about Mom pounding me into annihilation. Tired of fighting the desire inside me that hoped she realized - wherever she was - that it was her that made me smile for the first time in a long time. *But now I had to fight that, didn't I?*

My brain was numb while I thought about these contradictions. It didn't seem like the mechanic's peace, still. *Was that how you felt after you changed?*

Something caught my eye. My room. My room's door. It was open. A darkness that didn't fit the current time of day was inside. I got up and ventured over, the darkness almost getting darker. At that point, my footsteps were shuddered. Hesitant. I could no longer distinguish if what I was fretting over was a vision, or something worth more of my time.

When I opened the door some more, the answer didn't surprise me.

Dan. A freshman. Maybe a sophomore. His black locks had lacked their definite tone, just hastily frayed over to the side. His eyes were stuck on a piece of notebook paper. Nothing was on it. Yet his pupils never moved. Like a glue, just stuck to the back of his head. The only part of his stature that told me he was alive was the pencil, cradled in his right hand. With his middle finger and thumb, he twisted it over and over.

I stayed silent. No action of mine could affect anything in front of me, but something about this image was stuck in my head. A familiar foe I was somehow supposed to know but didn't.

The frequency of his twitch stopped. Slowing down, something swelled in his ears. The bawling began. Childish. Adolescent. A high-screeching definition at its core. Tears, begging for someone else to wipe it, rained down on the table with no alternative.

Dan's head jerked towards the door in an instant. My heart fluttered with the initial thought that he knew somehow, I was watching this. With a flurry of movement, he wiped his face dry with the sleeves of his shirt and did the same to the desk. Through my chest came a smaller me. Damp rain jacket galore.

It took me a hot minute to realize when this was. But I was just more curious as to why he'd never say this to me. I'd asked him that day, what happened. *He chose not to tell me this. He's been lying to me for a long time.*

Did I do this? At the hospice, it seemed like I was beginning to accept the fact that I needed to change. But now I was seeing what I actually had to change.

It wasn't a good feeling, my stomach still trying to conjure up some delectables to throw up. The best it got was a warm soup mixture of granola sliding up my throat.

I barged back out into the living room, the vision disappearing. There was no use staring at the spiteful sight.

Shannon exited our tiny pantry out of the corner of my vision.

Wait. I stopped. Dead in my tracks. *What?* My thoughts spun wildly until she noticed me too. She stopped in her tracks. In her arms was a laundry basket. The basket was blue. Light blue. Fist-sized holes encircled it.

About three paces from me she stood. Her face changed, trying to look impartial and unbiased. She didn't say a word.

Shannon tore her attention away from me and went inside Dad's room. A slight wooden thud and she walked back out with a fresh basket. This one was a dull red.

She strode back to meet the washing machine. My brain began to outline a thought process as to what she was doing here. *I never brought her here. For her sake.*

For a while, there was no noise besides my thoughts trying to come up with possible theorems and explanations.

But the theories limped to the background when my eardrums were finally able to pick up on something. Sniffling. *Sniffling.* From the tiny laundry room.

Was she crying? My dress shoes regained their rigidity - which I ignored up until that convenient moment - and made it harder to move forward into the hallway. Still, I trudged over. When I got closer, it was as though I was walking through mud.

Each step was slow. Afraid, even. Not knowing what else they might uncover.

Resumptions of Rot

For the first time, I was happy to be transported elsewhere.

The darkness was the only thing around me, initially. But it soon began to shape and form into actual objects.

The first was a pristine windshield. Everything else around me was also top-of-the-line. A peach leather interior created itself, with a glossed wooden dashboard fitted with all the tech a luxurious car could hold. A seatbelt wrapped itself around my chest, keeping me from exploding back out into reality.

Outside of the car, everything was devoid of detail and anything of value. I hadn't dreamed of this memory for a long time, so it made sense. This remembrance was already awkward. Clunky. Alien. The methodologies I had to inherit back then became visible inside my skull once more. The superiority threatened to drunken my mind with each passing moment, all part of a sense I hadn't felt for a long time.

But it went away, as I reminded myself that I was too broken ever truly to return to this feeling of fearlessness. I was still broken enough to think and reminisce over all that happened, yet in denial to reminisce over what didn't. What it meant for me. For us. *Was this part of the "Why" too? Why?*

It was a drastic rise to stardom I'd experienced at Gilbert. The car and its silvery matte finish were one of the many byproducts while I furthered my role - and my connections - there. Nevertheless, I desired more.

I did get what I strove for. Hitching a ride with my expectations, I noticed more drive from everyone else the further I went at Gilbert. No complacency was allowed into our schedules. It compelled me to push my body and mind past what it was previously used to. Luckily, Mom died, so I had something that needed distraction from. Plus, I no longer had reason to go home and waste my time getting into arguments with Shannon. She never liked the work culture I was embedding myself into. But it didn't matter what she thought. Gilbert knew me as the fun-loving perfect individual, and they loved me all the more for it. So did everyone else in Corporate Chicago. Even if it was all fake.

Then I got promoted once more. That was around the time Shannon quit her job. Another call of rejection. I didn't know why, but it quickly became her own problem. I wasn't even there to hug her, another party taking up my time. I didn't have time to object to that because this higher echelon either, and the aura it emitted was different. Ivy League alumni. Sons of CEOs, bankers, and investors all occupied this space. I knew I'd have to save face a lot more to stay here. For my job. For Shannon. Even more so as we didn't have that second income.

One of the ways I had to do it was to attend their parties. I had to. Shannon never understood that fact. Yes, all they did was bring their girlfriends or wives or mistresses to show off like exhibits. Yes, it became necessary for everyone there to drink. Even I felt a slight bit of disgust. But I needed to do it. *I needed to.*

The money was used well at my house. Upgraded bathrooms. Granite countertops. Higher quality hardwood flooring and varnishes comprised the many paychecks we spent.

The ones we had left over were spilled onto everything else. We made it a regular thing to watch a movie in theaters on Friday. We ate out every night. Price didn't matter anymore.

It was a degradation into unhappiness for Shannon, however. Her complaints and queries never stopped. It was all especially thunderous that week. She didn't like the movie I insisted on watching the night before. The party today - to celebrate my newest promotion, even though it'd happened some time back - ended in a triumphant crash when Shannon almost reduced the celebration into a brawl. Apparently, someone's hand grazed up on her. The guy apologized immediately, yet Shannon wasn't convinced.

Her voice brought me back to the car. The leather steering wheel became more touchable by the second until it was undoubtedly real.

Pretty soon, everything luxurious detail settled into how it was supposed to be. The only darkness that remained was of the foreboding type that overtook the night around us, not letting me more than a few meters.

Shannon was leaning into the window, cross-legged. Her nails were pink. She wore the same blue satin dress as in my other memories. *I've never seen such beauty, even by her standards.* Yet her face was filled with dried tears. "You don't have to go. No one forces you. It's your decision in the end." She sat up straighter as if it would drive the point home with the extra emphasis.

Her face curled into a frown. "And you decide to bring me along."

"What, you don't like it?" I joked, yet the face she glared at me with was enough to cut the grin I had formed. I was decidedly more unconcerned. My blue three-piece suit and brown loafers, which I was adamant to wear, were starting to resemble cardboard.

I shifted, trying to tip the see-saw in my favor. Nevertheless, not a worry in the world was on my face when I glanced in the rearview mirror. There were specks of drunkenness along my dilated pupils and my drooped lips. "Look, they wanted you to come. He did whatever, and he apologized for it. No worries." I defended myself, taking one hand off the steering wheel and placing it on my chest. "I'll worry about that. Alright?"

Shannon shook her head. "You can't just say he did whatever. You have any idea how scared I was?" Her lips were pursed after that. Tightly. *Why didn't she understand?* Even if something happened and I said something, I could say goodbye to Gilbert. Everything I had fought for. "I don't like the way they look at me anyway." Her face was red like she wanted to say more. Much more.

Why am I not looking at the road? I looked back. There was no space on the right of us with some heavily wooded claustrophobia. Half the car was off into the oncoming traffic lane as well. The ingredients for disaster all came together when a motorcycle barreled around the curve. I jerked the wheel back into my respective lane, which caused Shannon to fly into the side of the car.

After I recollected the car, Shannon scooted back to the edge of her seat. Her chest fluttered up and down, and her hair sat wild and crazy around the headrest. "How drunk are you? I can drive."

Does she have any idea who I am now? Does she think I'm weak enough not to handle a couple of drinks? Does she think I'm still that little kid who couldn't save Mom, who just stood there with his mouth open while Friede practically disowned me? "I'm fine." I turned to her in assurance, hiding the ego for now.

Despite that, she hissed. "Well then keep your eyes on the road." Her tone was aggressive, yet fearful.

"Ok. Ok, I'll slow down." I tipped my foot off the accelerator. My voice went down some decibels as well.

"Well, that too." I looked over and saw her white grip on the overhead handle being infused with a hint of color.

My eyes got caught in the tempting web of hers. It hurt to see tears in them. "What'd I just say?!" She snapped and pointed to the windshield.

I turned immediately. The road was clear. No lights, no signs, no cars.

"We're fine. It's okay."

Her head bobbed over to the left when I turned sharply. "So, running a red light's okay now?" A sarcastic laugh followed.

My mind couldn't figure out what she was talking about. "I'm sorry. I didn't see it. I'll make sure you get home tonight, I'm not that stupid. Alright? Is that what you want?" I quickly apologized, but the seething nature I felt towards her came out regardless.

Something was wrong. Beyond the groping, however ashamed she felt about that. Even my drunk state sensed her apparent distraught. "You alright? You were kinda off yesterday, too. And the day before that too." Another curve swerved up to us. I made sure to conquer it at a slower pace. "You can talk to me, you know that right?" Another smile formed on me. "Man to woman. Husband to wife. If you want, I can make it up for you in another way when we get into bed." I leaned over and gave her a nudge with my shoulder.

"It's more than that, Cal." She spat me away.

"Well, maybe you aren't going to come then, next time." But it wasn't out of anger.

"Good." She murmured, though it was loud enough for me to hear.

It was silent for the next few turns. I let my past version focus on the car while I focused on the drowsiness that began to sit on my eyebrows. Luckily, the various villas and vineyards that started passing us as the forest gave my eyesight something to focus on. The forest then opened to showcase a residential neighborhood. *Ours.*

The skyscrapers were still visible, their twinkling lights standing in the distance. But the entire atmosphere was so much more elegant and perfect here. There, we couldn't turn one corner without seeing walls plastered with graffiti back in the city. Here, we couldn't go a turn without having our breath snatched from under our mouths. *It'd been a while since we went on a walk.*

Out of nowhere, Shannon chirped. "Cal, you chug everything they hand you. Everything. I thought that was a one-time thing the first time. But it wasn't." I felt her shift in her seat. "I need you to get a hold of yourself because I genuinely can't trust any of them."

This was where the anger started. There was a point in our arguments, where a simple squabble turned into something more. Sometimes it was me. Sometimes it was her. Usually, it wasn't until after everything settled down that we realized it didn't matter in the end.

I almost hit the brakes right then and there, fighting the urge with a tempered control. *She was questioning me again.* I cycled through how much I drank just a couple of hours ago. My fuzzy mind neglected my desire to provide the exact number. Either way, I knew I could count on it with one hand. *Maybe she was the one drinking a bit too much.* I didn't say that out loud, for fear she might windmill on me.

"Sweetie, I drank like three or two, that's all." I reasoned, taking my hand off the steering wheel to emphasize it more. Inside though, the anger was starting to rise. She'd veil the accusations as care. But I saw through that.

My reasoning only annoyed her more. She placed my arm back on the steering wheel with a heavy thud. "You don't remember? And that's fine with you?"

A red stoplight ran up to our bumper. I stopped the car a few yards off the white line and faced her. "Listen, I'm not drunk. I know what it can do. I am better than that. So, you don't need to worry." I turned to face the road as the light turned green. It most likely grew impatient like me at the moment.

"It's not about whether you're better, it's about control." A pause. I felt her hair shift on the leather as she turned to me. "Wait. What do you mean by that? You know what it can do?" The words stung.

"It's nothing you need to worry about."

She scoffed. Shannon probably assumed that I was going to break and fess up to what I was alluding to when I slipped up. The fact that I didn't seem to frustrate her. Bitter undertones had latched onto some of her syllables. "I've known you for how long? Our fifth anniversary was a week ago, and that's only since we've been married."

I recalled our anniversary dinner. There was an argument there as well, that my drunkenness was displayed on full show in public. "I think I deserve to know what you're keeping from me. I'm good enough to know." Now it was her veiled insecurities beginning to show. Her voice grew with every enunciation, yet I remained silent. I hoped not to draw any more attention to the matter.

The "Cherry Hill" sign flew out of the darkness, almost blinding me with its whiteness. After another twist in the road, we entered the bend to the neighborhood. I punched in the gate code, twisted around the community, and entered our driveway smoothly. *Yeah, and I'm drunk.*

As I pressed the garage door opener, Shannon opened her mouth. "You want to know what I think it is?" The garage began rumbling open. My foot ate the gas and I started to park the car in the orderly space. Until I realized it wasn't as orderly as I'd assumed. I couldn't see the various obstacles and messes that were scattered until the car got a little closer and its headlights illuminated the garage as a whole. I switched to the brakes with a heart-stopping thud once I saw the mower only a few inches away.

Shannon grabbed the overhead handle and almost leaped out of her seat. Our organs resettled back into our bodies after a few seconds. My heartbeat slowed to a tortoise's walk.

I didn't see her shake her head in the darkness. The garage door rumbled and screeched to a halt.

I backed up and settled the car onto the driveway itself. Lucky for me, Shannon parked her red sedan at the end of the cul-de-sac's curve. *Or she might've gotten on my back about that too.* Turning off the ignition, the indoor lights shone for a good minute before extinguishing itself, like someone snuffed out the candle. The singular lights that illuminated us were the faint solar-powered lamps on each side of the garage door. They soon went off too.

"I'm guessing your family had some alcohol issues?" I turned and looked at her with a slight surprise. Somehow in the darkness, she saw said surprise. "It wasn't that hard. You don't talk about your family, you don't talk about your experiences with alcohol. Whatever they are. They'd be connected then. Right?"

I sighed, a feeling of dismissal. Inside, I saw an emotion I didn't want to see: Regret. Both versions of us stopped that track of thought for the train to steam over before I could regret anything else. That would amount to something only for one of us.

"I never tried to make it hard. I just don't care about it anymore." A lie.

She proclaimed. "Look, whatever you're trying to forget, I can help-"

A growl got caught in my throat, which escaped into my words. "You know nothing about what I have to forget. About I'm saving you from." I turned and faced her. Shannon's expression turned from curiousness and worry to a slight fear. I calmed my expression, not knowing what mask I was wearing.

"And good for you for figuring all that out. You want a fucking medal or something?" Anger still grasped my words and didn't let go as I grabbed my phone and pulled at the door handle. Yet, the door didn't open.

Her voice was soft. At that moment, she seemed so caring. She was trying to identify with me. But all that came to mind was that picture of her perfect family. *How could she ever know what I was going through?*

She sighed. I heard her hand feeling around in the darkness. Moments later, the car doors unlocked with a soft click. "I don't want a

194

medal; I want you to talk to me. Even if I may not get it. Tell me what's wrong, tell me what I have to do. What I can do that you can't." Shannon's words had desperation.

Yet her frown turned into a smile. "But you won't."

As she closed the car door and walked inside, I sat there. My drunken sweat, my seatbelt holding me in. It was thoroughly uncomfortable.

I sat for a while, ruminating in my thoughts. Both sides argued whether their egos were damaged enough to justify not giving an apology. When I got out, the internal rumination stopped upon realizing the mower had gotten closer than I thought. But the mechanic would have to wait. I had no patience left to fix the issue right then and there.

I met her upstairs. She'd already changed into her white silk nightgown and was on her side. Her hands were under her head, creating a sandwich with the pillow and her hair. Her eyes were closed. I knew she wasn't asleep though.

I took off my sweaty clothes and waded into the closet. I then walked over to my cardboard box and fished out the first pair of shorts I bothered to find. In the light, I wasn't even sure what they were. But I was satisfied, nevertheless. I didn't care enough to find a shirt.

I kicked the clothes I'd worn before near the laundry basket. I'd figured that she'd put them in it. She always does. I got in bed, pulled the covers over myself - my legs had been begging for comfort ever since I chose to wear those brown loafers - and was about to put my arms around Shannon when I stopped mid-motion.

Whenever I hugged her while we lay in bed, that sinking feeling in the bed was brought up inside me. But this was always a welcoming action, not one out of fear. I wanted to bury my face deep into her sweet neck and feel her warmth on my cheek. My arms always wrapped around her tight, but not too tight. *I never wanted to hurt her.* Then I'd kiss her neck.

I couldn't see her face from where she was twisted. However, I didn't think I needed to see her to know how she was feeling. Betrayed.

Hurt. I still wanted to hug her, yet for the first time I thought she wouldn't want me to. It held no great distinction in my mind, and I wasn't ready to argue with my feelings with this tremendous exhaustion that'd taken over my body.

The dormancy had lapsed inside me. *Don't do it, you fucking idiot.* I didn't know what side of me thought that.

But it didn't matter. I chose the easier option, and I retreated to my side of the bed.

Rot's Culmination

As soon as my head hit the pillow, I noticed its iciness. The indifference had manifested into a block of ice my head was resting on. I closed my eyes, doing my best to ignore it, hoping that I'd wake up back home.

But now I was standing in our kitchen. The tiles were more slippery. Less clean. The blue cold haze sauntering from the closed blinds made the environment look more desolate. Stubble was grown on my face, gnawing at my teeth underneath my skin. Dishes overflowed the sink onto the countertop. The coffee maker lay without use in the corner of said countertop. The living room was empty. Sure, it had furniture. But the silence it screamed was loud.

An overall emptiness was apparent. My mind refused to remember the specifics of this day at the moment. Except for that specific shade of blue.

My eyes were fixated on our calendar, which was attached to the outside of our refrigerator. It was all dried up from the various things we planned together in the infant years of our marriage. An address was the focus of my eyes.

The more I stared at it, the address made sure I remembered much more than that specific blue.

Oh no. We'd fought sometime back. On a particularly hot night. Nothing too bad. No plates were broken this time. It was about how I came home too late from a meeting the guys at Gilbert had.

I told her it was a meeting. That was what they said to me when they extended an invitation. Even if I secretly did know it wasn't one, I hadn't gotten a promotion in a long time.

Unbeknownst to her, I controlled myself a lot that night. The guys split off, like two seeds growing further from the tree.

Unfortunately, I got stuck with the wild crew. At around eleven, they took me to a strip club.

Through all of our shenanigans over the years, they never took me there. Never that far. They knew it was never my type of activity, even if I was "wild" around them.

Plus, I didn't want to risk anything. No matter our instability, my bond with Shannon was too important to me. I waited outside, while the others went, cued in by the usher. The moment that door opened, the loud music, cheering, and beer bottles clacking hit my ears. It was like someone threw cold water on me. That side of me surfaced, begging me to go in.

All the fights that me and I had were brought up. The torture I faced under Dad was glossed over as well. That part of me felt like I deserved it. But the other part of me won over. I was relieved not to find out what was behind those doors.

I told all of this to Shannon, hoping she would understand what I did. Instead, the fact that I reeked heavily of alcohol and came home in a cab that had a shot window was where her attention was placed. She kept nagging about how I was sacrificing my safety for my friends, which I wasn't. *They were never my friends too.*

The whole debacle was relatively quiet, yet the scars remained. Once I woke up the morning after, I could sense her eyes being open. Yet our backs remained turned to each other. For the first time in our marriage, we didn't want to wake each other up.

She left shortly after that with the red sedan. Softly. Quietly. The only thing she took was her pink rain jacket. It wasn't even raining.

I'd run around the past few days, asking whoever we both knew for some kind of hint. Our neighbors knew nothing about it, though they didn't seem to want to participate in the conversation. Our therapist suggested that I take some time off to let her process whatever had happened. I assured him that nothing occurred, but he insisted. Then he told me to get out of his office which I barged into despite the receptionist telling me he wasn't in at the time.

I relented and decided to let her free. *Not for the last time, unfortunately.*

Pretty soon, a week had passed, and I was still scraping the bottom of the barrel, sifting through the wood chips to see if anything held value. Our neighbors still knew nothing, and our mutual friends didn't bother to return my calls.

Oh no. This moment was when I'd find her. A couple of days into my search, my paranoia shooting through the roof. So much so that I was debating calling the police. In the heat of things, her best friend was moving into her new apartment. Shannon had circled the date she was going to help her out on the calendar. It didn't matter why she wrote it down or circled it.

Because it was today.

I was now in my car.

Yet no cars were on the road with me. The stoplights all were black. The streets of Chicago proved to be emptier than my heart and mental will would be after all this. I didn't bother to remember all those details. I didn't care. *Not now.* Not when it happened. Not even when I've dreamed this before. All my thoughts were on her.

The elevator in the apartment complex was broken. The stairs were multitudinous, increasing in incline with each step. Yet, despite my right knee begging for mercy, I pushed myself. Regardless of whether she wanted to talk to me for the time being, I just wanted some confirmation that she was safe. I'd forgotten about all the hateful words that flew out of my mouth for the past few months. I remembered the love I set aside just for her. It seemed like a good thing.

Finally, I reached the seventh floor, and stood still for a second, breathing heavily. The "7" turned into "38" before I could blink.

What? I burst through the stairwell door into the yellow hallway. My eyes swam across the apartment numbers. I couldn't remember back then what the number was, resorting to banging on everyone's door and asking for Shannon and emulating every madman's behavior. But walking down the corridor, I spotted the anomaly without that much pain. In between "211" and "212", was a door numbered "38".

Why that number? I couldn't hang onto the fact. I banged on it. Hard. I didn't care. Her disappearance worried me too much.

Shuffling and crashing muffled their way into my eardrum. So did a quiet voice. *Wait, that-*

Shannon's friend opened it. The same one that accompanied us on our dates. Julie was her name. *Was it?* Around all the things I'd been in, her name was shoved into the background.

Her face loomed in the gap. Short, piercings across her nose. A dragon tattoo across her left hand. The black hair and black eyes seemed to bore into my skull. I could see the prosecuting prowess Shannon had elaborated on so much.

Julie's face didn't loom over the entire gap, however. I used that diminutive advantage however I could. Her apartment was full of boxes, the furniture in the background covered in them. *Okay.* The kitchen right by the door was full of opened, empty cupboards. *What else?*

In that short millisecond, I looked around wherever else I could. Yet, all the clutter and diminutive size of the apartment wasn't what finally took use of my attention.

It was a light pink rain jacket. Propped on a chair. Hints of blue ran along its sides and sleeves.

Julie looked behind me, and immediately closed the door until I couldn't make out anything behind her and her body. "You always come to someone's home without asking them first? Or did you lose your manners down the stairs somewhere?"

I paused, the directness of her words pulling the symbolic rug from under my feet. I looked down to make sure the rug was still there, a welcome mat in its place. It was the mat Shannon made for Julie a couple of years ago, for her birthday. "Julie" was embroidered, with a pink background, and a dog chasing a bee on a grassy hill.

My words sputtered out at lightspeed. "I'm sorry. You're right, I just-" I moved my head out to the side to see her jacket again, to make sure I wasn't seeing things.

Julie had other ideas, as she blocked my view with her body and banged the door into her hip. It seemed painful, but she glared at me with any change in her expression. "I know I'm right." She looked around the corridor we were in. Besides a couple entering their apartment a few moments earlier, there was nothing.

"Alright, what do you want?" Julie asked, relenting the tiniest bit. I was shocked to see she could do so, standing there for an uneasy few seconds before she gestured her hand out to me. "If you have anything to say, speak fast because this door's closing bud." She started to bridge the door's gap some more.

It was enough to send words out of my mouth. "Okay. Okay." I held my hands up, and she stopped closing the door.

"Tell Shannon that-" My mind grasped for whatever words came up, as I realized my lack of preparation for this encounter. "I'm willing to talk about whatever she wants. Tell her that I know that the past few months have been hell, but we can fix it together." I took a breath. "Tell her whenever she wants to talk to me, I'm ready. And I'll be waiting."

"You know, if you see her." In her eyes, I caught that she knew her efforts to hide Shannon were in vain. I walked off, however, not waiting for her response. My heart felt empty like something was missing. I didn't know what I'd done to deserve such treatment. Not being able to see her beautiful face again was a torture I hadn't faced before.

Torture was the most prominent word in my mind as I drifted down the stairs.

Now, I had a phone up to my ear while my back lay in bed. I'd just woken up. It was two in the afternoon.

The call had come a few days after my encounter with Julie. Until then, the word most appropriate to my behavior around the house was moping. I rarely left my bed, only to eat and piss. The shower was often forgotten. Other than that, the backyard saw attention once, when I was feeling more lonely than usual (a sick spontaneity). Our secluded location - or as sheltered as you could get in Chicago - was always filled with the sounds of birds, chirping to each other in a constant annoyance. I waited until ten, straining my ears and trying to hear them. I couldn't.

It was as though everything was ignoring me, pretending that I didn't exist. Or the smell reeking from my shirt was driving them away.

I expected some news earlier, but I was still glad I got a morsel now. The happiness lasted only for a few seconds, as I picked up the call and listened to the muffled monotone voice that called me to one of the high-rise buildings just a few minutes away. No mention of Shannon, yet I knew she was behind it. I hurriedly washed all the muck of my skin that could be washed away and put on the closest thing to socially acceptable I could find in my pile of clothes.

I was back in my car as I shoved into one of the parking garage's spaces. My car's wheels almost came out from under it with a screeching halt.

Once again, I didn't care. I jumped out of the car, almost forgetting to take my keys, turn off the ignition, and close the door. I wasted precious seconds doing so. Soon, I was running out of the parking garage, trying to catch the time slipping by just in front of me, yet being wary of my smell, trying not to push it too far with additional sweat.

A few feet away from the entrance, and my right knee acted up again. Just be normal for once. I closed the gap with a limp.

Bursting through the door into the lobby, I was to be surprised once more.

Behind the receptionist's desk, behind a crowd of people, walking and jostling around one another with papers and whatnot in their hands, was a name. A name of a law firm. I knew it very well, yet I couldn't attach the name and the address given to me together. My brain also struggled to figure out why I was here.

Then it hit me. *No.* I didn't want it to hit me. I wanted it to get me out of the dream before anything else.

Still, an explosion of sound, color, and more color was sucked out of the world. My mind attempted to ease itself, grabbing a nearby chair's armrest to balance my unbalanced emotions.

It was done. *Everything.* Something had happened, and she thought it was too far. Reluctantly, I joined the line to the receptionist. Even more reluctantly, I called my lawyer. Old. But it was worth a shot.

Reaching the desk, the receptionist mispronounced my first name somehow. I didn't bother to correct her. I just listened to the directions regarding which floor I needed to go to and sulked into the elevator. It was gleaming bronze, and I was able to see my reflection without doubt. It was far too clear, as I saw myself aged beyond my actual time on this Earth. The khaki shorts and blue shirt I wore weren't as formal as they should've been. Luckily, I didn't imagine anyone else in the elevator alongside me to heighten my elevated insecurities.

The elevator opened and led into another reception area, occupied by three. It was smaller, and there were fewer seats than the one downstairs. There were people in the other rooms, but I forced them all to empty themselves. Except for one by the end. Like them all, this room was glass-paned with a large oval oak table with a bunch of office chairs and a small Peace Lilly in the corner. *What the fuck's my deal with Peace Lilies?*

I gasped. Shannon occupied it.

As soon as my eye caught her, it was like a kid finding candy in his pocket. I grasped at it. The shoulders in front of me, though few, were pushed out of the way. The receptionist was left behind in the wake of my dust, or so I thought. But as I opened the conference room door, she appeared behind me. "Sir. Sir!" The lady kept poking and prodding at my attention, but I didn't give her the satisfaction.

My eyes were on Shannon, at the other end of the table, wearing an all-black dress like she was attending a funeral. Behind her, not at the table, was Julie, tapping a large binder. She stopped when she took notice of me. Her eyes were relaxed, just observing my figure with her elbow on her chair. With a quick nod, I felt the receptionist behind me disappear. Any outside noise was then shut off.

I turned around. A man left the door and walked to the table. He looked forty. Tufts of gray and black hair signaled age, but nothing too old. His round, thin-rimmed glasses were simple. As was his outfit. Black, with a white undershirt, and a blue tie to top it all off. The man motioned for me to sit at the chair closest to the door. "Mr. Collins." His voice was similar to the scene. Morbid. Serious. *I need to wake up.*

The man took a seat and began talking. "As Mrs.-" He stopped himself. "As Ms. Sander's legal counsel, all questions, and all statements will be referred to me."

I nodded. "Good, 'cause a lot of people want to disregard that. And if you choose to, Mr. Collins, we will terminate this meeting and your divorce papers will be served without any consideration."

Inside, I winced. *The word.* The roughness and lack of mercy which he said made it hit home. Hard.

"If you've called your lawyer, tell him that there's no need to drop by since this is off the record." Julie slid the large binder to the man who opened it and began sifting through the papers.

I raised my hand, like a nervous student having a question. The man looked up and motioned for me to proceed while his hands continued to caress his binder. The words came out without a sound. A garbled, nonaudible mess, different from the loud corporate jargon I was used to in similar offices, in similar high-rises.

I took a deep breath and steadied myself. Here, I wasn't trying to prove anything or kiss up to anybody. I just needed Shannon. "It's just, being someone else's lawyer's office, with no real sense of what's going on, and with no legal help on my side-" I let the statement hang in the air.

The man seemed to have found his appropriate papers, as he closed his binder with a satisfying thud. "I assure you. There will be no need for your lawyer."

I still wasn't satisfied. "Do I have a choice here?" No one answered.

"Have you been through a divorce before?" I winced; my jaw clenching shut. My teeth started hurting, but the sadness I felt needed to stay inside, for now. I nodded. "Not me, personally."

"You know the basic responses to a divorce?" I shook my head. Under my insistence, I refused to have any part in Mom and Dad's divorce. If I did, judging from the stories I heard, I didn't know if I would've been sane.

He sighed as if my lack of knowledge had made his day more excruciating. I was just a burden and a painful one at that. "When someone serves you, you can agree to it. Accept the charges, and it becomes more mutually accepted. I would strongly recommend this option because there's just less for everyone to deal with. And everyone can go ahead and go to the allocation of assets, and after that, you're both free to do what the heart wishes."

"Or?" I felt one coming.

He sighed once more. "Or, with your legal counsel, you could combat the charges. Once you've done so, you have two options. Divorce trial. Or a mediation. I think the trial speaks for itself, but with the mediation, a third party needs to come in, until both parties have reached an agreement." His words were stretched out on purpose. Slow, like I was too stupid to understand his words.

I waited. He smiled and looked at Shannon. Her eyes were still stuck on the ground. The man then turned around and looked at Julie. I didn't like the glance they then exchanged. "I don't think you get what we're trying to say here."

He clapped his hands and set them on the table. "With an uncontested divorce, besides the two thousand you have to pay to initiate said divorce, you pay very little else. Maybe another grand to your lawyers, and some more here and there. Plus, at most, the final divorce decree occurs in ninety days." He shrugged. "Sounds simple."

Their piercing gazes began to take a toll on me. I couldn't look at them anymore. The pores on the plant piqued my stellar interest at the moment.

"But when you contest the divorce, you need to pay for your lawyers, the divorce trials, the mediation, and whatever else may happen." He drew a large circle on the table and stuck his finger in it numerous times. "You will not like it."

"I'm supposed to just trust-"

"And when you contest a divorce, those mediations and those trials will persist until both parties agree. Who knows how long those will last? I've witnessed many that have lasted years. One lasted a decade." *Well, maybe you just weren't good at your job.*

At that point, Julie had stood up. Her arms were crossed, and she was clearing her face of her long black hair falling in front of her. She put one hand on the man's shoulder, who then closed his mouth. He was unhappy as if he wasn't finished.

"You can quote me on this, but if you contest this divorce, I will personally make sure it will be absolute hell for you." Her stormy eyes scared me back into my chair, even though I was scooted back already.

I shook my head. "Look, I don't want to cause any pain, suffering, or money to anyone. But whatever problem Shannon and I have-" Frantic, the words spilled out. I gestured between us, and Shannon flinched. "It can be solved without a divorce. So, Julie, just let us-"

I stopped talking. Julie let her hand fall off the man's shoulder, and joined her other hand on the table, as she leaned towards me with precariousness. "Who the fuck are you calling Julie?" As if on cue, Shannon's head fell, and her gaze remained stuck on her thighs as Julie let her anger boil to the point that I expected her to leap over the table and choke me with her bare hands.

"I need you to calm down-" The man tried to calm Julie down by putting his hands on her shoulders.

"Get your hands off me before I make you, Gary." Her gaze remained on me, as she yelled at Gary through gritted teeth. He listened.

She took a deep breath. "Call me Julie one more time, dipshit-" Julie's finger pointed at me, but Gary brought her finger down.

"Hey, you can't do that." Gary decided that she'd gone too far and stood up. Julie's attention was drawn from me to him. I was grateful, as I felt like the sun was within a few feet of me, burning the skin off of my flesh.

Even though they brought their voices down to an inaudible whisper, the tension in the room never lessened, tiring everyone. Shannon thought the same, as she perked up. "I have a better idea. Why don't you let us settle it? Cause clearly, nothing's happening so far." She swirled her chair around, and faced them, who stopped to face her.

Gary seemed content, yet Julie didn't. "Shannon-"

"Charlotte." That was all she muttered under her breath. At that point, I was wondering why she was calling her Charlotte. *Unless I was the one calling her the wrong name.*

Shit. The more I thought about it, the more I knew that if that assumption was correct, it wouldn't look good on me.

Something in Shannon's voice must've ticked a box, as Charlotte and Gary walked out. The door closed, and the silence that filled the room was uncomfortable. All the while, I tried to figure out who Julie was, if it wasn't her friend.

The dog. The bees.

"Julie's the dog, isn't it?" I asked, my voice bleeding with hesitance. The sustained silence confirmed my suspicion, with a sudden remembrance. Julie had gotten stung by a bee and died. The mat was a way to ensure she wasn't forgotten. *Oh god.*

Shannon started. "Nathan. Gray. Braithwaite. Corey. Elijah. Oliver."

The pause she took between each name felt like someone was stabbing me. My thoughts were drowned by her increasing voice, as the anger she felt came tumbling out. More and more names, all of them people I knew, introduced to her, or even mentioned briefly in a story. Some of them, even I'd forgotten about.

"James. Noah." Shannon finished her voice almost at a screech-yell. It wasn't earsplitting, but loud for her. "I know every single one of them, what they do, how you know them, and the most useless-" She stopped. "And you can't even remember her." She knocked the chair she was sitting on over as she stood up with incredible velocity.

I took a breath. "Let's calm down, and-"

"Don't ever tell me to calm down again!" She waved me off and walked over to the window, before walking to one of the room's corners. As she masqueraded around the room, her hand remained on her hips the entire time. "You know what, this was my bad. I thought this could be civilized. But no. You had to mess it up. And if we're being honest, this should've ended months ago. Not that you would've noticed, anyway. "

My voice was quiet, reflecting a very calm demeanor that I struggled to keep up on the outside. But I didn't want to break this rift even more. "Before you say anything else you'll regret-"

"Nuh-uh. No sir. I will not regret anything I say. You know why? It's because I'm right, and you know it. You do. You and whatever conscience you have running around in your head, for some odd reason, can't even think of making one mistake in your life." It was as though she knew about the two souls inhabiting my body. Either that or the fractured bits of them that each provided their impetus into my life.

207

Shannon's face became red, like a ripe cherry. It seemed that she hadn't taken a breath through everything she'd just said. "Well, let me fix that. Since you're so happy not caring about me, you don't have to call me sweetie anymore."

"No-"

"No?! No. Shut up. I can't. I just can't. I have to look out for myself-

"And me? What about me? You said that you'd look out for me."

"No. You said that." It didn't seem like she believed it. She just wanted to break any possibility of us getting back together. Don't let it work.

"And you still said yes to me. Unbelievable." This time, it was my turn to stand up. "Okay fine. I've made many mistakes. Alright? Is that what you want?" I waited with my hands up like I was getting arrested. "But whatever it is, we can talk through it. I was worried sick over the past few days. You were all I thought about. How stupid I was over the past few months. I know. I realize that. Don't let divorce be the solution. Don't make that the answer." I let the hands fall back down.

She shrugged. "It already is!"

"Shan-"

"So all this started in the past few months?" Shannon smirked. "Nothing before then? If I wanna do something, I always have to see how you feel. But so help me, if it's something you wanna do, it doesn't matter how I feel about it. I'm done trying to care about you while I'm juggling all that stupid-." Shannon let her hands fall to her hips, her shoes tapping against the soft-carpeted gray floor.

"Please-"

"You made divorce the only option left." Her voice lowered to a growl, her throat straining under the depth. "I shouldn't have to leave to make you care. Maybe I'm wrong to want you to care the way I want to be cared for. But I'm too tired." Her eyes followed her to the floor.

"And believe me, this is the last thing I wanted." Her voice was the quietest I think I'd ever heard it.

She looked up. One hard stare at each other, and I realized that during her rant, I'd forgotten to even think. I was like a brainless sponge, just taking her information in. *Was this happening?*

After intense glaring, Shannon motioned for the two to come in. I turned around and saw them open the door and sat back down in the empty seats between us. Only me and Shannon stood standing, still looking at each other like one of those Western standoffs, seeing who'd flinch first. She was the first to sit down, but my heart didn't know if that counted as a victory.

"Alright. I hope that little talk was productive." Gary wanted to continue, but it was Charlotte's turn to put her hand on his arm, stopping him from talking. They both looked at Shannon, and all the attention had, for once, gone from me.

It took her a few seconds to realize as such. Even then, she took her time answering. "We're okay. We'll be okay." *No. We wouldn't. She had to know that.*

Shannon didn't say another word, yet a question floated rose into the air. Like a hive mind, they all turned to me and shone a bright spotlight. Seeing what I'd make of the situation, and what my decision was. Cornered, against the corners, with two walls touching my shoulder blades and an impending, intimidating, and relentless darkness pushing me further back.

I tried to find her eyes, maybe for the last time. They were in a glacial stare, looking into my soul. The hurt that spawned at that moment hurt to realize that a lot of our moments together were our last, yet I didn't get the chance to properly let them go. It hurt me more to realize that this was going to happen. No matter what I wanted, I couldn't do anything about it.

The conference room slumped away.

Now I was back in my backyard. My hands were at my side. It was that early morning chillness that bit my forearms. The overcast clouds scrutinized me with their harsh light. I was looking down, the weight of the air pushing me to the ground. I wouldn't have been surprised if my spine crumpled under the wreckage.

My phone was in one of my fists. It was brand new. Something I bought for Shannon to celebrate the seventh anniversary of our wedding. It arrived a day late. I'd christened it by calling to let Gilbert know I wouldn't be working for them anymore. I asked someone to bring me my stuff. I wasn't prepared to face anyone at the moment.

Maybe it was because my heart was cut open. That was when I realized that grief is love persevering. Love one half of the soul keeps, but the other half never receives. Love. Destined for two people but kept wholly by one.

It hurt to keep all that love. But I still wanted to.
Before I left the room that day, they told me she wouldn't be returning to the home anymore. I was tasked with gathering all her belongings, which were already condensed down to a list. Everything that meant something to us was now just words on paper. The peace lilies. All of them. Even the coffee maker.

I spent the days after that collecting everything. My thoughts were empty, mostly because I didn't dare to think. If I did, it'd be about her. I'd cry, and I didn't want to break that promise too. Of course, that was also difficult because it felt as though nothing made sense without her.

I remembered keeping the boxes with her stuff on the driveway yesterday. At twelve, a red sedan rolled around, and a shadowy individual picked it all up to put it in the trunk. My eyes were still open, and my mind ran amok around the house, so it wasn't long before I sprinted through the front door to figure out the source of the noise. Hearing the door slam open and my breath in the quiet night, they turned around and stared at the house. I knew they couldn't see me as well, but the connection was still in the air. Whatever was left of it. It was severed when they swerved off into the night.

Fuck me. When all these dreadful thoughts came, it came all at once. I couldn't help but, with my left hand at my hips, grip my eyebrows with my right. Everything felt too heavy to do anything else.

I closed my eyes. I knew what'd happen next. I'd thought about it over the years when I was in the shower or driving to work. They were just throwaways, distant fears figured would never come to fruition. Leading up to that meeting, the terrors drew closer, but I still managed to dust them off as the result of overthinking. But as my eyes waded in the water of my mind, I knew they'd become true in a matter of time.

I'd never leave my family behind. The memories would start plaguing me, leaving me with no freedom left in my life except for the bliss of sleep. It'd encroach on my sleep patterns soon enough, however. It would then get much worse, as the only thing that was second in pain to my past would haunt me: The dreams of what could've been. Our potential kids. Watching them grow up would be a double-edged sword that we'd never get the chance to hold or swing at our own will. *No.* Now we were at the mercy of her decision to let go.

I couldn't even think about letting go. I'd refuse it. No matter how unjust, how unfair and groundless the pain was, I'd shove it in my pockets before it too left with Shannon.

I knew that the hate would soon expand long past my breaking point. The hate for her. Every time I heard her name out in the wild, I'd leave the area. I'd never be able to even think about her name or face without the past digging itself up from its grave to haunt me endlessly. Anger would cover me in its blindness, and I would often regret letting her control me. It was easier to live that way.

Maybe you were wrong to want more. Stupid prick. Why'd you go back? Why did I go back to the same book expecting a different ending? I should've known better than to indulge in a relationship built on spontaneity rather than maturity, for they not-so-spontaneously combusted without fail.

What type of fool was I?

A fool in love.

Despite that hate, I knew deep down I'd still love her, which did more to supplement the anger than the actual rage. Every once in a while, a breeze of the wind would be her honey-drenched voice that'd slime and drip over the walls of our house. I'd run around, trying to find out where she is. Panic, fear, happiness, and dread would conquer my split mind while I did so. Then reality would set in around my depraved lunacies, and the lack of her presence around the house. The hate would overtake me even more, by the fact that I'd still love her years later. The fact that I'd have to make her into the villain of my story. I'd ignore the latter to still love her regardless.

I knew that it would be hard to let go of her. I'd still grieve over her. It would feel weak and wrong to grieve over someone who wasn't

211

dead. It felt wrong to keep loving someone who didn't love you back. Of course, my stupid brain still did it all. It hadn't known anything else for so long. That love of mine would still scarily twist itself.

I did love you. I always will. I loved her with all the broken shards of my heart. Now, my heart had to resort to breaking itself just a bit more to keep loving her.

To appease my hate, that love would disappear into my mind's depths, leaving room only for the utmost resentment. I'd know that I needed to find a way to move on. I'd understand that I needed to take a shower and brush my teeth and not live like a crazy hermit on the skin of his teeth. But I wouldn't care.

I'd only text her on her birthday. I'd wait in nervousness for her reply. Sometimes, she'd forget to text me back. I preferred that over the "Thanks!" she sent me. I knew that was one of the text suggestions that would pop up. *She didn't even care to type something out.*

I knew it would seem as though she didn't care about our memories enough to work through the differences. The memories that seemed to only exist for me. My happiness. *Were they that bad? Was I really that easy to let go of? Did you even love me?*

For years, only a hollow husk would remain of myself. I'd watch movies at twice their speed to get through them faster. I couldn't enjoy them like I did, so I'd get it over with faster. I'd watch them while the crumbs of food fell into my chest hair. That disgusted me. But I wouldn't change it. That'd disgust me too.

I knew the days would be emptier. Colder. Bluer. The purpose of my existence would be just to try and wake up the next day feeling better. I'd be waiting for the day when my first thought didn't involve her. The day I finally forget the pain.

But I knew it'd all be for nothing. My mind told me that the wait would be eternal. I wouldn't truly be able to heal my soul or restore it to what it was. *How could I? She took my heart along with the coffee maker.*

Even now, with my present self embedded in my past body, I knew this wasn't the "Why". *Shannon took everything but that.*

Maybe you already know why. Greg did help you a lot.

No. Even his words started to feel wrong. *Everything feels wrong.* I'd know all my feelings would be wrong. I'd know everything I did felt wrong in some way, shape, or form.

But what else was there to do besides feel wrong?

Enigmatic Misfortune II

The opening of my eyes brought me back to the present. My mind felt denser with the two memories now re-crammed into my brain. The transition felt seamless, nevertheless. Seamless enough for the worry to carry over without much difficulty.

Get back in the car. I shuffled forward still.

I reached the doorway quicker than I wanted to. Once Shannon entered my view, I stopped. The basket she'd just carried was off to the side on the floor, already half empty. The dryer door was open, the blue glow streaming out from it ricocheting off the walls and providing the only light inside the house. That too went off after a couple of seconds of inactivity.

Shannon had her hands on top of the open washing machine. Her eyes were peering into the empty jaw at the clothes inside. Tears streamed down her face; her mouth contorted in pain. Her back - per her chest - fluttered with awkward hesitation, almost freezing and jolting into action without any set pattern. The sniffling grew louder.

"Oh god." With a dull red face, she grabbed her chest. Her bracelet clanged metallically as her hand shifted around the washing machine until it held her balance. Like she had no legs.

My hate stopped. All the thoughts I had about her betrayal, the evil venom she spewed to the world. It all ended. As I watched her hold back her tears, I couldn't help but realize that unfortunately I still loved her. *I didn't want to see this.* Not just because she was in pain, but because of what it meant for my feelings. The emotions I'd built and reinforced, the people I'd shut out after the divorce. The hate I gave myself and others in the years after. *Was it all for nothing? Are you prepared to lose her while you change? For good?*

The butterflies when I saw something I thought she'd like, only to turn around and see that she wasn't there to see it. The mere thought

214

caused some pain in my chest as well. I didn't want to feel the carnivorous vines that were these complexities, seeking only to destroy me from the inside. Starting with my soul.

Nevertheless, I surged forward. "You need something?"

Shannon's head dropped when she heard my voice. "I don't need you right now." Despite what I wanted it to do, my heart kept on beating. She looked at me with those tearful scared eyes. No. Through me. She sped into the hallway and began closing the door to Dad's room. Her hand bent around the door and a click was heard before the door closed completely, before I could even begin to think why she was doing so.

"I just need some coffee." She barged out of the room, brushing my shoulders in the process. *Our first touch in a long time.*

I saw her arms motioning something as she walked into the kitchen, but I couldn't recognize what it was though. Shannon grabbed the coffee maker, and her hands moved with a familiar precision.

After Shannon started the coffee maker - which looked eerily familiar - all motion within her stopped. Her eyes fixated on the drip of the machine for a moment. Then, she snapped into motion and opened the refrigerator. Her hand disappeared and exited the fridge with the milk. Throwing the carton onto the counter, she opened the cabinets and brandished an empty mug. *How does she know where everything is?*

I walked over to the counter. Her head was bowed down with quiet, focused diligence like she was holding something back.

The machine finished its work, and Shannon poured its contents into the mug. The milk followed it.

Shannon swirled the mug, drops of coffee jumping out into the tortured freedom that was the world. She took a sip and put it on the countertop with an exaggerated exhale. She rapped her fingers on the wet granite. From her pocket, she drew her phone and texted something to someone before pocketing it moments later.

I only watched her with a patience I didn't know I had. It was all very normal. Even the tears had mostly dried up on her face, which found its color once more as well.

There was no catalyst, no drastic movement form my part. Yet in a flash, Shannon slapped her hand down on the mug. It went through it and smashed the countertop. There was a huge burst of noise as the mug crumpled and flew into the walls. I was far away enough to avoid anything hitting me. Apart from some of the coffee.

Her face trembled, the dull pink shirt she wore was now brown and distasteful. Wisely enough, I took a step back. "I said I don't need you right now." I looked down at her hand to see red liquid flow from it. Shannon dusted off a few fragments from her hands, grabbed a towel nearby, and wiped it out of sight.

My attention turned to her face. Her eyes. The ones I never thought I'd see again. I realized that no matter what she still had the softness in her eyes. *I always loved the softness.*

"I love you."

It came out in a flash. I wanted to slap myself so badly. *No, you don't.* I wanted her to embrace me once more. *She broke you.* She *promised to care about you, and she didn't.* I wanted her to put me back together and break me all over again.

Silence ensued for the next few minutes. The blood kept dripping from her hand. She didn't bother to use the towel again. We found something else to look at while our thoughts and reason caught up with the emotion.

A smile widened on her face, and for the first time, I didn't want her to smile. "You know why I fell for you?" Her emotions - seemingly - had won the race.

I forced myself to unfreeze and shook my head. Her hair touched some of the blood on her hand. The red gleamed in the purple hair. The colors it conveyed alongside her blonde hair made it homogenous to the morning grass covered in dew somehow.

"Yeah, I don't know either." The smile widened even more. "Maybe because you felt safe. Or I thought you were cute." She spread her hands out. The blood leaped onto my shirt. "I never found a need for a reason."

Shannon laughed. It'd been a long time since I heard her speak from the heart.

"Sorry." It was soft, but not like when she was angry. This was all said out of care. *Stop there. Don't give yourself that hope.* "Too poetic."

216

"Mm," I grunted. *Was I supposed to say something about that? I scratched my beard, hoping I wasn't making everything more awkward. I probably was.*

Shannon's mouth fell open. Her hands reached out to my beard, pushing mine aside. "You know I don't like facial hair. So, why'd you grow it, if you do love me after-" The smile of hers continued, unlike her sentence.

Every time I pick up the razor I think of you. "I didn't think you'd ever love me back." A fragility in my voice, like I'd never witnessed. Not exactly a whisper, but something loud enough that could still cradle and lullaby a whisper to sleep.

Her smile dissipated. "So, after everything we've been through, you just gave up?" She shook her head immediately in regret.

"Well, if I'd known that there was a way you wanted me to react, I would've done it. How am I-"

"Yeah. Yeah. I know. I'm sorry. I know-" With each word, her voice quieted down impossibly, to the point of inaudibility.

"No. I don't know. I don't know anything anymore." She shook her head more rapidly. With each motion, I became diminishingly sure it was directed at me. *I knew the feeling.*

"Well, can I do anything to help-" She looked back up into my eyes, and my words stopped once more. Nothing on her face told me to stop, but still, I obeyed her. The effect she had on me still was astronomical. Another reminder of the control she had over me. Another reminder of the love I had for her that let her control me.

"You can't help. No one can. This is mine." She pointed to her chest, but I knew she wasn't referencing her heart. "No matter how many people I go to, I always have that hurt inside me. I'm too broken to feel anything else besides the pain, even if there's something else that wants to be felt."

"But this is what you wanted-"

"I never knew what I wanted, 'cause I never fricking got what I wanted. Joseph. My friends-"

"Me?"

Shannon didn't respond.

Let it go. It's too small. "Ok. Ok. I'm sorry. I get it. It's ok. It's fine, we can-"

She nodded to herself, but the tears came out still. "No. You don't know how weak I feel right now. Just because I divorced you, I'm automatically supposed to act a certain way now." Shannon looked down at her hand.

In a flash, the bracelet was in her hand which catapulted it into the wall. It landed next to her feet. "I thought I could escape that." Dejection drenched her voice while her eyes looked with a vengeance upon the bracelet. *She never did talk about her family.*

I circled the counter, into the darkness that was happily created by the sun's afternoon angle. An omen I couldn't fully ignore. But I ventured into the darkness, nevertheless.

I didn't think it was ok to hold her again. Yet I still wanted to try and alleviate some of that pain, even though my thoughts raged inside me like never before. *Just like that, you forgive her? Was all the pain she caused you worth it?*

Yes. "Listen, it's ok. Let it out." I reached out to touch her hands. It trembled in the air, scared of what it might feel like after all the years apart.

Her pinkie came out of its hiding place and drifted over to my fingers. There was no nail, just a reddish-brown area of soft skin. I couldn't begin to decipher how such a grotesque act happened. Yet I touched it. It was still warm. She flinched initially, but her hands closed the nonexistent gap millimeter by millimeter.

"No!" She screamed and scooted away in a flash. I shot back a few steps, the loud bark jarring my senses and shoving the hair along my shoulders into the air. Her hands shot up to her ears but hovered over them without blocking her hearing. "Why don't you understand? I don't need you right now."

I shook my head. *She can't leave. Not now.* "You don't want me back? At all?" Confusion racked me, Shannon's conflicting words running wild inside. "Because I can't move on. I have tried. And it sucks 'cause it feels like everyone's able to move on easier and faster than you." I laughed. Nervously. "I mean, yeah, sometimes I feel better without you."

"But I don't want that feeling." I shook the smile away. "For once in my life I don't want to be mature or right. I want to be loved. I want to be in love with you."

I can change. "I can change. I know that now. I am trying to change. I'll try to change. Just tell me what needs to change." *You're desperate. Change can't be the end all be all.*

No. It has to be. If it wasn't for the blood that was on the floor, I would've knelt at her feet. "I've changed. Please. I'm trying."

"Good for you. But for me?" Her smile disappeared. "I don't want you to change. I want you to leave." *How could I stay back now?*

Shannon laughed. "You want to change? Just like that?" A pause, as if the questions were being asked to herself as well. "You have no idea how much I want to believe that. I don't think I do either." Her hands flew up and down like she was trying to fly away. I wished she could, so she could carry me far away from this place and everything else that causes us so much pain.

"Yeah, you were amazing sometimes. But you weren't sometimes too. And something still wants that hopelessness back for some reason because that was when I felt the closest to you, no matter how much I lost myself." I wanted to tell her heart to keep going. *Keep talking. Don't let the brain take over.*

But it did. Shannon shook her head again. The confusion on her face turned to steely resolve. "No. No, you made me feel like I was nothing. Even if that small part of me wants you and wants to believe that you will change, I have to keep telling myself you won't. I have to keep trying to convince myself that I don't need you."

"Until you don't." I finished her thought. It was easy. My heart stopped, though.

Shannon made sure her voice was softer. "Listen. I'll always care about you. More than everyone else. You know that."

"Oh yeah? Then why'd you leave like everyone else?" I loathed the fact that I thought she'd be different.

"Did you want to just live miserably for a couple more years? Let me guess, all you remember were the good times. The times we woke up together."

"Yeah, 'cause they were fucking amazing."

"Well, what about the times we didn't? When you or I woke up on the couch? You forgot?"

"No-"

"I did care. I cared enough to end the relationship before I left you like Robin."

I laughed, my hatred doing its best to rise from the depths of my mind and have some say in the conversation. "Just like that, am I supposed to forgive you?" *No. I spent years being the only person able to forgive myself. You feel the pain for once.* "And don't bring Robin into this. I've had enough of her relationship advice."

"Yeah." Shannon crossed her arms. "I heard."

"Oh really? Good. Good for you." I could barely formulate a word, the lava bubbling and rising. "Good. God, I love how this town's so small for everyone but me. Y'all couldn't wait a day before you talked behind my back?"

She raised her arms in apology. "I'm sorry. I know I'm not making sense. I know I'll never be okay; I've accepted that." She pointed to me. "Maybe once you move on it'll be for the both of us."

"No. Don't you dare put that on me." *I don't want to move on. That's why I didn't yet.*

"Please. I'm trying, but it's not working. I'm not that strong."

I softened my voice. "You are." *I didn't want her to be.*

"You don't get it." A deep breath. "Every time I see something that reminds me of you, I want to tell you about it. But I end up losing you all over again once I realize that I can't. It hurts. Cal, it hurts."

The night at the gas station. *She wasn't there for Robin.* I sighed. "Don't give that to me."

No heed was paid to my desperation. If it was possible for her to look into my eyes more, she achieved that impossibility. Shannon moved closer, then back a couple of steps once she realized what she had done. "I know. I'm trying. But it's not. Working."

"I want to wander around in circles." She took a deep breath.

"All the lessons I've learned from us, that I've given to other people. I hate it all. They all talk about my maturity, but inside I'm stabbing my guts because it feels so wrong to be mature." *Because you don't want to let go of the pain. The pain is the only thing left that makes you feel alive.* We knew each other too much for the words to be said out loud.

Her heart continued to pour out of her mouth. "I know that once I finally, truly, really let you go there's no going back. All those years together will be gone. You'll be a memory. And I'm scared I won't be able to forget."

No. You can't let her get away. Not again. "I understand. It's ok. I'll be here for you." I tried to move closer.

"NO!" Louder this time. "Leave me. Let go of me. I'm telling you this to let me go." Her broken eyes told me that even she could see the absurdity of her rationale. "You have to let me let you go. Because I'm not sure if I'm strong enough anymore." Still, her eyes pleaded with mine. Our eyes continued a conversion for a bit that not even our brains or hearts knew of.

"Yeah. You were right Dad. And Mom. And Hannah. I am weak."

I shook my head. "You are the strongest woman I've ever known."

"Yeah? I can't even load the washing machine without freaking out. Explain that." Shannon thought out loud while caressing her hair with that bloodied palm of hers. More purple was tinted with red. "So even if-" She let the statement hang in the air. "How do you expect to go back to normal?"

"Well, we have to try, don't we?" My arms gestured out, almost trying to reach for her face. "We don't know unless we try."

She shook her head. "We already did. Don't do that to me. Don't give me that." The fact that we said the same words, the fact that we were fighting the same demons inside flustered my organs.

"What, I can't give you hope? I'm not allowed to love you? I can't care? Why? What's wrong with caring?" I objected. "Half the people in the fucking world don't have anyone to care for them, so why is it so wrong to care? Why can't I care for the one person I actually want to care about?" *Why do you have to care for my care to actually mean something?* My hands flew around more, conducting an orchestra on my right side and holding up a traffic stop.

Shannon only chose one of my questions to answer with a laugh. "This isn't hope! It's a delusion."

"So what? We can't handle a bit of delusion?" My arms fell to my side, and it was my turn to smile. "The delusions are the only thing keeping me happy right now, so excuse me if I want some right now."

"It's not making you happy, and you know that. I know that too." Shannon argued. "It's madness."

Her words didn't make sense. *Or maybe they do. I just don't want to admit it.* "Pick one! Is it madness? Huh? Or delusion? Or maybe a bit of both?" I smiled wider. It hurt inside the more my grin widened. "As if we aren't confused enough as it is."

Shannon spun around, just now looking at the mess she made. She shoved the mug shards aside a bit more and hopped up onto the kitchen counter. I don't know why she did it. I doubted that she did too. She brought her hand up to her mouth, eyes eyeing what was left of her nails with a starving intent. In the blink of an eye, she slammed it down with a purpose.

Her legs swung, and for a moment she looked like her teenaged self. The same nervousness that overtook me at Junior prom resurfaced. The nervousness that the universe would give me sign that it wasn't meant to be.

I'm scared. Even if I told Greg all my fears, new ones kept popping back up. I was scared. Just as I was back then, I was scared of being proven right. That the hurt I felt over her would eventually amount to nothing.

Shannon's choppy breaths slowed down, but her legs swung faster. "Even now the only reason you want me back is because of yourself. You're too stubborn to accept that we can't be together. For my sake. You don't want to feel lonely inside, no matter what that means for me." We knew that the statement applied to her as well.

"Don't make that the answer. Make me the answer. Cause I would." I was aware of how weak the desperation made me look. Still, I begged. "Don't make that true."

"It already is." Her voice was still soft. "Somehow. Somewhere. I don't know anymore." The accusation she made caused my heart to squeeze itself once it saw the truth in the statement. Yet she didn't seem angry.

The coldness drew away from her face for a mere second. "What are we even talking about anymore?" The ice broke, but the atmosphere was still frigid.

"I think we're just trying to get our thoughts out before we leave," I answered. Before we leave ourselves behind. I didn't think much about it, but as we stared into each other with the thought bouncing off the walls of our minds the truthfulness of my words began to take form.

"I don't want all this. Trust me. But I can't do anything else." *You can't give yourself the choice of accepting anything else either.* I wanted to argue with her. But nothing came to mind. *For once.* "If it helps you, you should know a small part of me will probably always doubt that."

"You doubt yourself too?" I asked, my voice inquisitive and cradling a certain softness. Still. I felt the need to join her on the counter. But that bubble I thought had exploded a long time ago returned. I still hopped onto the counter with the sink as a natural divider. We were a good distance away from each other. A distance that I was starting to realize would never lessen again, no matter how hard we subconsciously pulled each other to ourselves.

Shannon nodded. "Yeah." Her face bent down to her hand while her teeth fought to find some nail to nibble on. She lifted her head when she couldn't with a sorrowed gaze. Those in grief attributed their sadness to everything around them that they possibly could. *I did that too.* "Probably 'cause I don't know what's real anymore."

Visions of her beauty crossed the hardwood in front of us and I knew I wasn't the only one seeing them.

"Whether I still feel for you." *The day we got married.* Her dress was beautiful. I'd deduced that when I sneaked into her room the previous night. I couldn't help myself. The excitement had overwhelmed me, and I wanted to see her dress so badly. Still, when I removed the veil from her face to kiss her, I couldn't believe someone could be that gorgeous.

"Or if I hate you." *That cold room.* Her glacial stare as I signed us away. It seemed like we hadn't found where I banished our souls to quite yet. "Of course, none of it matters if I'm lying to myself about it all." I finished, our roads leading us back to square one.

Our eyes found each other. We smiled. Jaded. We laughed. Even more jaded. Quiet, but loud enough to take notice of.

"We'll always be together. Just not in the way we expected." Shannon nodded and bit her lips once more. Her smile lessened a bit, but it was still there.

"Is that supposed to comfort me?"

"I mean, we've always wanted something along those lines. Didn't we?" The syllables broke apart before she could finish, but I knew what she was saying.

I realized this was as close as our connection would get. Those words she uttered cartwheeled us back to Robin's wedding, the day those words were invented. The way our youthful innocence connected then.

We looked into our eyes, and we both saw the same brokenness as we tried to wade through our deep memories, trying to find each other. Where we lost each other. Picking up the pieces of what was left of us.

Tears started to well up. It was hard to stop it from collecting the momentum to fall on my cheeks. Partly because I'd never felt so heartbroken. I thought I did, but Robin's voice came to mind. *Guess not.*

The floor took up my attention after a while. The very same floor that Mom kept so spotless, and clean. Shannon's blood was scattered everywhere.

A warmth hit my hands. I looked down to see the coffee - that was spilled all over the countertop - reach my immediate surroundings. It'd permeated over to Shannon as well. She ran her fingers along the liquid like she was drawing something meant only for her eyes, and then brought up her pinky to her mouth. She licked it and nodded to herself as if it still tasted good.

Curious, I ran my fingers in the liquid as well while my knuckles sifted through the broken shards of the mug. There was a coldness under the warm surface, which I hoped wasn't from the dirty sink water. I hesitated to bring it to my mouth, almost afraid of what it would taste like. But I shoved my index finger into my mouth without another thought and closed my eyes. Even though they were closed, *I winced. It wasn't dirty, which I was thankful for. Just* too bitter.

Shannon was sitting the closest to our cabinets, which she opened. Her hands retrieved something from the darkness.

A jar of sugar. Half empty.

I didn't ask for it. Shannon slid it across the countertop anyway. It teetered over the edge of granite, but it somehow made its way over to me. She didn't look at me while she did so.

I grabbed the jar and opened it. A plastic spoon was inside, which I used to scoop up the sweetness. Once I moved the jar over to the side, I realized that I didn't know what I was going to do with it. Eventually, I settled on sprinkling it over the countertop. I watched as it metamorphosized into brown cave-like structures and entire ravines. Valleys and mountains were decimated by my fingers as they scooped up some of the coffee sugar - I didn't know what else to think of it as - and put it in my mouth.

Wow. I closed my eyes in amazement. I opened my eyes and saw Shannon look at me. A smile grew on her face. Small. Aged. Mature. The smile that grew on mine would've probably echoed that, though I couldn't see myself, so I wasn't sure. *What were we doing?*

We smiled at each other for some time without finding an acceptable answer. She was probably doing it to prevent any more crying. I didn't know why I was smiling.

It didn't matter as our feet were getting sucked into the deep, ceaseless whirlpool. And we couldn't swim.

A rumbling outside. Both of our heads swiveled to the main door. Dad's truck. The noises stopped, and a rapid succession of footsteps crept to the door. It swung open, and Dan entered. Panting, his legs trembling like he'd been running.

His face, on the other hand, was a bit more obscure. Surprise. Shock. Anger. Fear. All in one coalescing emotion was worn on his face. Dan's face. Directed at me. Then a glance at Shannon.

It all began forming in my head. *What was she doing here?* Dan's family, and his lack of a wife. Or so he ushered into my head. My smile lost its foundation as I looked back at Shannon, and then at Dan once more.

The secrets. The coffee maker. The red sedan.
No.

Deeper IV

Dan filled all of my eyesight. Then he filled all of my thoughts.

It wasn't long before he filled all of my rage. Rage that I forgot I had up until that moment. Rage at the world, I always seemed to have more control over my life than myself. The world, the same one that couldn't let me figure out the "Why", no matter what evils I endured.

What? Something snapped inside. It happened so fast, yet so loudly I couldn't begin to fathom what it was.

The noise quieted, and the thoughts emerged. *Fuck the "Why".* The betrayals I'd faced from everyone, the rejections. The way I was let go of so easily. *Fuck them all.*

No. Change for the better. That's all you can do.

No. I'd been searching my whole life to find the answer to the pain. The reason for it to all occur. *I did.* So many years ago, when I first left Gaines.

There was nothing to be salvaged from the pain. No relationship was left. The dreams were there to reinforce that. *And the pain was there to be let go of.*

I had to let go of Gaines. *This time for good.*

"This isn't what you think-" I surged forward. My fist pummeled itself into Dan's head. He crashed into the hardwood before the thought could be finished.

I fell to the hardwood and began smacking his body. I regretted my initial punch as I realized it could've caused some damage.

No. I needed to feel his flesh writhe. He needed the pain.

Shannon's hands grabbed my back and pulled me off of him. "Stop!"

My head hit the black couch, and I landed on my butt. Adrenaline filled me, but I stayed on the ground.

I watched Dan groan and sit up. Wincing, he touched his head which started to bleed. A single slimy stream began to mix in with the sweat that permeated all over his forehead. It sank to his chin, and a drop hit the floor.

"How could you?" I muttered.

Dan showed no reaction and just wiped the blood sweat off his face. "How could I what?"

"You know exactly what." My hand, which was keeping me upright, slipped on my sweat, which started drifting across the floor. My head hit the head. Groaning, I tried bringing my head up, but I let it rest on the ground out of exhaustion. "She's the one, isn't she?" Shannon was by his side, and it reinforced my anger more. "You're fucking."

The laughter that followed made me hate him even more.

"You knew what she meant to me!" I roared.

The laughter stopped just as fast. "No, I didn't. If you'd let me meet her, or even bothered to tell me about her, I might've known." Dan's voice dropped. "No, I wasn't good enough for you."

"I just needed a place to stay. Robin didn't have any space left." Shannon's voice entered the fray, quiet but quick. "There isn't anything between us, I swear."

"Fuck off!" My throat grabbed itself and wrangled every single amount of effort it had to scream. My teeth began gritting each other, to the point where my head started to hurt. But not as much as this. All the words she'd just said to me. She didn't care. She didn't.

"No. I'm serious. I'm not lying. I'm helping your dad. And I just use his minivan from time to time. That's as far as it gets. And I'm working at the mall, and they don't pay much but I'm still trying to save up and-"

Shannon stopped once she saw the message in my eyes - my trembling eyes - and she scrambled to the underside of the TV mount before she finished her thought.

"Don't talk to her like that," Dan grumbled. "She's been through enough."

I waved my hand at him, my head still too lazy to get off the ground. "And there's nothing between y'all? Yeah, I'll believe that. Good for you. I never knew you loved the older ones like that." I spit at him. It

227

flew out and completed a beautiful parabola before it landed by Dan's legs. *Shit. I missed.*

I turned to Shannon. "He's why you came back here? He's that good in bed?"

She shook her head with slow caution. "You were the only thing left in Chicago." *That makes sense. She's making sense.*

"Sure." *No, she isn't.* I caught sight of the hallway. "You wanna let me know if you have anyone else hiding back there?"

Silence. "Yeah. I'll be the one who everyone thinks they know. The one who left, who has no one else in his heart. Yeah. I've only ever cared about myself." My finger was pointed against me. I wanted to prove them wrong. But I couldn't find anything inside that'd do as such. "I think after everything I'm entitled to be a bit selfish."

"Cal-" Dan spluttered.

"No. I ask the questions now. Like why everyone suddenly cares that I left when everyone left me behind. Why should I care for you? Why is it so wrong to care about myself?" *What does it matter? Can't I just live my life how I want to? Can't you accept that? They were fine with leaving me behind, but now they decided to have a problem.*

"That bitch." I pointed to Shannon, but Dan didn't react. "That one, right over there. She left me. Left. Without even trying. She was the selfish one." A lie. But I didn't correct myself. "And you. You, Dan. You of all the people in the world. Where the hell were you when I needed you?" I was on my feet at this point. My toes wanted to jump out of my shoes and kick them both. *Kick them until they scream for mercy.* My fingers, the nails that wanted to tear into the shades and tear them apart. *Let them see.* I wanted everyone to see that I was done trying to find answers. I wanted no more. Yes, I solved a lot of questions. But for others, I made my answers. If anybody were to judge, I wanted them to join Dan at my feet. I wanted them to taste the dirt on my shoes.

At that second, I conceded that the evil I was forced to face here was me all along. *You were the monster.*

Fine. I didn't care that it was evil. That was all I felt. That was all the world gave to me. All it allowed me to feel. All that drove me to kick Dan. Again, and again. Blood flew into the air, almost like it was trying

228

to draw my attention. Even my right knee protested and screamed. I didn't let it change me.

His eyes, bearing defiance and other emotions began to soften. I stopped kicking him.

"You can't blame anyone else for this." Dan sprayed out some more blood. *He's right.* "And I will do whatever it takes to preserve my family, even if you never meet my kids. I don't care anymore if you agree."

Shannon entered my eyeline as I looked up for the first time in an eternity. Her hands were in her mouth, teeth nibbling happily. was robotic, her teeth and mouth moving together in an uncontrolled tandem.

"Dad?" A voice. Wholly out of place. Soft. *Childlike.*

I followed the voice. *A mistake.* A face, peeping out of the dark hallway. I'd never seen Dan's kids up close, so the puzzlement continued in my head.

Her face was wrought with despair with eyes that seemed beyond concerned. Like it was impossible to grasp what was happening. I'd seen it all before. In my eyes, when Mom and Dad fought in those inescapable dreams.

Now it was me and Dan fighting.

It almost broke this trance, this machine that was taking me over. For the first time, I looked down and truly saw Dan. The blood around his head. Some of which were on my shoes and pants.

A shuddering step back, I took. *No. No.* Anger rose once more but at myself. Only a couple of hours before, I promised to fix things. To be better than Dad, or whoever the malicious spirit in our house was. Yet here I was, the hate I'd kept in from everything coming out at last.

For a moment, I thought Dan was dead. His eyes hadn't opened in a long time. He then spit out a gallon of blood and laughed. "You left long before you ran away that night, Cal."

In the corner of my eyes, Shannon rose to her feet and ran into the hallway before disappearing with Dan's child. "Shut up," I muttered, looking back down at him.

"Yeah. Like I like saying that." He opened his mouth, but nothing more came out.

I fell to my knees and grabbed his shirt collars. With a heave, I twisted his face towards me. Not out of anger, just fear. The words of his that were entering my bloodstream were poison, rotting my mind into something else. Everything he added would only make it worse. "Stop." *He needed to stop. He needed to understand.*

Dan smiled more. "I moved into your room because I needed you. I needed you too." Barely a whisper, yet loud as a yell.

I shook the thought off, and let his head fall to the ground. He groaned in pain, but my headache was unbearable enough. With my left hand at my hips, I gripped my eyebrows with my right and closed my eyes. The mechanic's words were long gone, his wisdom no longer applicable here. Perhaps there was a chance, a way for me to start living once more. I suspected that it was when I met Dad.

It didn't matter what I suspected now.

I looked away. Shannon was back where she was sitting moments before. In the darkness, away from the action. Her eyes told a peculiar story. There was care, but it was veiled. Veiled heavily. But there. I didn't know who it was directed to. The defiance she was also showing me was intertwined with a drop of hope. Hope, misguided as it was, that I'd stop this madness.

She closed her eyes before I could see anything else. Water escaped from under her shut eyelids.

They're only living together. I refused to hear it. Dan never told me much about his kids, and I wasn't in a place to defend him. I didn't know him anymore, or what he was capable of doing and how he could hurt me.

Yes, you do. No, I didn't.

I screamed, holding my hands up to my ears. The voices were turning hostile. The ravings of a madman provided to me at that moment would've been akin to what my mouth threatened to utter. I cried again, my fears coming through once more. The difference now was there was no going back from this.

Dan was still on the ground. Deathly still. But the voices continued. *I need some air.*

I stepped over the blood and crashed into the door into the moonlight. A slight moonlight, not yet setting deep into the roads or into my mind. Still, no one was around. I took a deep breath and waited for my mind to fall quiet. Alas, I was mistaken.

Sniffling. Sniffling. From behind me. I turned around, and Shannon was over Dan. Shaking him. Trying to elicit some response. Even she seemed confused as to what she was doing.

"Don't call the cops. It'll ruin his life."

"Stop worrying about that-"

"I came as fast as I could." He muttered, but it was loud and clear.

The crying began. "I just wanted to help you." Sobs reached my ears, but no tears came out. His body didn't have the willpower to conjure up any.

Shannon hugged him. "I know honey, I know. I'm sorry. I don't know how she got out of the room."

Dan held his hand up. "Go see if she's alright." That was all he said. After that, he tried to point to the hallway, but his fingers trembled under the duress. So much so that Shannon brought his hand down.

"Yeah. Relax. I got it." With her heavy breathing, heavy enough that I didn't know if that was meant for her or him. Nevertheless, she stood up and was about to close the door when she stopped.

Shannon turned around. Her eyes met mine. Pain enveloped her pupils. She didn't want to do what she was about to do. But she had no choice.

"Fuck off, Cal." *I've never heard her curse.* Shannon never gave me enough time to ponder if this moment was somehow worse than the divorce as she closed the door.

But I didn't have to ponder to know this was the last time I'd see her eyes.

The light from the living room had all subsided. Except for a few strands from the open blinds. No, from the lack of blinds entirely. *I actually tore them open?*

I looked around at the silence. No one was outside. Yet I knew our neighbors were in their homes, watching and listening in horror. Hugging their children as I, the curse of this town, lived and breathed. Even the Gargoyle statue looked at me with contempt.

I felt around for the keys in my pocket. At least they didn't fall out. I got into my car and turned on the ignition. It rumbled to life, somehow even more jerkily than before. To my right, the plastic water bottle lay empty. I didn't want to throw it away. In the backseat, my clothes had fallen out of their suitcases. I didn't want to put them back in.

I left my shoes inside as well. But the excuse wasn't worth it to go back inside.

The pain.

I stumbled my way back to the entryway of the neighborhood as the pain resurfaced. The same neighborhood that gave me a heart and a place to call home. The same pain that came from the fact that it wasn't only the pain I was leaving behind.

Aubrey.

Why the hell did I come back home? And to what end? What cruel entity lay above my head and decided this was for the best? Or was it finally me, who decided to take matters into his own hands? It was all almost destined to take my last chance at salvation away from me. All those splinters crept deeper into my skin, almost fighting my body to squeeze through my veins and swim to my brain. My heart and my thoughts still refused to let go of what was taken from me, what I'd lost, and what others had lost because of me. *Not again.* These were people I'd loved. Those people latched onto my ventricles, and I had a feeling they wouldn't be let go. I'd never be able to escape my family. Not with Shannon. Not by myself. Never. No matter how far I drove.

Dad.

The winding roads implanted another knife in my heart, each stroke of asphalt on the earth seemingly longer, as if someone was extending the brush further and further and further. This was my punishment: to be stuck in the place that destroyed me.

Mom.

I passed Robin's old house. The burdens there were there to stay. Never retrieved ever again. I took a glance at it, and my eyes went back to the road. My mind stayed on it for longer though, thinking about what could've been. Maybe we could've gotten closer. The memories could've been multiplied, and more appreciated. As I passed it, more and more people were coming to the haven. Maybe I needed such a place until I got back on my feet. But I didn't want to admit it.

Robin.

Gaines Elementary. Gaines Middle. The abandoned train tracks. Aspen Boulevard. Tellermen's Plaza. Aubrey's. Placid Lane. The hidden sandwich shop. The lake. Drophead. A couple of Burgervilles. Even the Italian place, though I refused to pay attention to it. It all passed so fast that the minuscule stop sign hit my eyesight at the last moment. *Who the fuck would place a stop sign here?* My reactions kicked in. One ear-destroying screech later, and I stopped moving. I was in another neighborhood. No cars were around, no people. All the lights inside the houses were shut off. Even my car seemed to sense my calmness and its environment, as it hushed itself and allowed me to hear its heartbeat. Mine was audible as well.

Shannon.

I accelerated through another stop sign a few intersections away from the first. I didn't care anymore. The guilt was multiplying in the surrounding silence. I didn't know whether I liked that the empty space kept growing and growing.

Dan.

I drove while the thoughts expanded. Soon, the sign for the town of Gaines illuminated the window, highlighted by my headlights. *I still need to eat something.* My eyesight wavered from the lack of energy. Still, the white letters burned bright. The words that were going to be bore into me if I stayed burned brighter. The madness, the recurse, the repulsion of the people I lived with for so long. I never needed to talk to them to know. I'd failed them, the promises I made to Dad, and the people I wanted to keep with desperate desperation. All gone.

Me.

I thought I didn't deserve a happy ending. I did. Somehow. Someway. But it was clear now I just didn't allow myself to have one. Digging myself deeper and deeper. I couldn't blame anyone but me. Like Dan said.

Me.

Oh god. I didn't want to drive. I needed to crash the car into the nearest tree and curl up into a ball to wait until the ambulance could take me. At least then I'd be taken care of. More than I took care of myself.

The hurt.

I didn't want to be like this. This state, where the painful dreams and memories were somehow better than reality. Even the fake ones, the normal ones everyone else seemed to have. I didn't want it. I wanted to take away any power from those dreams. I could've. Yet here I was.

The hurt.

Amidst all this, the torturous story I had created inside had a beautiful complexity. A beautiful agony.

The hurt.

The hurt grew as I realized I didn't truly know if I wanted to go back or if I wanted to leave.

The sign for Gaines fell to the foreground, only visible in my rearview mirror after a few seconds. Pretty soon, that too was not visible. The cars buzzing turning into a roar while picking up speed on the highway. My ears rang along with it. Loud. The headache resumed at an intensity I couldn't even imagine.

My thoughts faded into an unreachable oblivion. Misunderstood by everyone. Understood by none. Experienced by none. Except me.

The fears tried to resurface from the dark depths of my soul. And they succeeded.

Because nothing was proving them wrong anymore.

Author's Note

If you feel confused about whether you want to like the ending or not, then I've done my job.

Hello. It's me. The author. I know no one reads these anyway (I always skip them in my books) so it's fine if you don't want to read this. I'm not entirely convinced anyone's gonna buy this book anyways.

The feelings of loneliness, pain, anguish, and regret I've explored were tough to put into words. Some might say that the fact that everyone's experienced one or more of these feelings makes it all easier to describe. In reality, it does the opposite because those emotions rarely fit one mold, often breaking said molds within every person. Even with my pure intellectual capability, it gets tough to write these heavy concepts.

It's hard to even sit here and just *explain* the words that I've written. But I'll do my best.

The type of pain that comes with no mercy is one of the main reasons behind this novel. (Yes, I'm aware that this isn't the longest piece of literature you've ever come across, and according to some sources online it shouldn't even be considered a novel. Word count, among other things, dictate what pieces of fiction should be classified as. But I still call this a novel, because of the grand scopes that I attempted to emulate.) A ruthless force with no escape except for change. Anyone who's anyone knows change is difficult, which makes the pain worse.

You may be sensing the reeking pessimism here. That's good. When I first introduced this story to the world, my mom was on the receiving end. I told her what this novel was and what I wanted to accomplish. I had no concrete idea as to who the characters would be or the actions undertaken would entail (Obviously, I had bits and pieces), but I knew what I wanted everyone who sets their eyes on these words to know. Upon hearing it, she was worried. Not about the fact that I was attempting a monumental task, but on the fact that I was creating such a monster. A monster, an entity devoid of any real happiness or comfort. A monster with a certain vulgarity - not just with words and phrases but also actions - that even I was scared to fully explore. A monster, present in all of our lives. This was going to be depressing, for all those who experienced it, even if we've all seen the monster. Even I, to some extent, got sucked into the darkness that was this book more times than I'd care to admit. Unfortunately, the darkness likes to do that.

That pain without mercy, and the other feelings and themes in this novel have been attempted to be the primary driving forces of this story. This is mainly because I consider fiction that drives itself forward as some of the best. I hope this can be considered among them as well.

When reading, you will realize that the conception of right or wrong in all of these characters have been skewed in one way or another. This is because I find this to be true in real life as well. The real reason that everyone is different is we've all seen life in a different way. Inversely, life's offered to us various gifts and detriments as well. Almost like a symbiotic relationship. Of course, those who see those lessons in a different way will beg to differ. That's due to the fact that perception is the ultimate word on what we take from our experiences. Perception is the vehement key to everything.

Again, I've wholeheartedly accepted the fact that not many people are going to buy this. In that case, working on this at 3:43 on my birthday may have been for nothing. I've understood that most people's first artistic works aren't their best. This won't change that narrative. But I'm happy that I get the chance to showcase my talents to the world. I've put countless hours into making this as perfect as possible, so I thank you for taking the time to actually give this the attention it deserves if you've gotten this far.

I hope you enjoyed the book. You may not support some of the motivations or events that were taken. Sometimes that response was purposeful, sometimes it may be of your own accord. That's fine. Even I don't support some of the motivations or events that were taken in my own book. I only seek a sense of understanding. I hope you understand the plot, characters, and everything about this book. Especially Cal. I know I gave you guys many reasons to both love and hate him. It doesn't matter what side you fall on, as long as you understand him.

I also hope that the pain you feel in this book paves a path to the beautiful memories enclosed in these pages. Because the truest source of beauty is struggle. And if I had a scar for every form of pain inflicted on me, I would be covered in them. So I'd like to take a moment to thank those scars for what you are about to read.

What I see as part of the beauty of this book is the fact that anyone can interpret this however they want. I wanted to really foster the neurons that fire in our head, the connections tht constantly form and disintegrate in our mind all the time. If you read this book again, I feel like you can enjoy it even more with the details I've spent years perfecting. I like my stories like that, and I hope you do to because I've tried my best to craft a worthy reward for those types of people.

This isn't meant for those who want an escape from reality, because I try my best to wrestle it back into the back. I know this is a tough read. Believe me.

I'm sorry haha. I'm kinda rambling all over the place here. Still, thanks for reading.

I don't have an "About the Author" section. Just know that I'm seventeen and I do a lot. Follow me on social media for any updates (Put my name in and it should pop up).

Oh, and by the way. It may seem like I hate my town but I love it.

Anyway, peace. And again, thanks for reading. I hope you remember this experience. In a good way.

Made in the USA
Columbia, SC
26 October 2024

45113377R00148